HOT KISSES

"Emily, wait."

"You wanted something, Mr. Cutright," Emily said in her frostiest voice.

"Are you angry because I kissed you?" He almost grinned at the way she stiffened. Unable to resist taking it further, he gave her a long, slow smile. "Or maybe you're angry because I stopped."

She gave him a puzzled look. "No, I wouldn't say my feelings were that strong."

He took a step closer to her. Her eyes blazed a challenge he was almost afraid to meet. Almost. Cutter had never been able to resist a challenge. He took another step closer. She sidled away until her back was against the cabin wall. Cutter put a hand to the wall over her shoulder, effectively trapping her in place.

He leaned closer and could almost feel the heat of her body. She had ripe, full lips—lips that were meant to be kissed, he thought. Cutter tried to push that thought away. A thought like that made the game Cutter was playing dangerous.

Very dangerous.

"What is it you wanted to give me, Mr. Cutright?" she asked in a choked voice.

"What do you want from me, Emily?" He wanted to kiss her so badly he could almost taste it. "Did you want me to kiss you again?"

"No," she said in a voice so soft he barely heard her.

"I don't believe you. Come now, admit it, Emily. You need me to kiss you."

She swayed toward him.

BOOK YOUR PLACE ON OUR WEBSITE AND MAKE THE READING CONNECTION!

We've created a customized website just for our very special readers, where you can get the inside scoop on everything that's going on with Zebra, Pinnacle and Kensington books.

When you come online, you'll have the exciting opportunity to:

- View covers of upcoming books
- Read sample chapters
- Learn about our future publishing schedule (listed by publication month *and author*)
- Find out when your favorite authors will be visiting a city near you
- Search for and order backlist books from our online catalog
- Check out author bios and background information
- Send e-mail to your favorite authors
- Meet the Kensington staff online
- Join us in weekly chats with authors, readers and other guests
- Get writing guidelines
- AND MUCH MORE!

**Visit our website at
http://www.zebrabooks.com**

KENTUCKY KISSES

Deanna Mascle

Zebra Books
Kensington Publishing Corp.

http://www.zebrabooks.com

ZEBRA BOOKS are published by

Kensington Publishing Corp.
850 Third Avenue
New York, NY 10022

First Printing: December, 1999
10 9 8 7 6 5 4 3 2 1

Printed in the United States of America

Chapter 1

Cutter ducked through the narrow doorway of the company store and let his eyes adjust to the dim light within.

He should never have agreed to do this.

Leaning his long rifle against the uneven cabin wall, he studied his quarry. Emily Keating sat at the rough log table, the very picture of spinsterhood. He didn't know her, but she was exactly as he'd imagined.

Her dress was buttoned tightly up to her chin, her hair was drawn back severely into a bun, and a pair of reading glasses were perched precariously on her nose. He could see why she'd traveled all the way to the Kentucky frontier. Even she might find a husband in a place where men outnumbered women ten to one.

Cutter shook his head. Why did Silas McGee want this woman for a wife? Mack must be out of his head. She was a poor example of femininity, not to mention a bit long in the tooth. Maybe she had some hidden qualities, somewhere beneath all that starch and whalebone, but he couldn't imagine it. He grimaced at the thought.

He shut the heavy door with a thud and immediately regretted it. The cabin seemed even smaller with the door closed. He wished the cabin had a window so he could at least see out, but the blockhouse was built for defense, not comfort. There were only rough-hewn logs enclosing the room with a simple wood door and a stone fireplace at one end.

He shifted his weight uncomfortably as he waited for her to look up. The sounds of fort life drifted in from outside. A boy called to the cows as he led the animals out to water. A group of women chattered around the washtub on the common. Inside, the only sound was the scratching of her pen.

The musty smell of the room's contents made his nose twitch. The stale scent of poorly cured furs and the sharp, pungent odor of gunpowder filled the air. He caught the faint scent of lavender and looked for its source. He was certain it didn't come from the stiff spinster woman.

Whatever it was, it smelled of civilization.

He longed to be outside again in the crisp fall air, where he could take in a deep breath and not worry about inhaling a lungful of dust. It was always a shock to return to Fort Boonesborough after days and weeks of surveying the wilderness with only his pack mule for company.

He liked living in the open. Once he was inside a building the four walls closed in on him. Even when he grew more accustomed to life in the settlement he rarely chose to stay indoors.

Then there were the people. He could not abide living in such close quarters.

He wouldn't be here now if Mack hadn't asked him for this favor. Silas McGee had a great deal to answer for.

Cutter rested one leg on a barrel and rubbed at a worn spot on his buckskins. It was time to see about having a new pair made. That was one advantage to having a wife, but having your own seamstress was hardly justification for taking on such a burden.

What was she doing that was so all-fired important, anyway? Adding up the day's receipts couldn't take this long. There were few goods on the shelf to sell anymore. Cutter tapped the barrel under his foot and nodded at its hollow echo. Empty, just as he'd thought. Not a customer in sight. The fort's small store was hardly a going concern and surely couldn't provide enough work to keep a clerk busy.

Cutter cleared his throat. The sound bounced off the back wall of the small room, louder than he intended, but still she did not look up. He shifted his weight irritably. He had better things to do with his time than to stand here and watch some woman pretend she could do a man's work.

Finally she sighed and laid down her pen. She sprinkled sand on her work, blotting up the excess ink, and looked up at him. "I'm sorry to keep you waiting, but Mr. Cooper's rather unique method of bookkeeping requires my full concentration."

When she raised her eyes to meet his, Cutter forgot his irritation. Her eyes were the bluest he'd ever seen, like the deep blue of the Kentucky sky on a hot summer day. For a moment he lost himself in their depths.

"May I help you, Mr. Cutright?"

The barely concealed impatience in her voice brought him back to the stuffy cabin with a jolt. He frowned. How did she know his name? They'd never met. It seemed once again his reputation preceded him. Let Daniel Boone take on the onerous duty of legend. Boone was welcome to it. Cutter refused to let the other settlers put him up on a pedestal just because he was one of the first white hunters in Kentucky. He hated the man who had been Stephen Cutright back east. He much preferred the Kentucky man the Indians had named Cutter.

However, it was not his past that he was concerned about

today, but his friend's future. After this was settled, Mack
owed him.

"Please call me Cutter. We hardly need such formality
here on the frontier." Cutter gave her a warm smile even
though he rarely wasted such effort on other people. He
wanted to accomplish this favor for Mack and be on his
way.

"I hardly think that would be proper, Mr. Cutright."
Her voice was cool as she folded her hands neatly in front
of her. *The perfect lady,* Cutter thought with a grin. He
couldn't imagine what attraction she held for Mack, who
always before had seemed to prefer the bawdy to the prim.

"I think the proper thing would be to give a customer
what he asks for." Cutter winked at her and was pleased
to see her blush. She was almost pretty with a hint of pink
on her cheeks to complement the beauty of her eyes. "It's
the least you can do for keeping me waiting."

"I'm sorry you had to wait, but I must get back to my
work. Please state your business."

Cutter put on a sympathetic smile. "I can imagine that
Cooper is a hard taskmaster. You must long for a home
of your own so you're no longer beholden to him."

His reward was a brilliant smile that lit up her plain face
and made her eyes positively shine.

"I want that above all. I've been waiting for news so I
could do just that."

Her voice was husky for a woman's and surprisingly sensual for someone so prim and proper. Astonished by the
flare of desire it raised in him, Cutter figured it had been
too long since he last spoke to a white woman.

Now it was Cutter's turn to smile. "I have the answer
you've been waiting for."

"They finally agreed to give me my land grant?"

He answered her with a nod and was given another
smile.

"Thank you, Mr. Cutright. I was beginning to think they would never uphold their promise to my father."

She stood and slipped around the table. Tall for a woman, she nearly looked him in the eye. To Cutter's surprise, she reached out and touched his hand. It had been a long time since anyone had touched him so gently, a long time since anyone had touched him at all. It felt good. When she smiled at him her eyes were so blue and beckoning that Cutter lost the trail of his thoughts again. There was a moment of awkward silence.

"You're in the right of it. It was only a matter of time. Your father paid for that land. As his only child you're entitled to it. I told the council so myself after I understood you were to marry Silas McGee," he answered genially, basking in the glow of her gratitude.

Maybe Mack's choice was not so bad after all. She was no great beauty, but not so ill to look at. Mack could do worse for a wife, especially if she knew how to sew. "When you combine the land you both own, you will be very well off indeed."

At his words the smile disappeared from her face as quickly as it had appeared. The brilliant blue of her eyes clouded over as she pursed her lips and set her hands on her hips. "I am not going to marry Silas McGee."

"Mack said you two had some differences to settle, but he really is a fine fellow. You could do worse than to marry him." Cutter tried to keep the tone of his voice congenial.

He really was not in the mood to argue with the woman. He'd had more than enough of that from his mother. People always demanded more of him than he was willing to give. That was the reason he'd come to Kentucky in the first place: so he wouldn't have to deal with people, especially women.

Imogene Cutright Clark had ruled two husbands with an iron will and would rule her son, too, if he allowed it. That was another reason why he avoided his home as much as possible. He wouldn't even be in the fort today if his mother hadn't insisted he bring her in to restock supplies.

Cutter didn't know why his mother wanted to come to the fort. She'd been here only once before and claimed she could not abide such close quarters with common folk. That at least was a sentiment Cutter could agree with. Fort life was too stifling for him. Too many people. There were few enough people he could tolerate, Mack being one of them, although after dealing with this woman on his behalf, Cutter wasn't so sure anymore.

Cutter fixed her with a determined glare. "So can I tell Mack you'll marry him?"

"I already told Mr. McGee I wouldn't marry him. I don't understand your purpose in coming here today, Mr. Cutright."

Her cold words and the continued use of his formal name set Cutter's jaw on edge. He didn't like reminders of his past. "I came here today, Miss Keating, because I have a high regard for Silas McGee and thought to help Mack press his suit."

"You have done so and failed. Now you may leave."

Cutter clenched his jaw. He'd dealt with stubborn women all his life, and there was only one way to handle them. It would have been easier, though, if he could just kick them the way his mule struck out at irritations.

"If you've heard of me, Miss Keating, then you know I never fail. I'm not leaving until you agree to marry Silas McGee." He was rather pleased with the stern tone of his voice.

"Suit yourself." She shrugged and moved behind the table with a stiff rustle of petticoats. Without even looking at him, she sat back down behind the rough table and turned her attention to her work.

Cutter was not used to being dismissed so easily. He was not through with Emily Keating, not by a long shot.

Cutter shoved his way past a pile of furs. He loomed

over the infuriating woman just as she picked up her pen, ignoring him still. He placed a large hand spread-fingered across the ledger.

She slowly set the pen down and sighed deeply.

"Yes, Mr. Cutright. What *is* it?" she asked quietly.

He had the urge to wrap his fingers around her slender throat and throttle her, but a Virginia gentleman did not handle ladies like that—even a lady as stubborn and willful as this one. Instead he satisfied himself by clenching his fingers into a tight fist, crumpling the page beneath his hand and smearing the ink on it in the process. Her cry of outrage gave him satisfaction. At least he could prod a reaction out of her.

"That page represents more than a day's work." Her eyes fairly shot sparks at him as she angrily spit out her words. "I hope you are satisfied with your petty revenge, Mr. Cutright."

Anger, even more than pleasure, made her eyes radiantly beautiful. How could a woman anger and attract him at the same time?

Her mouth tightened before she spoke. "I'd been led to believe that you were a better man than that, but now I see that once again rumor has grossly exaggerated the truth. You are a boor, Mr. Cutright, as well as a thief."

"A thief! Believe me, Miss Keating, you have nothing I want."

"What else can it be but thievery when you men conspire to take what is mine?"

"We are taking nothing."

"Then I may have my land grant?"

"Of course not, but we are hardly stealing it. We are withholding it for your protection."

"Was it for my protection that you destroyed my work?" She waved a hand over the ledger book.

"You won't need to bother yourself about Mr. Cooper's books when you're married," he shot back quickly. He'd

planned to apologize for damaging her work—after all, it
was a childish revenge—but now he thought better of it.
A thief and a boor! Well, she was a shrew. It was her
infuriating manner that drove him to lose his temper. He
was damned if he would apologize.

"For the last time, Mr. Cutright, I will never marry Silas
McGee." Her voice was low and soft. She enunciated each
word slowly and surely.

"What's wrong with Mack? A shrew like you should consider herself lucky to find a husband."

Surprised to find himself shouting, Cutter smoothed his
hands over his buckskins to calm himself. He rarely lost
control of his temper. Usually it was only his mother who
could drive him to that. Just like his mother, Emily Keating
did not seem bothered at all by his loss of control and
merely raised her eyebrows.

"I have nothing against Mr. McGee. As you said, he is
a fine gentleman." She spoke conversationally, confusing
Cutter even more than ever. The woman wanted her land
and needed a husband. There was only one explanation
for her refusal to marry Mack.

"Then tell me who you plan to marry in his stead."
Cutter clenched his teeth and suppressed the urge to shout
again.

"I do not intend to marry at all, Mr. Cutright."

For a moment her cool answer left him doubting his
ears. Every woman needed a husband. It was as simple as
that. Surely the woman was not stupid. She must understand her situation.

No woman lived alone in the Kentucky wilderness. A
woman needed a man's strong back to hack a home and
fields out of the wilderness and a man's skills to hunt food
and protect her. There were few enough settlers to band
together against the frequent Indian attacks. It was a struggle merely to survive.

"Most women would be glad to have a man to protect them."

"I'm not most women."

No woman could hope to succeed where so many men had failed, dying in the process. It was too much for Cutter. He lost control of his temper again.

"What is wrong with the institution of marriage, Miss Keating?" Cutter shouted. If he kept his anger bottled up he might explode. The woman was infuriating. "Its success has been proven for thousands of years."

"Very simple. It may be a success from a man's point of view, but not from a woman's."

Her smile was so condescending that it raised Cutter's inner temperature still higher.

"Really. I must be too simple to understand. Please explain yourself." Cutter's condescending tone matched hers perfectly.

"I subscribe to the views of Mrs. Abigail Adams, who said, 'Deliver me from your cold, phlegmatic preachers, politicians, friends, lovers, and husbands.'" Her expression dared him to question her further. "Especially deliver me from husbands."

Cutter rubbed his chin thoughtfully. "*Mrs.* Abigail Adams. Obviously she took part in the sacrament of marriage herself."

"Yes, she is married to the statesman John Adams." Her tone implied that she did not expect him to recognize that name, although any patriotic American knew that Adams was essential in their struggle for independence from England. "She requested that her husband and the other framers of our Constitution remember the ladies when writing the code of law for our country."

"Remember the ladies?" Cutter arched an eyebrow, intrigued by this unusual woman despite his irritation with her. He couldn't remember the last time he'd been challenged by such an entertaining conversation.

"Yes, I can read you her exact words if you'd like."

She was already reaching for a slip of paper folded into the ledger and unfolding it almost reverently.

"Please."

" 'In the new code of laws, which I suppose it will be necessary for you to make, I desire you would remember the ladies, and be more generous and favorable to them than your ancestors. Do not put such unlimited power into the hands of the husband. Remember all men would be tyrants if they could. If particular care and attention is not paid to the ladies we are determined to foment a rebellion, and will not hold ourselves bound by any laws in which we have no voice, or representation.' "

She set the paper down and looked up at him with a smug expression.

"So you consider yourself a rebel, Miss Keating?"

"Yes, I do." She held her head up proudly and dared him with her eyes to mock her.

"I'm a rebel, too. We're a land of rebels. I happen to know Mack doesn't tolerate tyranny himself. So why not marry him and rebel together?"

She narrowed her eyes.

"Why would I choose to commit myself to serve some man who is my intellectual inferior just to give him a free servant? Why must I subjugate myself to a man's will in all things? No, thank you, Mr. Cutright. I choose to make my own way in this world."

"Intellectual inferior?" Now it was Cutter's turn to raise his eyebrows. Emily Keating had a very high opinion of herself indeed. Someone needed to teach this woman her place in the world.

"Just because you can read and write does not make you superior to a man who cannot, Miss Keating," he said, and chuckled, feeling some of his anger drain out. He might be able to salvage Mack's courtship yet. "You would do better to learn some modesty."

"What you want of me is false modesty," she retorted hotly. "I can do most things a man can do just as well, and there are a good many things I can do even better. Name one reason why it would be to my advantage to marry."

"Let me be the first to tell you, Miss Keating, that if you intend to inherit your father's land you will have to marry someone," he said triumphantly. "There is no way you will be allowed to live on your land without a man's protection."

"Of all the ridiculous notions, that is obviously one only men could conceive." Now she too was shouting. "I am just as capable as any man and smarter than most. I am well able to take care of myself. I can shoot a gun straighter than most. You'd best get out of here, Mr. Cutright, before I demonstrate that fact."

Chapter 2

Apparently agreeing with her, the insufferable man stormed out. The door slammed so hard behind him the entire cabin shook. Emily heaved a sigh of relief. As she raised a hand to steady the pile of furs Stephen Cutright had knocked askew in his stormy exit, she noticed her hand trembling. It was not fear, she reassured herself fervently, only anger.

She'd been angry a great deal of late. After her initial grief for her father had passed, Emily took strength from her anger at him. She'd been angry with him from the moment he gave up his position at William and Mary to find adventure in Kentucky.

She hadn't seen it coming, not even when he became more and more fascinated with the new territory, seeking out anyone who'd ever been there. By the time she realized what he intended it was too late to change his mind. Who could have expected that a middle-aged scholar would suddenly decide to become a frontiersman?

She should have known that her father, the dreamer,

would never conjure up anything practical. It was one of the most lovable things about him. That made her grief almost overwhelming. After all, he was all the family she had had. It had been more than enough for the first twenty-five years of her life. He died before they even reached Fort Boonesborough, leaving her to cope in this wilderness alone. A single hot tear slid down her cheek and Emily wiped it away impatiently. She would not allow herself a show of weakness. Tears were a weak woman's weapon, and Emily Keating was nothing if not a strong woman.

She could very well cope on her own, Emily asserted. No matter what certain men thought! Stephen Cutright. Just thinking about him made Emily's lip curl.

She'd heard a great deal about Stephen Cutright since coming to Kentucky. Until she met him today, she'd thought him an admirable man. She should have known a man wouldn't live up to his reputation. Mack had talked about his friend at length. Emily had encouraged it rather than be forced to reject Mack's repeated advances. In truth, there was nothing wrong with Silas "Mack" McGee, except for the fact that he wanted to marry her. Emily envied Stephen Cutright the other man's friendship. She could do with a friend right now, Emily thought as she tucked a loose strand of hair behind her ear. Instead she'd only made an enemy of Stephen Cutright.

She'd thought him the epitome of everything admirable about the breed of men who came to the Kentucky wilderness. One of the original long hunters, he was a leader in their small community, and the other men listened to him with respect. He was a renowned hunter and a skilled land surveyor. She had heard about Stephen Cutright, called Cutter by his friends, the first day she arrived at Fort Boonesborough a few weeks ago. She knew he lived with his mother and son in a remote station and that he was not married. She hadn't known he was also handsome.

Emily sank back down on her stool as she thought about

Cutter's long, lean body and noble face. His face was too
long and angular for traditional tastes, but Emily liked
the way his prominent cheekbones created hollows in his
cheeks. Those green eyes of his made her think of Kentucky's many forests. Emily rubbed her eyes quickly to clear
her memory of Cutter's image. She'd never dreamed about
a man before. Why now?

Loneliness, she told herself.

It was all Stephen Cutright's fault. He'd shaken her certainty that she could craft a life for herself here, just when
she couldn't afford any doubts. Emily had always been
certain of her ability to make her own way, but it was not
as easy as she thought. It was more difficult here where
she knew no one, and it seemed that few of her skills were
of any use.

"There's not much call for Latin translations here," she
said aloud, surprised to note the tremor in her voice. It
seemed that Cutter had upset her more than she wanted
to admit. She stood again, then began to pace in the narrow
path beside her desk.

She didn't have any interest in hunting and trapping,
but she could farm. In her mind's eye she could see neat
rows of corn growing in a field, an orchard of apple trees
in blossom, and chickens scratching in a yard.

Then she imagined Cutter laughing at her dreams.

"Damn him!" Emily slammed her fist against the pile
of furs. That brief descent into profanity made her feel a
little better, and Emily allowed herself a small smile. Why
was it that men, attractive men especially, seemed to think
that their wishes were all important?

A lifetime spent beneath her father's benevolent tyranny
and watching her friends one by one fall sway to men's
charms, and then to their domination, had been more
than enough to make her decide that she wanted as little
to do with men and marriage as possible.

The one time she'd been tempted to give up her own

control had been enough to convince Emily that spinsterhood was the only choice for her. Just thinking about
Nelson Jeffries made Emily cringe. She was no longer that
young, foolish girl. She was not going to marry Silas McGee
or anyone else just to get her land, Emily promised herself
fervently.

"Well then, Emily, what will you do now?" she asked
herself out loud and sighed heavily. Good question. However, now was not the time to attempt to find an answer.

She had to finish the work that Cutter had interrupted
and redo the page he'd destroyed.

Men! They were nothing but a lot of overgrown children.
At least you could discipline an unruly child, but one could
do nothing but tolerate a man and then clean up the mess
he left behind.

If Nelson Jeffries hadn't jilted her at the altar and run
off with her dowry, would her father have been so determined to come to Kentucky? Maybe, if she'd married Nelson, she would now be a content wife and mother, with
her aging father dozing by the fire.

Probably not, Emily decided. If he had married her, Nelson probably would have left her pregnant and alone, and
still taken her dowry.

A baby. That was her one regret about her decision not
to marry. A baby was the one thing of value a man could
give her.

Emily seated herself behind the table with a sigh of
regret. No use dreaming about things that were already
done. She had work to do, even if it wasn't very difficult.
Papa always said she far exceeded the abilities of most of
his pupils. Yet now the only skills she found useful here
in Kentucky were writing and sums.

Even so, who knew how long before Mr. Cooper found
a man to perform this task and she had no job at all? Emily
turned to quickly survey the empty shelves behind her.
Men were not the only threat to her position. It might be a

long time before Mr. Cooper could bring in more supplies. Soon there would be no need for a clerk if there was nothing to sell, no records to keep.

"In the meantime, you still have a job to do, Emily," she reminded herself sharply and set to her task.

When the cabin door opened again, Emily glanced up with some trepidation. Relieved that it was not Cutter returning to rouse her temper, she rose from her seat out of respect for the older woman who entered with the stiff carriage of gentility. Her jutting chin indicated a formidable character.

"You are Miss Emily Keating, I presume? I am Imogene Clark."

Emily nodded slowly. She recognized the familiar patrician tones and knew this woman was one of Virginia's landed gentry. Emily had once entertained women like this in her parlor at home, the mothers of her father's students and the wives of the other faculty members. She had not regretted leaving that duty behind her in Virginia.

Emily wondered what brought this woman of obvious breeding to the wilds of Kentucky. *Probably some boorish man,* she thought rebelliously. Whenever a woman was uprooted, there was usually a man to blame. And Cutter wondered why she did not choose to land herself at another man's mercy. Look where her father had led her! Just the thought of Cutter's condescending tone and persistent arguments raised Emily's ire, and she barely heard the woman bid her good day.

"It was," Emily grumbled beneath her breath.

"I beg your pardon?" Mrs. Clark looked at her doubtfully.

Emily realized her rudeness. Cutter's behavior had rubbed off on her.

"I am so sorry, but I have just heard some bad news

about my land grant." She gave a polite smile and tried to look attentive. "Pray tell me what I can do to help you today?"

"I am sorry to hear you're having some difficulty," the woman said, although she did not sound sorry at all. "However it does fall in very well with my plans. I believe my proposal may alleviate some of your worries."

"You are the second person to tell me that today. I hope that your solution is more to my taste than the last."

"First, tell me, Miss Keating. Did you indeed study with your esteemed father at William and Mary?" The older woman gave her an intent look that made Emily conscious of her appearance. She resisted the impulse to sit up straight in her seat while she tolerated the inspection.

"I did not attend classes, but I was given extensive tutoring at home, and in recent years, I helped prepare my father's lectures," Emily answered with confusion.

Mrs. Clark smiled as if pleased by the answer before continuing her interrogation. "Then you are familiar with Latin and Greek?"

"Yes, and I am also conversant in French and Italian. Please, madam, tell me what this is all about?"

"Oh, this is splendid," the woman answered with the first show of warmth Emily had seen. "I want my grandson to attend William and Mary. He will be of an age to go in a few years, but his studies have been woefully neglected since we moved to this godforsaken wilderness. When I heard Professor Keating was coming, I hoped to entice him to tutor Tad. So you can understand my dilemma. When I heard of your abilities I realized that fate had once again intervened on my behalf. We would of course provide you room and board at our station."

Mrs. Clark gave Emily a tight-lipped smile. For a moment Emily marveled at the woman's selfishness. Mrs. Clark seemed to think Emily's father had died just to inconvenience the woman, Emily thought in outrage. There was no way she wanted to agree to anything this woman said. Then Cutter's face flashed before her eyes and she knew that opportunities like this one would not come very often.

Emily consoled herself with the thought that at least this woman's husband was probably an influential man in the territory. She could not imagine Mrs. Clark marrying anyone who was not. He might help her obtain her land grant. That would put a stick in Cutter's wheel well and good, she thought angrily.

"It would be a pleasure to tutor your grandson," she said emphatically, and even managed a smile of her own.

"Good. Our station is some distance from the fort, but we do not leave until tomorrow morning, so that gives you time to gather your things. I will send someone over to collect you at first light. He does so like to get an early start."

"That will be fine," Emily answered. "Who should I expect?"

"My son, Stephen Cutright—surely you know of him. He is going to be our representative to the Virginia legislature, you know," Mrs. Clark said proudly and then swept out of the cabin, leaving Emily to stare after her. It was several minutes before she remembered to shut her mouth.

The next morning the common was empty except for one sleeping pig. It was snoring. Emily wished she was too—sleeping, not snoring. She'd slept little the night before while trying to come to terms with her change in fortune. The long night had not given her enough time to prepare for the man waiting beside the loaded horses.

"You're late."

Stephen Cutright was obviously an unhappy man. Emily pressed her lips together to bite back her sharp reply. He was also intolerable, but he was her employer, or at least his mother was, she reminded herself. She had to control her temper.

It wouldn't be easy. How could a man who was so attractive be so unpleasant? Cutter was handsome, with those high cheekbones and haunted eyes. She liked the way a curl of his thick brown hair fell over his eyes until he brushed it away irritably. Unable to resist, Emily strained her eyes in the predawn light to get a better look at him before answering and then wished she hadn't.

He stood there, looking her up and down, with a sour expression on his face that set her teeth on edge. It was obvious that he did not like what he saw. That was nothing new to Emily; men had been giving her looks like that all her life.

So why did it bother her when it came from this man? She had been hired for her brain, not her appearance, she reminded herself. Still, she smoothed back her hair nervously and wished she had taken more time with it this morning. At the time simply braiding it back from her face had seemed a sensible choice for riding through woodlands. Now she was not so sure. It was not like her to be uncertain, and Emily did not like the feeling. Yet another thing to blame Cutter for.

"Is something wrong, Mr. Cutright?" Emily hated the sweet inflection she had forced into her voice, but sometimes she had to use whatever weapon came to hand.

"What are you wearing?" he asked, disapproval heavy in his voice.

"Surely you recognize buckskin when you see it," Emily said pointedly. "You're wearing it yourself."

"I recognize buckskin, all right, but I never saw it on a white woman before." He glared at her and Emily lowered her gaze so he would not see the anger in her eyes.

"Leave her be, Cutter." Emily flinched at the sound of Silas McGee's deep voice. His presence was all she needed, Emily thought with a small sigh.

"I think she fills 'em out just right." Mack whistled between his teeth as he joined them.

As much as she wished both men were miles away, Emily straightened her shoulders and gave Mack a smile in greeting.

"Good morning, Mr. McGee."

"Em, I would purely love to see you wearing those buckskins every morning of my life—"

"Mack, load Miss Keating's things onto a mule while I speak to the lady," Stephen interrupted.

Emily did not like the tone of Cutter's voice, but she had to admit his timing was superb. She was not in the mood for any more of Silas McGee's blatant flattery. She wished he would take no for an answer and leave her alone. She hoped he wouldn't stay long at Cutright's Station or she might be forced to set him straight—again, she thought with a sigh.

Emily supposed some women would be flattered by his attentions. He was handsome and had a physique that made all the women at the fort giggle when he smiled at them. He would have no trouble finding a wife back east. Despite his obvious attractions, Emily could not find the man pleasing, even if she had been in the market for a husband.

Mack's blond good looks were no match for Stephen Cutright's dark, brooding intensity. If she did marry, it would probably be someone more like Cutter, Emily mused. *In looks, not personality,* Emily thought, barely managing to keep a straight face.

Emily, stop this foolishness. It hardly mattered which of the two men she found attractive, because she was certainly not marrying either one of them.

"You wanted to speak to me?" she asked Cutter pointedly when the silence became oppressive. The expression on his face was disapproving, but she could not see how she had offended him already this morning.

"Your clothing. Get rid of it immediately. I do not want to see it again."

"Mr. Cutright, I went to considerable time and expense to make this clothing. I will not destroy it simply on your whim."

Disapproval turned into anger in his eyes, but he maintained a firm control on his temper. Emily admired his discipline even if she felt challenged to break it.

"Miss Keating, it is no whim. You saw how Mack reacted. Do you expect other women-hungry men to be more tactful?"

"I never expect tact from a man, Mr. Cutright," Emily said sweetly. "That would be too much to hope for. Do not worry about me; I can protect myself."

"I will not tolerate—"

"Mr. Cutright, you already said we are late," Emily interjected before he could say something to really set off her already flaring temper. She longed to tell the man exactly what she thought of his overbearing manner, but she could not do it until they were well away from the fort. Otherwise it would be far too easy for him to dismiss her on the spot.

"I think that means we hardly have the time to debate fashion and I hardly have time to change my clothes. You can't mean for me to ride naked. That would be sure to incite your women-hungry men. I made these clothes because I thought they were much more suited to wilderness life than long skirts. I am sure they will come in handy when I am living on my own land."

"You still cling to that plan?" He raised his eyebrows and gave her a questioning look. "You don't know when to give up, do you?"

"I don't give up; I make my own way." Emily gave him a challenging look.

"Your way could get you killed."

"That is not your problem, is it?"

"It is now. You are in my charge. It's not a care I accept

gladly, but I take it very seriously," he said sharply. "I do not need yet another dependent, but I tolerate your presence at my mother's request. I am only looking for an excuse to ship you back east, where you belong."

"Mr. Cutright, I promise you that I will provide you with no such excuse, even supposing you have the right to make that decision." Emily pointed in emphasis. "It was your mother who hired me.

"I was hired to tutor your son and I have no doubts about my ability to perform that duty. You are my employer, but that entitles you to question my ability only within that capacity, no more, no less," Emily said firmly. Her control on her temper slipped as he narrowed his eyes, giving his face a dangerous expression. "You are not my husband, my father, or my brother, so you can forget the notion that you are in any way responsible for me."

Emily got a little carried away in her vehement argument and jabbed her finger into his chest.

Cutter's brown hand quickly caught hers.

The jolt of the contact felt like a bolt of lightning. She saw shock flash in his eyes, and he released her hand as if it burned him.

"God forbid I should have the responsibility for you, Miss Keating. That is more than any one man should have to face." He took a step back from her, and Emily took some comfort in the knowledge that what had just happened disconcerted him as well. "I can only think that Mack's guardian angel was watching over him the day you ensured that he was not saddled with a sharp-tongued virago for a wife. Now saddle up."

As Emily mounted her horse she sighed with relief. It had not gone as badly as it could have. After she found out that Cutter was her new employer, Emily had been sure that her tenure would be the shortest in history. Obviously his mother held some sway over him. It was not much, if the icy looks he sent his mother were any indication. At least now Emily knew that she was not the only woman who set him off. The man had obviously taken to the wilderness because he was a woman hater.

Chapter 3

As they rode deeper into the profound humid green shade of the forest, the ancient trees made a canopy overhead. Cutter much preferred this roof to any other. He shaded his eyes to admire the lush meadows and dark green treetops of Kentucky spreading out before him, welcoming him home.

Cutter felt himself relax as the forest closed in around them. The fort was far behind them, and there had been no sign of human habitation for miles. There was only the rustle of the trees talking. The layers of fallen leaves and pine needles absorbed the horses' hoofbeats. He took a deep breath, glad to be away from the smoke and stench of the fort. He loved the clean, fresh air of the forest.

It was a relief to be away from the crowded, tense atmosphere of the fort. He had come to Kentucky to avoid the press of people living on top of each other.

Cutter knew that most of the other settlers missed the trappings of civilization. They wanted roads instead of narrow paths used by animals more than people. They wanted clapboard houses in place of log cabins. Cutter missed his books, but he'd learned more about life since coming to Kentucky than he had learned in all his years as a student and lawyer in Virginia.

He'd learned that there was another way of life than the constant rush in the cities and the drudgery of working for another. He'd learned to depend on his own abilities. He'd learned to find peace within himself.

Every trip he took to Fort Boonesborough reinforced those lessons. Cutter did not always agree with Daniel Boone, but he had heard Daniel say that when he could see the smoke from his neighbor's cabin it was time to move on. That was a sentiment he could agree with.

He was grateful that his mother was not afraid to live in their isolated station despite the increasing Indian attacks. It was becoming more and more dangerous to travel away from the larger forts in Kentucky, and many of the settlers living in outlying farms like his had abandoned their homes in favor of Harrod's Town, Fort Boonesborough, and Logan's Station.

Cutter was not sure that the larger forts were any safer. An assault earlier that spring on Boonesborough had left four men injured, including Daniel Boone. Just last week an attack at Logan's Station had left at least one man dead and several others injured.

Despite the fact that some families had been burned out and even killed, Cutter felt more confident of his ability to protect his family than he did of the safety of any of the forts. He would rather rely on his own abilities than be dependent on another's.

Even if he did not, Cutter was not sure he could bear to live in the confines of a settlement ever again. Living among so many people demanded too much from him, more than he wanted to give. He didn't want to care about other people. That led only to pain, and he had had enough of that to last a lifetime.

The arrival of his mother and son in Kentucky had been enough of a disruption to his fragile peace. The time he spent scouting and surveying made it somewhat easier to accept their presence in his life.

It would not be so easy any longer. Increasing tribal unrest demanded that he stay close to home to protect them. That didn't suit the life Cutter wanted. He'd tried to talk his mother into staying at the fort, but she refused steadfastly, insisting that her place was with him. She said Tad needed his father, but Cutter did not know how to deal with his son. Tad brought back too many memories, memories that were a threat to his peace.

Glaring at Emily Keating's back, Cutter knew she was another threat. She rode well, Cutter admitted grudgingly. She said she could shoot, and Mack concurred. She was well educated. She was determined to make her own way in the world.

He should admire her for these qualities, Cutter knew, but instead she unsettled him. Against his will Cutter found himself intrigued by the woman, almost anxious to see the flash of temper in those luminous eyes, to see the stubborn lift of her chin. It was an interest that had no place in his life.

No woman had touched him as this one did, not since Caroline. Even so, no woman could be more different from his wife than Emily Keating. Where Caroline had been soft and gentle, Emily was sharp and prickly. Where Caroline had been beautiful, Emily was not. . . .

Beautiful or not, there was something about her that caught the eye even when he couldn't see those remarkable blue eyes. Her hair was a wonderful whiskey-brown color that caught the sunlight as it filtered through the leaves overhead. Curls escaped from the loose braid that hung down her back and made Cutter's fingers itch to run through them.

She did fill out those buckskins well, Cutter thought, as

he eyed the way the pants fit snugly. Mack had been right
about that. As he watched that round bottom just ahead
of him, Cutter's mind filled with images of her riding
naked as she had threatened. His own buckskins became
uncomfortably tight.

Cutter ground his teeth together as he realized that
Emily had done it again. She had managed to disrupt his
peace. He would not tolerate it. She would have to go.

It would have been easier if he could have left the whole
passel of them back at Boonesborough, but Imogene Clark
was a stubborn woman. Emily Keating had already proved
herself stubborn. There was definitely not room in his life
for two stubborn women. Either he would have to send
Emily back east or she would have to marry Mack. That
was all there was to it.

Just the thought of Emily and Mack together made Cutter uncomfortable. They would never suit. In all fairness
to his friend, Cutter assured himself, Emily would just have
to go back to Virginia. Cutter couldn't inflict misery like
that on Mack.

The sound of a shot ringing over his head had Cutter
fumbling for his rifle, glancing quickly about him for the
source of danger. He breathed a sigh of relief when he
saw Mack point excitedly and ride off to collect the rabbit
he'd just shot. Cutter cursed under his breath as he felt
his heartbeat gradually slow to normal. He could not
remember the last time he had been so unaware of his
surroundings. Damn Emily Keating for the distraction she
was.

The shadows were deepening and the forest had grown
ominously quiet by the time they reached Cutright's Station. Emily was tired. She hadn't gotten much sleep the
night before. It had taken little time to pack her meager
belongings, but she'd been up late reassuring the Calloways

that she appreciated their hospitality but it was time for her to move on.

After they finally went to bed, she'd lain awake worrying about her future. She refused to believe that Cutter was right about her inability to make her own way in Kentucky. Still, he had planted doubts in her mind that would not go away.

This morning she'd awakened with a thick fog in her head. Her confrontation with Cutter had been invigorating, but the long ride had drained her strength. Despite her exhaustion, she managed to look about her with interest as they approached the high walls surrounding a few log buildings. This would be her new home.

Smoke drifted lazily over the settlement. The land surrounding the palisade fence had been cleared for crops, and the bright green stalks of new corn stood near waist level.

A gangly youth stood between the open gates of the small fort and waved excitedly. His marked resemblance to his father told Emily that he was most likely her pupil.

Someday he would be as handsome as his father, Emily decided. The boy hesitated at the gate for a moment before turning and running back into the station. He quickly reappeared, followed by a black man and woman who immediately began to unload the pack mules as Cutter and Mack led their horses to the low-roofed stable. Emily pressed her lips together in anger.

Of course Stephen Cutright was a slave owner, Emily thought scornfully. One more reason to dislike the man. Emily did not know why she was surprised. After all, he was a Virginian. She was too, but slavery was one of the many despised institutions she'd thought she'd left behind in Virginia.

It just couldn't be right to own another human being, and it struck too close to the bondage that women were held in for Emily's peace of mind.

Emily dismounted stiffly and was jolted out of her thoughts when Mrs. Clark brought her grandson to Emily's side. The boy gawked at her with a wide-eyed stare that made Emily distinctly uncomfortable. Maybe the buckskins had been a mistake. They were not exactly made to inspire awe in a new student.

"Tad, come meet your new tutor, Miss Keating." Mrs. Clark wrapped an arm around her grandson's shoulders but he shrugged her away impatiently.

"I don't need a tutor," Tad said with a scowl. "I'm going to be a long hunter. Learning is just a waste of my time."

"You will be no such thing," his grandmother said in a tone that brooked no argument. "You will attend William and Mary just as your father did, and that is all there is to it. Now I expect you to be polite to Miss Keating; you can learn a great deal from her."

"Yes, ma'am," he muttered sullenly and scuffed the toe of his boot in the dirt, stubbornly staring at the small mound he made with his toe.

Emily could almost feel the resentment radiating from the boy. She couldn't blame him. She hated it too when people forced her to do something she didn't want to do.

"Mrs. Clark, I am sure you have a great deal to see to after your absence," Emily interjected before the other woman made this first meeting with her pupil an even greater disaster. "Why don't you leave us to get to know one another?"

"Very well," the woman said curtly and left them alone.

"I don't need a tutor," Tad repeated petulantly.

Emily restrained the urge to smile. She did not want to embarrass him with her amusement. She understood very well how it felt to have your life beyond your control. She lost her inclination to smile as she remembered that this boy could cost her her own security if she did not find a way to reach him.

"Your grandmother is right. There is a great deal I can teach you."

"I don't want to learn anything a girl can teach me!" When he met her gaze head-on, Emily was struck anew by how like his father he looked. The angular planes of his face would gradually form into the strength his father's face presented to the world. The childish mouth would eventually resemble the sensuous lips of his father. . . .

Emily shook her head to clear it. What had come over her? She never thought about men. Never. Yet Cutter occupied her thoughts with disturbing regularity. With an effort she brought her thoughts back to her unwilling pupil.

"What do you want to learn about?"

"Nothing you can teach me."

"Try me."

"I want to learn to shoot," he burst out, and then bit his lip with obvious embarrassment. "No girl can teach me that."

"You are right; you probably should learn that from a man. Your father is reputed to be one of the best hunters in Kentucky," Emily said calmly. As infuriatingly male as he was, she could not lose her temper with this boy, or Cutter would surely use that as an excuse to dismiss her and send her all the way back to Virginia.

"He won't teach me. He's always too busy."

Emily heard the hurt the child felt at his father's rejection. She forgot her own worry in the need to comfort the boy.

"It so happens that I am a fair shot myself," Emily said quickly. "If you promise to study Latin, as your grandmother wants, then I promise to teach you how to shoot."

"You probably aren't any good," he said scornfully.

"I am very good," Emily said with a smile of assurance. "Silas McGee taught me and said I was as good as any man and better than most."

"Mack taught you?" Tad repeated in breathless awe. "He wouldn't teach me 'cause my pa said he couldn't."

"Well, that is one advantage of my being a girl," Emily said, quick to seize any advantage. "He won't think to forbid it of me. So do we have a deal?"

"Deal," he said with a quicksilver grin and dashed off before she could say more.

Emily gazed after him thoughtfully. He ran straight to his father's side as the men stepped from the stable. She watched as Cutter answered the boy's eager chatter with a curt nod and strode off, leaving the boy standing there with his rounded shoulders speaking eloquently of his dejection. It appeared Stephen Cutright acted no better as a father than he did as an employer.

The next morning the silence woke her. Emily stared at the naked rafters above her bed for a moment before she remembered where she was. A feeling of satisfaction swept over her.

This was the first day of a new venture, a new challenge. She liked having a goal again. It was a heaven-sent opportunity to prove to Stephen Cutright that she could handle anything the Kentucky wilderness could throw at her.

Then she noticed the absence of birdcalls and the stillness of the morning outside, and a chill of fear trickled down her spine.

The first lesson of frontier living she had learned was that when the birds sang it meant all was right in their world; no danger was near. Even within the fort at Boonesborough they listened for the birds before venturing out to get water or work in the fields. The bright trill of a birdcall calmed her fear for a moment. Then Emily realized that it had been no bird she had heard.

Indians.

A woman's scream ripped through the silence and confirmed Emily's fear. She had experienced a number of Indian attacks on Fort Boonesborough this year, but knew it would be far different here with so few men to defend the station. Every rifle would be needed.

Emily nearly knocked her forehead on the landing as she hastily scrambled down the ladder from her loft to the room below, where Mrs. Clark slept. As the fort's dogs set to howling and barking in the barn, Emily ran straight to the rifle that hung over the fireplace and hastily loaded the weapon.

"Where are you going with that?"

Emily paused on her way to the door and looked to the bed where Mrs. Clark still lay, clutching her bedcovers under her chin, obviously outraged at the intrusion.

"Don't you dare go out there," the older woman said in an imperious voice.

Ignoring her command, Emily gave the heavy bar holding the door closed a shove with her shoulder. She ran out of the cabin without shutting the door behind her. The gates to their small stockade stood open, framing a chilling tableau.

She could see Cutter's slave Reuben lying on the ground amid a circle of trampled corn with an Indian brave, painted and shining in the sunlight, standing over him.

The blade he held over Reuben was glistening with new blood, gleaming in the bright morning light. The black man lay so still that Emily thought he must be dead. The arrow protruding from his chest was an ominous sign.

Another scream rent the air and pulled Emily's attention across the field to where a second Indian dragged Cutter's slave woman toward the woods. The savage stopped their progress long enough to give Ruth a vicious slap across the face.

Ruth subsided into whimpering cries as the man pulled her along. Emily knew she had to do something, but she had only one shot for the two targets. There would be no

time to reload before the Indians either finished their
barbarous work or came for her.

Emily pressed her lips together in determination and
hefted the long rifle. She laid the cold barrel against her
cheek and swallowed nervously, still hesitating between the
two targets.

Before she could decide, a shot rang out from the woods.
The Indian holding the knife over Reuben jerked like a
puppet on a string and fell beside the black man.

She stared at the twitching body, then lifted her gaze
to the distant tree line, where she saw Cutter and Mack
approaching at a run. Mack paused and raised his gun to
aim at the second Indian, but his shot went wide. The
Indian did not even turn around or loose the woman he
pulled along with him.

Emily carefully sighted her gun at the Indian's back and
squeezed the trigger. Her shot was right on target. He went
down with a cry that made Emily's blood run cold. The
knowledge that she had just shot another human being
left her with a sick feeling in her gut.

"You really can shoot!"

Emily dropped the gun and whirled around to find Tad
standing in his nightshirt with a look of awestruck wonder
on his face.

"Reuben, my God! Reuben, don't you dare die on me
now." The anguish in Ruth's voice drew Emily's attention
away from her student.

Emily saw the woman fall to her knees beside the black
man's still form. The slave was not dead, not yet.

"Tad, get your grandmother. Tell her there are wounds
to tend." Emily did not wait to see if he obeyed her order
before she ran across the field. Maybe she could help until
more experienced hands took over.

Emily knelt in the dirt beside the black woman. She
noted with a grateful sigh that the arrow was in Reuben's

arm, not his chest, as she had thought. He moaned and his eyes fluttered open.

"Ruth, you be okay?" he asked in a hoarse voice that set the woman crying again.

"I am now. I sure am now." She cradled his head to her chest as she cried.

They deserved some time to themselves. Standing, Emily shook out the skirt of her nightdress. The hem was stained red from the blood near Reuben's side, and Emily's stomach rolled at the sight.

A piercing cry behind her made Emily whirl about in panic. She stumbled in surprise when she saw the bloody Indian rise up out of the corn.

She had thought his face hideous from the paint before. The river of blood flowing from the wound on his head made him seem more a creature from the land of the dead. He yanked a tomahawk from his belt, swinging it high, his eyes staring straight at her.

Breath catching in her throat, she froze at the murderous intention in his eyes.

A knife flew through the air, lodging in the Indian's chest with a sickening *thunk* that Emily was sure she would remember for the rest of her life. The Indian looked down in surprise and took another step toward her before he fell at her feet, spraying more blood on the hem of her white nightdress. One brown hand reached toward her and then went limp, leaving a streak of blue paint on her foot.

Raising a trembling hand to her throat, Emily stared at his still form, half expecting the man to rise and attack again. She took a shaky step backward to avoid the final touch of the Indian.

When someone touched her arm, Emily turned and cried out in panic, stumbling backward over the dead body of the Indian, nearly falling over him.

"What do you think you are doing?" Cutter's green eyes

were stern and his tone was brusque, but his hands were gentle on her shoulders as he turned her away from the grisly sight. "Are you aware that you are wearing only your nightgown?"

Emily stared at him for a moment, trying to understand his words. She could not believe that they had just survived an Indian attack and all the man worried about was her clothes. Yesterday she had thought the man rude and insufferable. Today she added *cold* and *unfeeling* to the list.

"I am so sorry that I did not take the time to change. I thought I might be of more use if I arrived before the Indians were on their path home," Emily snapped. "Although Ruth might prefer being an Indian chief's squaw to living with you."

"Do not act as if you are some grand savior," he said with a snarl. "We would have stopped him one way or another. One lucky shot does not make you a marksman."

Emily's heart was still pounding too fast. She didn't want to face another murderous Indian, but now that she knew she could perform in a pinch she would not let Stephen Cutright diminish that. She could not forgive him for teaching her that lesson so quickly.

"That was no lucky shot. I told you I could defend myself. It appears I'm a better shot than you. I would thank you for saving my life just now, but then if you had done the job right the first time there would have been no need."

Emily mimicked the tone her father used to dress down his students and she watched with fascination as Cutter's eyes filled with anger.

"You are a sharp-tongued, ungrateful—"

"Ease up, Cutter; she did fine. Don't be so hard on her," Mack spoke up, looking in confusion between the two of them. Emily expected he could see the sparks of anger that flew from her eyes.

"Mack, help Reuben back to the station. Miss Keating and I are having a discussion."

"Some discussion. I—"

"Now, Mack."

Emily was surprised to see the younger man do as Cutter ordered. She was damned if she would ever obey any order given in that tone of voice from this infuriating, ungrateful man. She crossed her arms across her chest and waited to hear what he had to say.

"So you think killing one Indian has prepared you for frontier life?" Cutter asked in a hard voice. He did not give her time to answer but gripped her arm with biting fingers and pulled her across the cornfield, away from the fort.

"Loose me at once. I am not one of your slaves to be ordered about." He ignored her protest, so Emily tried to pull her arm free and discovered that his grip would not be loosened. She stumbled again, and he barely paused long enough for her to regain her balance. She seethed inwardly, but gave her full concentration to keeping her balance while avoiding stepping on the sharper stones with her bare feet. She would deal with Cutter when he was in a more reasonable mood.

Emily forgot all about her sore feet when they reached the sprawled body of the Indian she'd killed. Cutter loosed his hold on her arm so quickly she nearly fell again.

He was so young, she thought irrelevantly as she studied the young warrior. Now the war paint did not seem so frightening. It was nothing but a brave mask. He was scarcely older than Tad, she thought as tears filled her eyes. Emily fought them back fiercely. She would not let Cutter see her cry. She would not.

Then her gaze traveled to the gaping red wound in the Indian's back and she felt her stomach rise in her throat.

Chapter 4

Cutter stood and watched the girl retch into the dirt beside the man she had killed. A series of powerful dry heaves racked her body. It was painful to watch. He told himself she had to understand the impact of what she'd done. He told himself he was only teaching her a much-needed lesson. He told himself that he was not being cruel—but he did not believe it.

It took him a few moments before he realized she was no longer getting sick. Now she was crying.

He hated it when women cried.

Finally she stood up and wiped her face, leaving smears of dirt on her cheeks that made her look younger and more vulnerable.

Cutter felt like a brute for doing this to her. Not knowing what else to do, he slung the leather flask off his shoulder and handed it to her. "Here, a sip of this should clear your mouth."

She thanked him softly and took a large swig. She gasped

and choked before she managed to spit out the liquid. Cutter couldn't help but grin at her grimace of distaste.

"Whiskey!" she accused him in a prim voice at odds with her unladylike appearance.

"Did you expect a man like me to carry water?" Cutter asked pointedly.

"Maybe if you did it would improve your aim."

Her words were hard but her hand trembled as she wiped her mouth. Cutter couldn't help but admire her struggle to keep her control even while she refused to look again at the body of the man she'd killed. She was more composed than he'd been after seeing the first man he'd killed.

"I will have to give it a try. I hate to be outdone by a woman."

Her shoulders straightened a little at the compliment, just as he'd intended, but Emily would not be distracted.

"I don't want to talk about that. I didn't know it would be so awful," she said in a small voice. "I didn't know. I feel terrible."

"Imagine how he feels."

The stricken look returned to her face at his reminder. When her lower lip started to tremble again, Cutter wished he could take the words back. He had meant them as a joke. It was the type of gallows humor that he and Mack enjoyed after a time of great stress. She was obviously not in a laughing mood just now. *Damn.* He didn't even know how to talk to a woman anymore. It was better that he stick to the woods and solitude.

"I can think of nothing but what I've done." She turned her face away from him, but the way her shoulders shook he knew she was crying again. It was his fault that she was so miserable. He'd hurt this brave, defiant girl just as he hurt everyone close to him. Cutter cursed under his breath.

Before he thought of what he was doing, Cutter pulled

her roughly into his arms. She stood stiff and resistant to his embrace, but he stroked her hair comfortingly.

"You did only what you had to do. We could never have stopped him from taking Ruth if you had not intervened. What you did was very brave, a sign that you are a true Kentucky woman."

"Truly?" She raised her tearstained face to look at him, those beautiful blue eyes made luminous by the unshed tears filling them.

Looking into those eyes, Cutter was very conscious of her body pressed tightly against his, and the fact that it was covered only by a thin cotton nightgown. Unable to resist he pulled her tighter against him. "Truly. You saved Ruth's life."

She stiffened against him, bracing her hands against his chest. "I am surprised you care about that. I would think you are more concerned about the loss of your property."

Cutter couldn't understand what she was talking about. "My property?"

"Don't act like you truly care about Reuben's or Ruth's personal safety. All you care about is that I saved you the loss of your slave," Emily said as she pulled loose from him. "I cannot believe that I took a man's life merely to save you some money."

"You are apparently laboring under several misconceptions about my life," Cutter said coldly, angry that she'd managed to get under his defenses once again.

He'd almost done something they would both regret. He wasn't sure who made him angrier: Emily or himself. He knew only that he'd had enough of Miss Emily Keating's sharp tongue.

"Ruth and Reuben are no slaves. I freed them when my mother brought them here. I did not think it right to ask them to risk their lives for nothing. It was their choice to stay on in my employ."

"Oh."

For a moment he thought he had effectively silenced her, but then she raised flashing eyes to his face again and opened her mouth to speak. Cutter could think of only one thing that would shut her up.

He pulled her roughly into his arms again and pressed his lips hard to hers. It was something he had longed to do since the day they first met.

Had it been only two days ago?

He wanted to silence her. He wanted to prove to her that she needed a man, that she could not live without one. He wanted her.

What began as punishment ended as a caress. He could not stop himself from testing the moist depths of her mouth with his tongue. He could not stop his hand from moving to caress her cheek. When she returned his kiss and a low moan escaped her, he knew he was lost.

Cutter buried himself in the taste of her mouth, in the feel of her body pressed against him. There was nothing in the world but the two of them.

A man could drown in such sweetness.

"Stephen! What is the meaning of this?" His mother's outraged voice brought him back to earth.

Lifting his lips from hers, Cutter was amused to see Emily flush with embarrassment at being caught in his arms. When she abruptly pulled herself loose and strode away with her head held high, he could only admire the picture of dignity she presented despite her bare feet and stained nightgown.

She did not even look at his mother as they passed in the cornfield. Cutter wished he could ignore his mother that easily, but instead he folded his arms across his chest and waited for her to reach his side.

"It is high time you took yourself a wife if you are reduced to seducing unattractive bluestockings."

"Emily is far from unattractive," Cutter said, staring after her.

His mother would not be ignored and waved a finger under his nose. "Stephen, do not dare interfere with that girl. I will not have it."

Cutter turned to look at his mother and was surprised to see her mouth pinched tight with anger.

"Interfere? Whatever do you mean, Mother?"

"You know very well what I mean. She is here for one reason and one reason only: to prepare Tad for William and Mary. If you want a woman I know several eligible young women who would be happy to be your wife."

"No, Mother, no wife. Not ever again. You are right though; I have no right to dally with Emily. It won't happen again."

Walking away from his mother, Cutter didn't find it as easy to avoid the bitter regret the words left in him.

Emily's trembling legs carried her as far as her loft before giving out. Lying down on the hard mattress, she pressed her hand to her chest and felt the wild beating of her heart. She stared at the bare rafters above her, barely blinking, afraid to close her eyes.

Whenever she did she saw the dead body of the boy she'd shot lying in the cornfield. Despite her efforts, she could not stop the charge of memories. She remembered the cold rush of fear when the other Indian rose up, charging to kill her, and the warm spray of his blood on her foot. Worst of all, she could still feel Cutter's arms around her.

Holding up her hand, she noted that it was still trembling slightly. Emily wasn't sure what affected her more: the fact that she'd just killed a man, or Cutter's kiss.

Who was she fooling? Emily thought as she sat up and breathed in a ragged sigh. Cutter's kiss had nearly driven all thought of the Indian attack out of her head.

She bit her lip thoughtfully as she undid her braid and

began to brush her hair. She was grateful that Mrs. Clark was intent on berating Cutter first. Right now Emily was in no condition to handle a confrontation with her; but there would be a confrontation, she was certain.

The older woman would eventually find her way to set Emily straight. Her sour expression spoke volumes about her disapproval when she had discovered Emily in her son's embrace.

Not that Emily exactly approved herself. She couldn't deny there was something between them, but that didn't mean she had to like it. She hated the loss of her control. She hated being so attracted to a man who despised her. He made his disapproval and disdain obvious. She felt the same way about him, Emily told herself fiercely. Still, Emily had never felt such a strong physical reaction to a man before.

Just the thought of Cutter's arms around her, his lips hot on hers, made Emily's stomach feel queer. The sensation was unfamiliar. She wasn't sure what caused it.

It was not as if she hadn't been kissed before. When she was younger some of her father's students had thought to gain her father's approval by courting her, and as she grew older one professor had sought to gain himself a second wife and secretary all in one neat package.

Then there was Nelson.

Her kisses had numbered fewer than a dozen, but Emily determined them sufficient evidence, combined with Nelson's betrayal, that she had no need of a man. The quick pecks, the sloppy tributes, the awkward fumbling left her cold and often irritated with the bother. Only Nelson's flight with her dowry and her father's trust had left her hot.

Nelson had insisted on treating her like a lady. He'd barely kissed her lips, rarely held her hand, never embraced her. She'd been so young, so foolish; she'd thought it was out of respect.

Although she thought him handsome and was flattered by his declarations of love, now that she knew what it felt like to want a man, Emily knew she'd never really wanted Nelson. All these years after his betrayal it was a relief to discover that final truth.

Now she finally understood why some women were willing to sell themselves into the bondage of marriage on the strength of a few kisses. Until today she'd never imagined what attraction there was between a man and a woman, but now Emily's imagination was filled with fevered images.

Cutter's embrace had been nothing like those others. Even now, after she'd been rejected by the man and humiliated by his mother, the simple memory of his touch set off a quivering response in her body that left her lightheaded. If she'd thought the spark ignited between them with a simple look was unsettling, then the effect of his touch was enough to change her world.

Emily's brush snagged a tangle in her hair. The sharp pain brought her back to reality.

"Change your world, indeed," Emily said out loud to inject the proper amount of scorn for the idea. "Maybe for some silly girl with thought for nothing but gaining a sweetheart. For a fool like that, a kiss might change her world, but surely not for Emily Keating."

Emily Keating knew better than to fall for any man's smooth words and sweet kisses, she told herself vehemently, and savagely brushed through the tangle. She'd learned that bitter lesson from Nelson, even if now she should thank him for jilting her. She knew it was only another way for a man to control a woman. Stephen Cutright was just like every other man she'd known.

No, that wasn't right. Cutter was as different from Nelson as two men could be. He didn't treat her like a lady. He treated her like a woman. Cutter never delivered smooth words.

It was laughable even to accuse him of being a smooth

talker. If anything, he'd done his best to drive her away with his words, and Emily, fool that she was, had fallen into his arms instead.

And his kiss had not been sweet. *Sweet* implied innocence, and there'd been nothing innocent about Cutter's kiss. *Sweet* was not a word Emily would ever use for Cutter. No, his kiss tempted, all passion and heat.

Heat. Yes, that was definitely the word. She could still feel his strong hands on her waist, their heat fairly burning through the thin cotton of her nightgown, the gentle caress of his fingertips on her face leaving a trail of fire she could still feel. For the first time in her life, Emily knew what it felt like to be a woman, to be wanted.

It felt wonderful.

Emily touched her lips, then felt the tender spot on her chin where his whiskers had scraped her. She'd always preferred the look of a clean-shaven man, thinking it made him look neater and more presentable.

Her former fiancé had been very presentable. Presentable didn't seem such an important thing for a man to be. This morning Cutter had looked anything but presentable. Cutter's unshaven jaw only made his sensual mouth more attractive. She felt her own lips curve into a smile as she remembered the way that mouth had felt on hers.

Then she remembered the smile he'd worn just before she turned away. Emily had seen that self-satisfied look on a man's face before, and she knew exactly what it meant. It was the look of a man who'd just won.

A heat that had nothing to do with passion flushed her face at that memory. Emily wouldn't put it past Cutter to use whatever weapon he could to prove his point that she couldn't do without a man.

If an Indian attack wouldn't do it, then the weak nature of a woman probably would, at least in his mind, Emily thought scornfully. He probably thought he'd already proven it, just because she'd been fool enough to fall into his arms.

Well, she would not allow him that satisfaction for long, Emily promised herself as she brushed her hair with renewed vigor. It had been only one kiss, and she would make sure there were no more. He might think that kiss proved she was nothing but a weak woman, but she would prove him wrong. She would.

Emily used the bucket of cold water she'd hauled up to the loft the night before to scrub off all traces of the morning's activities. She scrubbed off the mud, blood, and war paint. She scrubbed until her skin tingled, but she couldn't remove the memory of Cutter's lips on hers.

Time would take care of that, Emily promised herself. She'd gotten over Nelson quickly enough, and they'd been engaged. Dressing in one of her high-necked gowns, she looked longingly at the buckskin clothes hanging on the pegs by her bed, but she knew the image she needed to present today, and that image required a dress.

By the time she walked out of the cabin in search of breakfast and her pupil, Emily felt sure she was every inch the spinster teacher Mrs. Clark had hired. A deliberate message for Cutter—and herself.

Holding her head high, she swept across the dogtrot between the cabins and ducked through the doorway of the kitchen. It wasn't until she entered the kitchen and finally allowed herself to breathe that Emily realized no one had witnessed her performance except two hunting dogs asleep in the shade.

That's all right, Emily thought, and tilted her chin at a confident angle. *Begin as you mean to go on.* Sooner or later Stephen Cutright would see her. Then he would know exactly who he was dealing with. She was not some young miss whose head could be turned by a mere kiss.

The kitchen was hot already, even though it was still early in the day. Ruth bent over the little black iron stewpot that hung on a swinging iron arm attached to the stone fireplace and stirred its contents. Straightening, she wiped her face with the back of her hand. When Emily's foot scraped across the stoop, Ruth gave a small cry of fear.

Turning around, Ruth pressed her hand to her throat and managed to give Emily a weak smile. "Oh, Miss Emily, you shouldn't sneak up on a body like that."

Emily smiled weakly. "I'm sorry. I didn't mean to, but I expect we're all a bit jumpy after this morning."

"I'm glad to see you, miss, although not so glad as I was this morning when you brought that gun out. I wanted to thank you for helping me this morning. I hate to think what might've happened if you hadn't been there."

"I'm sure Mr. Cutright or Mr. McGee would have seen to your safety. They seem to revel in violence," Emily said serenely. "They saved Reuben, after all."

"That they did," Ruth said, and her eyes filled with tears. "I think I would rather have died than to live without him, miss."

"How is he?" Emily asked, but she barely heard Ruth's detailed account of how she'd bandaged her man and ordered him to rest.

For the first time in her life, Emily wondered what it was like to care so much about someone else that you'd rather die than live without him. She'd once thought she was in love with Nelson, yet she hadn't mourned his loss greatly. The memory of Cutter's arms around her and his lips on hers rose unbidden in her mind.

Unwilling to think about that any further, Emily waited for Ruth to pause and quickly asked, "Have you seen Tad? I think it's time we started our lessons."

"He's in the barn, seeing to the chores he ignored this morning. Then he'll be at your disposal."

The sound of Cutter's deep voice behind her made Emily's heart race. He'd only surprised her, she told herself, just the way she'd startled Ruth. That was all it was.

Emily took a deep breath to calm herself and then turned to face him.

He leaned against the doorframe. She'd never noticed before how broad his shoulders were; they seemed to fill the doorway and block the light. His large hands held a long rifle in front of him with a casual grace. She couldn't help staring at the gun and the long, tapered fingers that held it. She couldn't help remembering the way those hands had felt on her body.

"Is something wrong, Miss Keating?"

The mockery in his voice drew Emily's gaze to his face. He'd shaved, but the lack of a beard didn't make him any more presentable. The lean lines of his tanned face and too-long hair, not to mention the buckskin clothes, still made him look like the wild frontiersman he was.

She'd never seen a man who could stand so still and yet seem poised for action. Emily couldn't picture him in the formal parlor she'd owned back in Virginia, but she'd never forget the sight of him standing over the body of the Indian he'd killed to protect her.

"Miss Keating?"

"What?" Emily shook her head in a futile attempt to clear it. She couldn't allow the man to distract her from her purpose. "I'm sorry; my mind was wandering."

"You look disapproving." He lifted an eyebrow and gave her a questioning look. "Have I done something to offend you?"

"I don't know why you trouble yourself about that now," Emily said loftily. "You seem to have gone out of your way to offend me, sir, and it never bothered you before, Mr. Cutright."

"Can you not call me Cutter?"

The note of annoyance in his voice was music to Emily's ears. She needed to keep him annoyed with her, for her own protection, until she overcame this unreasoning attraction to him.

"It wouldn't be seemly," Emily said in her best school-teacher voice. Out of the corner of her eye she saw Ruth looking at the two of them with a broad smile on her face. Why, Emily didn't know, but blessedly the woman stayed out of it.

"Seemly or not, I would like you to use my name when you talk to me," Cutter said in that soft voice that sent shivers down her spine. "Call me Cutter."

Soft voice or not, Emily didn't like his tone. When would he learn she didn't take orders from him? *"Mr. Cutright* is your name."

The smile disappeared from his face, and Emily was glad. It was harder to resist him when he smiled, harder to remember what her purpose was here.

"Not in Kentucky it isn't. Here I'm known as Cutter." His voice was firm, as if he were speaking to a dull child. It irked Emily to no end.

"If you say so, Mr. Cutright," Emily said, just to needle him, and then smiled sweetly.

"I had something to give you, but now I'm not so sure I want to," he said as he stepped inside the room.

That single step brought him closer to Emily, too close for comfort. He smelled of pine needles and soap, a combination she'd never thought could be so heady. Simply breathing it in made her feel light-headed. Standing this close to him forced her to look up to meet his gaze, a disadvantage Emily wasn't used to, and she didn't like it.

"That is your choice," Emily said and shrugged. "I do not know that I'd want something from you."

It was a lie.

There were many things she wanted from him, even though she knew they would only hurt her. Eager to escape his company and regain her composure, Emily nodded at Ruth and moved out the door. She couldn't prove her point if she kept acting like a lovesick schoolgirl, Emily admonished herself.

She'd never needed a man in her life, and she certainly didn't need Stephen Cutright, even if he was more attractive than any man had a right to be. The sooner she had that straight in her head, the better, Emily thought, and breathed in the cooler air outside the kitchen, grateful to be away from Cutter.

Chapter 5

"Emily, wait."

She should have known escape wouldn't be that easy.

Emily stopped in the middle of the dogtrot. She closed her eyes and took another deep breath before turning around to face him. It wasn't until she saw the anxious expression on his face that she realized he'd called her by her first name. That wouldn't do at all. She couldn't allow herself to believe he might actually care about her.

"It's Miss Keating," she said in her frostiest voice. *Begin as you mean to go on,* she reminded herself. She certainly did not mean to get any more familiar with Stephen Cutright.

Handsome or not.

Her tone must have finally gotten her message across, because he clenched his jaw against whatever he'd meant to say. His eyes flashed his anger at her loud and clear, even without words.

Emily allowed herself a small smile of triumph. It was good to know she could unsettle him as easily as he unsettled her. "You wanted something, Mr. Cutright."

"I want you to call me Cutter," he said through gritted teeth.

"Well, we both want things we can't have, now, don't we?" Emily answered roundly. "Maybe if you saw fit to help me achieve my goal, I'd see my way to calling you the name you'd prefer."

The woman wouldn't give up, Cutter thought, and ground his teeth together in frustration. She was worse than a dog with a bone. Worse than his mother when it came to coming back to a subject he thought long closed.

After this morning she should have realized a lone woman wouldn't survive in the harsh Kentucky wilderness. With that thought, Cutter realized what had put the bee in her bonnet today, and it wasn't the Indian attack. "Are you angry about this morning?"

"Angry?"

Emily gave him a wide-eyed, innocent look that didn't fool Cutter for a minute, even though it still aggravated him.

"Why would I be angry?" she asked. "You saved my life, after all."

"Maybe you're angry because I kissed you," he said, and almost grinned at the way she stiffened. Oh, yeah, he was on to something here. Unable to resist taking it further, he gave her a long, slow smile. "Or maybe you're angry because I stopped."

"Angry?" A crease appeared in her forehead and she gave him a puzzled look. "No, I wouldn't say my feelings were that strong. I am a lady, but I never expected you to act like a gentleman, Mr. Cutright, so why should I be angry when you act like a lout?"

Oh, she was just enough like his mother to raise his temperature, and just different enough to make it interesting, Cutter thought as he narrowed his eyes.

"A lout?" he asked softly, and took a step closer to her.

"Yes." There was a slight tremble in her voice. Her eyes

blazed a challenge he was almost afraid to meet. Almost. Cutter had never been able to resist a challenge.

"I suppose a *lady* might think that," Cutter said.

He took another step closer. She sidled away until her back was against the cabin wall. Cutter put a hand to the wall over her shoulder, effectively trapping her in place. He didn't touch her, but they stood so close the delicate scent of lavender tickled his nose.

How could she smell like lavender? he thought irrationally.

"Are you a lady, Emily?" He leaned closer and breathed the words into her ear. He could almost feel the heat from her body. The memory of that body pressed against him, with nothing more than a thin cotton nightgown and his worn buckskins between them, filled Cutter with the aching need to pull her into his arms and punish her with his lips.

Cutter drew in his breath slowly and tried to push that thought away. Thoughts like that made the game Cutter was playing dangerous.

Very dangerous.

He couldn't afford to want this woman. It would only complicate his life, and Cutter wanted things simple. He needed things simple. He needed to drive her away, for her sake, for his sake. "You didn't act like a lady this morning, Emily."

She raised her face to his. "Miss Keating, to you."

She had ripe, full lips—lips that were meant to be kissed, Cutter thought. What was a schoolteacher doing with lips like that? How could he have ever thought her prim and proper?

"A gentleman would not remind me," Emily said quickly.

"Ah, but I never claimed to be a gentleman, now, did I?"

Her skin was creamy smooth, with a sprinkling of freckles

across her nose from the sun. As he stared at her Emily blushed. Fascinated by the flush of pink that traveled across her cheeks, he traced her cheekbone with his thumb.

"What was it you wanted to give me, Mr. Cutright?" she asked in a choked voice.

Cutter couldn't revel in his effect on her because after touching her he wasn't sure he could speak at all, but there was something he needed to know.

"What do you want from me, Emily?" His voice was so hoarse Cutter scarcely recognized it as his own. He wanted to kiss her so badly he could almost taste it. This morning she'd tasted dark and smoky, like corn whiskey; he wondered what lavender tasted like. "Did you want me to kiss you again?"

"No," she said in a voice so soft he barely heard her.

"I don't believe you. Come now, admit it, Emily. You need me to kiss you."

She swayed toward him. Just as Cutter was ready to pull her into his arms, she suddenly seemed to realize what she was doing and instead stamped her foot down hard on his. "I do not need you, and I certainly do not need anything you can give me."

Angered by the unfamiliar frustration, Cutter almost welcomed the pain in his foot. That would remind him not to be lulled by her again. The woman was a menace. He would do better to stay away from this source of frustration. "That's not true, and you know it. Don't tell me you're a liar too, Emily Keating."

"You're right; I need you for one thing: my land grant."

When those sapphire eyes flashed at him, Cutter had to admit she was beautiful, not that he'd ever tell her that. Cutter shifted his weight and almost dropped the long rifle he held in his hand—the rifle he'd forgotten about until now.

"There is one other thing," he said and gave her a cocky grin.

"No!" Emily said and took a cautious step backward. "Only a lout would force himself on a woman."

Cutter closed the small space between them with one step and took her by the arm. "I've never forced a woman, Emily. I don't have to, and I certainly won't force you. Just don't lie to me. You want me to kiss you, but that isn't what I have for you now. Although if you want the other all you have to do is ask."

"You can count on the fact that I won't be asking." Emily lifted her chin defiantly. "Now loose my arm, Mr. Cutright. I need to go find my student."

"First I have to give you this."

Cutter had to give her credit; she never flinched, and she didn't run away even after he released her. She stood her ground, trembling slightly, but she stood it. She even took the long rifle with only a slight stagger from its weight.

"You proved this morning you know what to do with it, and this spring has already been dangerous enough. We need every rifle ready. If you insist on living here, then I will have to insist you pull your weight."

"I will do that, Mr. Cutright; never fear."

With that she raised her pert little nose in the air and turned on her heel to march away. It wasn't until she disappeared into the stable that Cutter realized he hadn't proven to her she had no place out here, as he intended. Instead she'd distracted him from his purpose. Again.

In an attempt to push Emily from his mind and forget the unsettling effect she had on him, Cutter worked in the cornfield until the sun hung low in the sky and the trees pointed long, distended shadows across the field.

"I never took you for a farmer, Cutter, but you seem to have the knack for it."

Cutter grimaced in pain as his aching muscles protested his turn to face Mack. The woodsman had one foot resting on one of the stumps that lined the cornfield as he leaned an elbow on his knee. Mack wore an amused expression on his face. From his casual stance, Mack appeared to have been watching Cutter for a while.

"Isn't that what we're doing this for, so we can all be farmers?" Cutter wiped his brow with the back of his hand and looked down in surprise at the blisters on his palm. It must have been a long time since he had last worked in the field. There always seemed to be something else that needed doing.

"Not me, and I never would have thought it of you, until now," Mack said with a shake of his head. "I wouldn't believe it if I hadn't seen it with my own eyes."

"With Reuben bedridden for a few days someone has to take care of this. Last time I checked you enjoyed corn bread as much as the next man," Cutter said, and set aside the hoe to approach Mack. "I take it you found no sign of others?"

"No hide nor hair," Mack said. "I figure those two braves were just scouts, or maybe out hunting on their own. I checked with the Butlers and the Smiths and they hadn't seen or heard anything. I told them to keep an eye out just the same."

"As should we," Cutter said grimly, fingering the long rifle that was never far from his side. "I wish we had more men here. I would rest easier. We are so few and our neighbors so far away."

"That's the way you wanted it, and you know more men aren't always the answer. Remember that stations with more men than yours have fallen."

"Yes, and the last Indian sign we saw for months was in March. That is what really makes me nervous." Cutter scanned the trees that surrounded the field, but all was peaceful. There was nothing there to cause this unsettled feeling in his belly, but that feeling had saved his life more than once, and Cutter had learned not to dismiss it.

"Either there's action somewhere's else, or they're saving up for something big." Mack nodded.

"And we both know there is nowhere else. We've only got a handful of stations still manned in Kentucky." Cutter caressed the cool metal of his rifle barrel as he thought. "Something is going to happen. I feel it in my gut."

"We could always go to Boonesborough," Mack reminded him. "Stout walls and more guns. Probably be safer—especially for the women and the boy."

"No, I didn't come here to be cooped up in a fort. I will make my home where I choose, and not let it be dictated to me by a few Indians." Surprised at his own vehemence, Cutter looked away from Mack and back at the station. It was quiet. A lone drift of smoke rose above the kitchen where Ruth worked, and Cutter watched it until it disappeared into the blue sky.

He didn't want to leave his home, but he couldn't shake the feeling that they lived on the edge of danger. It had always been true of Kentucky, but this year promised to be worse than the others. He could feel it. He didn't mind the feeling for himself, but too many depended on him now. They looked to him for protection. He didn't like that feeling much either.

"I thought you'd see it that way," Mack said quietly. "But what of the women and the boy?"

"If my mother would go . . ." Cutter sighed just thinking about arguing with his mother again. "She won't, so we have no choice but to guard them as best we can."

"Can't say as I blame her." Mack shrugged. "I don't fancy staying cooped up in the fort all the time either. But we're not so few as all that even with Reuben laid up. Emily is a fair shot, as she proved this morning."

"Why do you want her for a wife?"

The question had burned in Cutter's gut all day and was part of the reason he'd half killed himself working the field. He hoped to work out his anger and frustration with one Miss Emily Keating. It hadn't helped. Now in addition to his aching head he had sore muscles and raw calluses from the unfamiliar work.

"Why marry Emily?" Mack said in surprise. "Why not?"

"She is nothing like the other girls you've chased in the years I've known you."

"That's exactly why." Mack took off his hat and ran his fingers through his sun-streaked blond hair. "It's no secret I'm attracted to a pretty face and well-placed curves, but not one of those girls made me wish to spend another minute with them once I'd gotten what I wanted. Emily's not like that at all. She's just different."

"That she is, but she has her faults just the same. She has a sharp tongue and is stubborn as a mule."

"That's my Emily, all right," Mack said with a wide grin. "Never a dull moment."

"That's what I'm finding out," Cutter grumbled. He didn't like the way Mack called her "my Emily." It didn't sit right at all. "I can see already I will have no peace with that woman about. Emily Keating has only one thought in her head: to get her land grant."

"She wants her home; surely you of all people can understand that," Mack said quietly. "You just said you would not let Indians drive you from yours."

"What I understand is that she's a fool for thinking she can make a go of it alone. We were just talking about the danger to us here with three grown men."

"She's no fool, is Emily Keating," Mack answered roundly. "I believe she knows in her heart she cannot do it alone, but she does not want to admit it. She wants that home more than anything, and that's why I think she'll eventually come around."

"Come around," Cutter laughed at the thought of Emily Keating ever coming around to another person's way of thinking. "I wouldn't hold my breath waiting. She's stubborn as a mule."

"Determination is not a bad thing in a woman making her home here," Mack said quietly. "Some of those pretty little things at the fort wouldn't have lasted through this morning, let alone stood their ground and fought like a man."

Emily had stood her ground, Cutter admitted grudgingly. He remembered the way she'd looked, her white nightgown barely hiding her full figure as she raised the long rifle to her shoulder and took aim. He'd seen the fear in her eyes, but she'd held her ground and been dead on the mark.

He shook his head. He couldn't admire a woman, and most certainly could not admire Emily Keating. That woman could spot any weakness in an instant, and he could not afford to let her under his guard again. That was more dangerous than any Indian attack.

"Yes, she is a good shot, but she is not a man, though I think she would like to be."

"You don't understand Emily at all," Mack said with a shake of his head. "She doesn't want to be a man. She already thinks she's better than a man."

"You would marry a woman so full of herself?" Cutter asked incredulously.

"I would marry Emily, for it is no false conceit," Mack said. "She is everything I've said and has a quick brain too. I couldn't stand a woman with no thoughts in her head and no plans for the future."

"You may have the right of it, my friend. I don't have much use for empty-headed fools, be they man or woman, but it just may be this woman has too many thoughts in her head for her own good, or yours."

"Nah, I'll take Emily over any other woman in all of Kentucky for a good wife. Maybe you should consider looking for a wife yourself, since you're so taken with farming," Mack teased him.

"The woman who can tame me hasn't been born yet,

and if I chose to marry it certainly wouldn't be Emily Keating," Cutter said with a shake of his head at Mack's foolishness.

"Well, you'd best find a way to deal with her, because she lives under your roof."

"That may be, but it is you who will have to live with her and you who will have to bed her," Cutter said and grinned at his friend to hide the strange twisting in his chest at the thought of Mack touching Emily.

Mack studied him for a moment and then shrugged.

"Not anytime soon. She won't have me, but I'm counting on your sweet temper to convince her differently," he said and slapped Cutter hard on the back.

"What do you mean?" Cutter asked stiffly.

"I figure after spending some time with you she will beg me to take her away."

"You must love her," Cutter said with a shake of his head. "Either that or that blow to the head this winter addled your brains. There's no other reason for it."

"No, I don't love her," Mack said as he stroked his chin thoughtfully. "But I respect her, and that's not a bad way to begin a marriage."

"Spoken like a fool who knows nothing of marriage or women," Cutter said with a half laugh. "Women care nothing for respect."

"That is where you're wrong," Mack said softly. "In Emily's case, anyway. She is out to gain your respect one way or another. What do you think this morning was about?"

"She risked herself for my respect?" Cutter asked, angry at her foolishness. "Then she is a bigger fool than I thought. I will not have her play such games with the safety of my people and my station again."

Cutter thrust the hoe at Mack. "Here, why don't you try your hand at farming for a bit? Who knows, you might find you have a knack for it."

Mack took the tool with a pained look and held it out

from his body as if it were a long-dead skunk. "Where are you going?"

"To have a conversation with Miss Emily Keating," Cutter said with determination. "I won't have her playing games with our safety. She needs to learn a proper appreciation of the dangers here."

"Cutter, when will you learn?" Mack called after him. "I think you need to learn a proper appreciation for the dangers of dealing with Emily Keating."

Chapter 6

Cutter ignored his friend's teasing warning and sought out Emily. He found her engaged in Tad's lesson. Angry as he was, he paused in the doorway to listen in. He told himself he wanted only to see if she could at least do her job well.

"I don't see how none of this will be any good to me," Tad said and pushed the book in front of him across the table.

Cutter recognized the look of frustration on his son's face. It was the same way he felt whenever he had dealings with Emily Keating.

"You don't see how *any* of this will *do* you any good," Emily corrected him. "You're wrong, you know."

"I want to learn to shoot and hunt and track," Tad said with a sigh. "That's what's important in Kentucky."

"You're right. Those things are important," Emily said with a nod. "But no knowledge is wasted."

"What good is Latin and Greek going to do me here?" Tad scoffed. "I'd be better off learning Shawnee."

"It is a proven fact that the more languages you know the easier it is to learn another," Emily said in a calm voice. "Once you learn the mechanics of language and gain a basic understanding of grammar and structure, I imagine you will find it easier to learn another language, say Shawnee."

"Geometry and logic, what about them?" Tad asked. The stubborn expression on his face reminded Cutter of Imogene Clark. "They just give me a headache."

"Geometry is one of the skills your father uses when he surveys the land. Logic is used in everyday life, from dealing with the Indians to where you lay your traps when you're hunting."

"But—"

"She has the right of it, son," Cutter said and stepped into the cabin. "But none of it matters a lick. She is your teacher and you will attend your lessons and listen to what she has to say. She deserves proper respect from you. I don't want to hear any more lip from you. Understand?"

"Yes, Pa," Tad said, and gave him that familiar sullen look Cutter had come to expect from the boy. Cutter didn't know what to do with the child most of the time. That was why Tad was better left to his grandmother's care.

"Good. Now I think you've had enough for the day. Why don't you go help Mack in the cornfield? There's still some hoeing to do and it's almost time for supper."

"Good-bye, Tad," Emily said softly. "You did well today. I think we will get along just fine."

"Yes'm," Tad said without looking her in the eye and shuffled out the door.

Emily followed Tad to the door and watched him for a moment before quietly closing the heavy wood door. When she turned around, Cutter was taken aback by the blaze of anger in her eyes.

"You are the most despicable man I've ever met. It is one thing for you to belittle me and treat me with no respect. I, at least, have the ability to fight back. But I will not have you treat Tad like that."

"I won't have my son be a whiner, and I won't allow him to be disrespectful."

"He was not whining," Emily said and stood before him with her hands on her hips. "He was doing what any normal, healthy boy would do, and that is complain because he is cooped up inside to undertake meaningless tasks while life seems to pass him by outside."

"They are not meaningless tasks. If they are then I am apparently wasting good money on you," Cutter said and raised one eyebrow.

"I know they are not meaningless, and you know they are not meaningless, but they are meaningless to a twelve-year-old boy. I was making some headway with him until you came in and ruined everything."

"I suppose you consider it progress to accept lip from a boy you're supposed to be teaching?"

"He wasn't giving me lip; he was questioning. I want to teach him to question things. It is useless to learn things simply by rote, because then you will never be able to adapt your lessons to fit changing circumstances."

Cutter watched in fascination as the spinster teacher changed before his eyes into a fierce wildcat. Her creamy skin was flushed from her temper, and Cutter could not help but think passion became her. Just the thought left him tongue-tied, but Emily was not through with him yet.

"I happen to think the best way to teach a child respect is to show it to him, not bully it into him."

Stung by her accusation and its truth, Cutter ground his teeth together. "I do not bully my son. I am strict, but that is important on the frontier. I cannot have my child run wild and endanger himself, as your father apparently did."

"You are a bully! Strict would not matter if you showed the child some love. Every time he looks to you for affection you slap him down or push him away. You are a cold, hard man, Stephen Cutright.''

"No," he protested, surprised that her judgment hurt. It was the image he'd carefully cultivated, after all. It was the way of life he'd chosen for himself, knowing it hurt too much to care. But he would not discuss that with Emily.

"It is not for you to judge my relationship with my son. I am surprised that a scholar such as yourself would jump to such a hasty conclusion. What can you know of it in such a short time?"

"I know he worships the ground you walk on and you can scarcely be civil to him," she said with a snarl, eyes flashing. "You order him about as if he were a lesser being and constantly belittle him. That is not a relationship; it is a dictatorship."

"It is neither your job nor your place to be concerned with my care for my son," Cutter said. "Your concern is with his mind, not his heart."

"As his teacher it is my job to be concerned about both his mind and his heart, for I believe they are one and the same. A hard heart can do as much damage as a thick head—something you would do well to consider yourself," she said. "Don't you remember when you were a boy how it felt to have your pride crushed?"

"Pride or false bravado? I think you have trouble telling the difference between them." Cutter felt some satisfaction in reminding her that she had faults as well.

"No, it is only men who cannot tell the difference. It is men who take foolish risks for the sake of their pride."

Emily's scorn for men was evident in her belittling tone.

"Foolish risks! My God, woman, that is exactly what I came to discuss with you until you distracted me with your blather."

"Blather—" Emily protested. She picked up the heavy

book lying on the table, and for a moment Cutter thought she might use it to strike him.

"Silence, woman," he roared, angry at her for being the distraction she was and angry at himself for allowing her to break his control. "You will listen to me and then, God help me, I will listen to you. You took a foolish risk this morning."

"I saved Ruth," she said with that familiar, stubborn lift of her chin.

"Yes, you saved Ruth, but after you made your shot, did you think about what would happen then? What would have happened if Mack and I had not been there? Would you have shared Ruth's fate, or Reuben's? Or worse?"

"Surely among us we could have handled one lone warrior scarcely more than a boy?"

She was still defiant, but Cutter noted a hint of uncertainty in her voice that gave him confidence.

"You did not know there was only one more," Cutter said, daring her to defeat his logic this time. "You still do not know if there was a horde ready to descend on the station."

"If there had been a horde I could not have withstood them with only one rifle," Emily argued.

"That is where you're wrong," Cutter said vehemently, glad to at last be on firm ground. "My walls are built so one rifleman can withstand attack for some time. But by leaving the gates wide open and wasting your one shot you did not use your resources wisely. What do you suppose that taught your student, Miss Keating?"

Cutter was almost amused at the emotions he saw cross her expressive face. Finally she bit her lower lip and gave him a stiff nod.

"I admit I was wrong to rush to Ruth's defense without evaluating the situation, but I think it was wrong only because I endangered others. I contend that I can and I will risk my own neck, because it is mine to risk." Her voice was meek, but her flashing eyes showed the depth of her anger.

Cutter felt his own anger return full-force. Emily Keating just would not admit she could not handle herself in the wilderness. She showed an unwarranted eagerness to put herself at risk. He would not tolerate it. "You will not risk your neck here, because I am responsible for it."

"I am my own person. You are not responsible for me," Emily shouted. "I do not understand why you are so dedicated to protecting me when I obviously do not want or need your protection. You take risks every day when you go off on your own to hunt or survey. Why is that different?"

"It is different because I am a man," Cutter said through clenched teeth. He would not get involved in another shouting match with this woman.

"A real man would not need to prove his manhood by dominating others."

"A real woman knows her place." Cutter forced his hands into fists behind his back and resisted the urge to shake some sense into her.

"You did not seem to question my femininity this morning," Emily reminded him.

Cutter did not need to be reminded. He felt the attraction between them as if it were a living creature. The desire to touch her was strong.

He barely resisted the impulse to stroke her slender, graceful throat and kiss it at the base where a small, blue vein pulsed. And that mouth—it was driving him crazy. Just the thought of kissing her again made Cutter ache. "A real lady would never have brought that incident up so boldly."

"What you do not realize, Mr. Cutright, is that I can be both a lady and a woman. A real woman. You say you do not like a bold woman, but your actions say differently," she challenged him.

"I simply meant to comfort you. I certainly did not mean to get so carried away."

"Carried away? By such an unfeminine woman as myself?" She raised an eyebrow to give him a disdainful look. "You, sir, need to make up your mind whether I am a delicate female in need of protection or an amazon you need to avoid."

"I don't want to protect you," Cutter said through gritted teeth. "I just want to save myself the trouble of having to rescue you when you get into a bind."

"And just how does your embrace fit in with your brand of protection?"

He knew her lofty tones were deliberately chosen to antagonize him, but he also knew he needed to push her away before he lost his control and pulled her into his arms again. The memory of how she had felt when he held her only made the ache worse. He put a sneer on his face. "It has been a long time since I've been around a white woman. I'm sure it won't happen again."

Cutter steeled himself against the look of pain in her eyes. He told himself he didn't care about her feelings. Hell, he didn't have any feelings about her at all. He didn't even want to protect her, Cutter reminded himself; he just wanted to save himself the trouble of having to rescue her when she got into a mess.

"It most certainly will not," Emily said, only the slight tremble of her voice, and the hurt in her eyes, showing her emotional turmoil. "I will make sure of it."

That stung. It was one thing for him to decide he wanted nothing more to do with her, but Cutter would not allow a plain-faced spinster to reject *him* out of hand. "Will you, now?"

Cutter narrowed his gaze and took a step closer.

"Cutter . . ." His name was soft as silk on her lips and sent a shiver of desire down his spine. Those full lips were tantalizingly close.

"Yes, Emily?"

He didn't need to say her name, but he liked the sound of it. He liked the way she blushed when he said it. Her cheeks were a delicious shade of pink. He wanted to taste them.

"Cutter." She touched her upper lip with a nervous flick of her tongue that was nearly his undoing. "You said you weren't going to kiss me again?"

"What makes you think I am?" For once Cutter couldn't wait to hear what she had to say.

"The way you look at me."

She was nervous and obviously unsettled by him. Cutter liked it that way. It felt good to turn the tables on her. She unsettled him every hour of every day. "How do I look at you?"

"Like a starving man gazing into a baker's window."

Cutter didn't like that comparison one bit. It struck too close to the truth for his comfort. Suddenly he knew he needed to get away from her before he made another foolish mistake.

He forced out a laugh. He needed to make sure he wasn't tempted in the future. "Now that is a joke I can enjoy, Miss Keating, for we both know you are anything but a sweet confection."

The next morning Cutter's laughter echoed in her mind as Emily prowled around the kitchen. It upset her more than she wanted to admit that Cutter had nearly kissed her again, and she would have let him. The only thing that stopped him was his obvious dislike of her.

Not that she wanted him to like her, Emily thought as she stopped in front of the wide stone hearth and gazed at the red coals and the licking golden flames. It was too hot to stand by a fire, but the blaze drew her just as Cutter drew her. She wanted nothing to do with the man, but she couldn't stop the thrill of feminine excitement that filled her when a flicker of desire showed in his eyes.

He didn't like her.

He didn't respect her.

He wanted her.

She wanted him.

"Miss Keating."

Mrs. Clark's sharp voice brought her back to the moist heat of the kitchen—and reality. Emily turned away from the fire. "Yes?"

"Will you sit down, please? Your pacing is making my head spin."

Emily sat down at the puncheon table, opposite Mrs. Clark and Tad, to finish her breakfast. She rinsed down a mouthful of dry corn bread with some buttermilk. She wasn't fond of buttermilk, but at least it offered more flavor than the corn bread. She was fed up with corn bread. They ate it at every meal.

Corn bread, hominy grits, and corn mush. Some days Emily thought she might turn into an ear of corn if she ate one more bite of johnnycake.

"Why aren't you eating, Tad; are you ill?" Mrs. Clark's voice was sharp with concern.

When Emily looked up the older woman was touching the back of her hand against Tad's forehead, but the boy brushed her away with an irritated look.

"I feel fine, Grandma. I'm just not all that hungry."

"You are always hungry," Imogene said, worry creasing her forehead.

"I'm so sick of corn, Grandma. Can't we eat something else?"

"I know. We're all sick of corn, but your father doesn't have time to hunt for any fresh meat."

"Let me go hunt, Grandma. I can shoot a deer; I know I can." Tad's eyes were bright with excitement, and he

almost bounced off the bench. His grandmother paled
noticeably at his request.

"No. You have too much to do here. You have to work
with Miss Keating to make up for all the lost time with
your studies."

"Tad's right; we need some fresh meat. Maybe we can
take the boy out with us later," Mack said, stepping into
the kitchen and snatching a piece of johnnycake from
Emily's plate, giving her a wide grin in return. "What do
you think, Cutter?"

"No, Stephen!" Mrs. Clark turned pleading eyes to her
son. "Tad isn't to learn how to hunt. Don't take him out.
He needs to study."

"Pa, please." Tad stood up, almost reaching for his
father but apparently not summoning up enough nerve.
"I don't want to spend all my time studying. I want to
learn to hunt. I want to learn to shoot."

Emily saw the child's need for his father's love and
approval in Tad's eyes, but Cutter's voice and expression
were hard, with no sign of either.

"You heard your grandmother. You need to study."

Tad sat down again. His head hung low, with his too-
long hair falling over his face, but she saw his chin quiver
ever so slightly. He didn't look up again and carefully
shredded every last piece of corn bread on his plate.

Looking up at Cutter, Emily was surprised to see a look
of tenderness on the man's face as he watched his son.
She hadn't thought he cared for the boy at all. She wished
he would show the child some of that tenderness. It might
make Tad feel better.

Seeing Cutter's sensitive side didn't make her feel better
at all. It was easier to dislike him and believe him cold and
hard. She didn't want to think about how it would feel to
have him give her that tender look.

"We have no time for hunting today either, Mack,"
Cutter said, still looking at Tad, who wouldn't lift his head.

"We need to see to things around here, but maybe this afternoon we'll have some time to go down to the river and do some fishing. Would you like that, Tad?"

"Yes, sir." Tad lifted shining eyes and smiled at his father.

Cutter didn't smile back. Now his face was stern, as if he were afraid to show any affection for his son. Stephen Cutright was a puzzle that Emily had yet to solve. Maybe that was the attraction he held for her. Maybe once she understood him she would be free of this disturbing fascination.

"Good. First you have to work hard at your studies. I expect to hear you've made good progress with both Latin and mathematics."

"Yes, sir."

"Does that meet with your approval, Mother?"

"I suppose it won't hurt," Mrs. Clark said grudgingly. "I wouldn't mind a change from corn bread myself, although I would wish for something sweet, if I had my choice."

"There are some berry bushes near the best fishing spot; maybe Miss Keating would like to go along and pick some berries as well."

Still confused by what she saw on Cutter's face, Emily agreed without thinking. The last thing she wanted was to spend more time in Stephen Cutright's company, but just thinking about sweet, juicy berries made her mouth water.

Berries and fresh fish. A feast fit for a king.

Chapter 7

"You've been eating berries," Cutter said from behind Emily, startling her so she almost dropped the basket of berries she was holding.

In the distance locusts unreeled their eternal dry shrills under the summer sun. The sun glinted off the water. A trickle of perspiration slid down her neck and between her breasts. The scent of pine filled her nose.

She'd been watching him with his son, teaching the boy to cast and trail his line along the surface of the river. She'd seen Tad blossom under his father's attention, and she knew this afternoon was a time the boy would remember all his life. Watching them together made Emily wish for something she knew she could never have.

She did not want a husband, Emily had reminded herself as she turned back to her berry picking. All it took was the sound of Cutter's rich baritone to send a sliver of pleasure slicing through her and make her wonder why.

Turning slowly, Emily stared up at him. His green eyes glinted dangerously and he wore a crooked smile. His gaze drifted over her in a slow caress that made Emily very conscious of the fact that she'd undone the top buttons of her dress in the heat. She'd put on an older dress for berry picking, and suddenly the bodice felt too tight, making it hard to breathe. Emily's mind was blank, yet her senses worked overtime.

Her skin told of the humid valley air with only the dank breath of the wet limestone lining the riverbed offering relief. Her ears told of the gurgle of the fast water on rocks and the soughing of a breeze in the treetops. Her mouth told her of the sweet, rich taste of ripe berries. Her nose told her of the moldy odor of rotting leaves overlaid by the sickly sweet scent of overripe fruit.

Then there was Cutter.

His dark hair was pulled back in a queue, but a single unruly lock of hair hung low over his eyes, giving him a rakish look. He'd unlaced his shirt and splashed water on his face. Some tiny droplets of water still clung to his neck, and he brushed them away with the back of his hand without taking his eyes off Emily.

"How do they taste?"

Taking a step closer, he tucked a lock of her hair behind her ear, barely skimming her face with his fingers. That so light a touch, so casual a gesture, could send a wave of desire through her shocked Emily back to reality.

"They are nearly perfect. Almost past ripe. Sweet, heavy on the branch. They almost fall into my hands." Emily knew she was babbling, but she considered herself lucky to form words at all. It was merely the combination of too much sun and too many berries, she told herself. It was not Cutter's nearness that made her head spin like this.

"Can I taste?" He raised one eyebrow as he asked.

"If you like." Emily almost forgot to breathe as he took the basket from her hands and set it on the ground. Instead of taking a handful of the plump berries, as she expected, he bent his head and kissed her.

If Emily thought her senses were overloaded before, now they went beyond anything she'd ever experienced. Only now she cared nothing for the land and water around them. Now every sense was concentrated solely on Cutter, the way he felt, tasted, sounded, smelled. The only thing that mattered was Cutter.

His hands cupped her face, raising it up to his. His lips tasted and tempted until Emily opened herself to him, and his tongue teased and tangled with her own. His fingers found the pins holding her hair and quickly undid them. He ran his fingers through her hair and let it hang unbound around her shoulders.

Unable to resist touching him in return, Emily tentatively ran her hands up his chest, reveling in the feel of his rippling muscles beneath the deerskin. Her hands stopped, trembling, when the tips of her fingers reached the thick vein at the base of his neck that pulsed in tune with the wild beating of her own heart.

He sighed against her lips; Emily thought she heard her name, and then he released her.

When he stepped back his green eyes were dark with passion. He traced the line of her jaw with his forefinger and rubbed his thumb across her lower lip. Emily almost swayed back into his arms.

"Nearly perfect. Ripe. Sweet. Ready to fall into my hands." His voice held the hint of a smile.

The heavy warmth that filled Emily turned hot with anger.

He'd taken something special between them and made it seem cheap and tawdry. Tears stung behind her eyelids, but she would not let him see. He did not need to know that she felt this way only for him. He did not need to know the secrets of her heart.

"How dare you?" Her voice shook with emotion. Anger, she told herself.

"What did I dare?"

"You said you would not kiss me again," Emily reminded him, folding her arms across her chest in a desperate need to protect herself and to keep herself from reaching out to him.

"You were the one who offered me a taste."

The corners of his mouth twitched, irritating Emily. He was laughing at her.

"I thought you wanted a berry."

"Why satisfy myself with such a small fruit when a more tempting variety is so close at hand?"

Emily narrowed her gaze at him, unable to deny the gratification she felt at knowing she tempted him. Although she wanted the man to respect her, to acknowledge her worth as a person, it was satisfying to know that she pleased him as a woman. A warm glow filled her as she realized that she was not alone in the attraction she felt. He felt it too. It was not enough, but it was a start. A start to what, Emily did not dare dwell on.

"This fruit has sharper thorns than the other. You'd best remember that next time you are tempted. You might find the penalty too high."

"Maybe I think it is worth it," Cutter said softly to himself as he watched Emily march off, her basket of fruit in hand. He heard Tad's shrill voice as the boy showed her the fish he'd caught. Emily smiled at his son, and Cutter felt something twist painfully in his chest.

She cared for his son. That was good. He knew the boy had little enough love in his life. It wasn't Tad's fault that his father was flawed, that his mother was dead. Watching Emily rub a smudge off Tad's face with a gesture as timeless as motherhood, Cutter wondered if she cared for him. A rustling in the trees made him turn away from the touching scene, instantly alert.

"If I'd been an Indian you'd be dead," Mack said with a low chuckle. "It's a good thing I'm here to watch your back."

Cutter flushed with guilt and wondered what his friend had seen. He knew Mack didn't love Emily, but the other man did intend to marry her. Just two days ago he'd been eager to help his friend.

Now thinking about Mack claiming the sweet lips he'd just tasted filled Cutter with anger and sadness. In the few days he'd known her, Emily Keating was making Cutter do things he'd never done before and rethink his entire life. It was not a comfortable thought.

Twice he'd kissed her. Twice he'd betrayed his friend. He hadn't gone to Emily for that purpose; he'd only wanted to check on her safety. Instead he found himself seducing the plain spinster hired to teach his son.

Worse, Cutter feared it would happen again. He wanted her. No matter that he knew she was a virgin destined to be someone else's wife. No matter that he had vowed never to marry again. He wanted her and was helpless to stop that wanting. All his life Cutter had struggled for control of his life, his body, and his emotions. One smile from Emily Keating broke through those restraints, and he didn't know what to do about it.

He would think on it later.

"It's time to go back. I don't want my mother to worry overmuch about Tad." He knew his mother feared for Tad every time the boy stepped outside the station gates. She coddled the boy too much for wilderness life, but Cutter knew there was little else in her life to give her joy. Let her find joy in her grandson; God knew she would not have it of her son.

"Cutter." Mack laid a hand on his shoulder, stopping Cutter in place. "You're not dead, you know. Maybe you should try living a little."

Tossing a berry over his shoulder, Mack walked over to join Tad and Emily. He whispered something to Emily that made her laugh. Her laugh was rich, deep, and throaty. A lump formed in Cutter's throat and he had to look away.

* * *

That night after supper Cutter gathered his family around the fire. He didn't want to be alone tonight. For the first time in years he dreaded his own company. He didn't want to think. He didn't know what to think. He knew only one thing for sure: Mack was right. He wasn't dead.

Cutter was never more aware of that fact than when Emily was near. The firelight made her hair glow around her face. The flames danced in her eyes. When she moved he caught the faint scent of lavender, but that might only have been his imagination. His imagination seemed to work overtime when it came to Emily Keating. That was another reason he didn't want to be alone this night.

He tried to tell himself his reaction to Emily was natural. She was the first woman who'd lived in his home since Caroline. No matter what he told himself, Cutter didn't believe it. His reaction to Emily was something more basic than that, something that went far deeper, but he wasn't ready to face it yet.

Cutter did his best to ignore her. He told Tad a story that left the boy wide-eyed and jumpy. He exchanged tall tales with Mack until they became so outrageous that Tad was rolling on the floor with laughter. Cutter sang "Barbry Allen" with his mother, creating a harmony so sweet she smiled dreamily into the fire long after, no doubt thinking about his father.

Still, Emily was there, drawing his gaze. The murmur of her voice as she talked with Ruth, the way she looked in the firelight, her giggle when Mack teased her, all conspired to force him to admit that he couldn't forget Emily Keating.

A quick look around the compound told Emily that Cutter was nowhere around this morning. She sighed, not knowing if it was disappointment or relief that caused the tightness in her chest. Emily found it difficult to assign specific emotions to the turmoil Cutter created in her.

She cast a look up at the sky, noting that the sun was almost at its peak. She never broke the rhythm of the beater as she worked the milk in the butter churn. Her arms and shoulders ached with the effort. Soon the butter would form and she could rest.

A quick peek under the lid told her she was finished churning. She skimmed the yellow globules of butter out of the buttermilk with a slotted spoon and placed them in a big burl bowl she'd brought out to the dogtrot for just this purpose. Setting the bowl just inside the kitchen door, Emily dragged the churn back inside the kitchen. She emptied the buttermilk into another bowl and straightened to find Cutter leaning against the doorframe watching her.

"I thought I was paying you to tutor my son, not become Ruth's kitchen assistant."

"Tad is working on his Latin translations. He works better when I don't hover over him." Emily fought the urge to smooth back her hair. She knew several strands had come loose while she was churning. She probably looked a fright, but it shouldn't matter. She did not care what Cutter thought of her.

"I'm sure you know best," Cutter said and stepped inside the room.

It must be her imagination that the room suddenly grew smaller and the fire suddenly burned hotter. Emily dropped her gaze and fiddled with the small bowl of berries sitting on the table. Cutter reached into the bowl, his hand barely whispering by hers, and selected a berry. Emily followed his hand up to his face as he bit into the berry. Her face burned as she remembered the kiss they had shared yesterday in the berry patch.

"Good berries, don't you think? Very sweet." Although he darted a quick look at Ruth, his smile was for Emily

alone. Those long, lean fingers plucked another ripe berry
from the bowl and slowly lifted the fruit to his wide, sensual
lips. His teeth flashed white against his dark skin as he ate
the berry.

"Good afternoon, ladies; as much as I'd like to spend
the day here, I have work to do."

Emily followed him to the door before she caught herself. She quickly scooped up the bowl containing the fresh
butter as a cover for her curious behavior.

"Infuriating man," Emily grumbled to herself as she
slapped the big burl bowl down on the table.

Ruth gave her a sidelong glance and allowed Emily to
see the sly smile on her coffee-colored face.

"What?" Emily asked sharply. She liked Ruth, but she
had had enough innuendo for one day. If Ruth had something to say, then she could just come out and say it to
her.

"Is he the reason you will not marry Mr. Mack?"

"How do you know about that?" The thought that everyone here knew about Mack's proposal and her rejection
embarrassed Emily more than a little.

"That man is always hungry," Ruth said with a shake of
her head. "When I told him he'd best get himself a wife
to keep him fed he said he was working on it. He told me
about you before you came to live here, but I don't see
you fixing to wed him."

"No, I'm not going to marry Silas McGee." Emily kept
her gaze fixed on the bowl as she used a wooden paddle
to work the creamy mass of butter along the bottom of
the bowl. She folded the butter over and over, pressing
the water out. She didn't want to see the look of skeptical
disbelief on Ruth's face that Emily had come to expect
from those who could not understand what a bluestocking
like herself meant by turning down a marriage proposal.

For a long time the only sound in the kitchen was the

crackle of the fire, the thump of dough slapping against a board, and the scrape of the butter paddle.

"He is a good man," Ruth said at last.

"Yes, he is." Emily waited for the lecture.

"You are not married."

"No, and I don't plan to be." Ready for battle, Emily lifted her head and glared at Ruth.

Ruth didn't comment on that, simply lifted her eyebrows in silent surprise and continued to knead the bread dough she was forming into loaves.

"Don't you want to know why?"

"If you would like to tell me, I will listen," Ruth said quietly.

Emily smiled at her bent head. In the few days she had been at Cutright's Station, Emily had already developed a fondness for the former slave. The other woman had an inherent wisdom and wry outlook that pleased Emily. Although she was uneducated, Ruth's life experience far exceeded Emily's own. On the surface they appeared very different, but in the end Emily did not think they were so different. They were both working to make their own way in the world. In the end, Emily thought she and Ruth had more in common than Emily ever would have with Imogene Clark.

"Ruth, I would be pleased if you'd call me a friend." Emily hesitated over the words, realizing she'd never had a close woman friend before, someone to share her innermost thoughts and fears.

Ruth smiled back at her. "I would like that too. Now tell me why you won't marry."

"A married woman cannot own property in her own right. A husband can beat his wife and there is no law against it. A married woman has no rights." Emily threw down the butter paddle in disgust and rose to pace the crowded kitchen. "Can you not understand why I want to avoid such bondage? I would think you of all people would understand."

Ruth wiped her flour-covered hands before turning to face Emily. "I have been a slave and I am a wife. I know one's not the same as the other."

"You say that because you love Reuben." Emily remembered the terror on Ruth's face the day of the Indian attack. "You said you cannot live without him, but that's not true. You could make your own way."

"I could, but it would be like living without my heart." Ruth's smile was wistful as she stared past Emily, obviously thinking about her husband.

"Oh, Ruth. Reuben is a good man. He would not hurt you, but what of the men who beat their wives, who do not support their families?"

"What of the men who love their wives and children? What of the men who give everything to care for the ones they love?" Ruth turned back to her bread dough.

"Men have all the power." Emily sighed as she pushed the wooden bowl away from her. "I do not want to give a man even more power over me than society has already given the lot of them."

"No. We let men think they have power, but it is not so." Ruth moved to the open door and stared outside thoughtfully. "Men travel to new lands by boat and horse and foot, yet when do they call these places home?"

"When the women arrive," Emily answered, still puzzling over Ruth's words.

"Who is it that sees that churches are built, schools are started, that the young are prepared for life?" Ruth prompted.

"Women," Emily agreed, but she was not satisfied. "Yes, but what use is all of this if the men wield the real power in the home and out?"

"Emily, you only say that because you have not had a

man love you. When he does you will realize that you hold all the power. You are the key to his happiness."

"What happens if you love him back?" Emily asked softly.

"Then the same is true of him. Neither wants to hurt the other, and so harmony is made. That is marriage, Emily."

"Bondage. How can it be anything else when someone holds your heart hostage?" It horrified Emily just to think about it.

"He only holds it because you give it to him, Emily."

"I will never give it." Emily scowled at the very idea.

Ruth touched her chin gently, tilting her head so their gazes met. "Do not speak so hastily, Emily. I see the way you look at Cutter, and the way he looks at you."

"No!"

"It is a good thing. He has been a lonely man, but since you came here he has smiled more. I think you make him happy."

"Well, he makes me crazy."

"That, my friend, is love."

Chapter 8

"No! I refuse to even hear of it," Imogene Clark said and stood up from the breakfast table. She pressed her lips tightly together and frowned at Emily.

Her expression told Emily the older woman obviously thought the discussion was closed, but one look at Tad's crestfallen face firmed Emily's resolve. The boy had been disappointed enough of late. Emily would not fail him as his father did nearly every day. She knew he resented his grandmother's overprotective attitude, and she couldn't blame him.

It was precisely why the boy's father made her so angry. It was up to her to foster Tad's independence and teach him to think for himself. His grandmother and his father certainly didn't seem inclined to do so. If she didn't, Tad would turn out either dependent on his grandmother or as disagreeable as his father. She had to show him that his grandmother and father could be reasonable people, or at least she hoped they were.

Emily had spent considerable time thinking about Cutter since her talk with Ruth. No matter how hard she tried to reason it out she could not come to an understanding of the man, or the disturbing emotions he raised in her. Of course, it was difficult to think when she almost always ended up daydreaming instead.

"There is no reason we cannot go into the woods today," Emily said quietly before Mrs. Clark could reach the door. "I am afraid I must insist."

"No reason!" Mrs. Clark turned around and marched back to the table to stand over Emily. Her chin quivered in her obvious rage. "I can think of a dozen reasons, but first and foremost there is the threat of Indians and wild animals. I will not allow it."

"Cutter and Mack have checked and rechecked the surrounding area, and there is no sign of Indians," Emily said calmly. "I am a good enough shot to handle any type of wild animal, even assuming one would attack us. We will not be so far from the station that help cannot reach us."

"Bears and wolves have been known to carry off children," Mrs. Clark protested. "Once outside the gates my boy will be at risk."

"Aw, Grandma, I'm hardly a child," Tad protested, his face flushing with embarrassment. His disgust with his grandmother's arguments showed clearly on his face.

Emily could sympathize with him. Mrs. Clark and Cutter seemed to treat Tad and Emily with similar disdain. Every time she thought to escape the station for a few hours Cutter intervened. He said it was for her own protection, but Emily thought it might be another way he sought to prove his domination of her. It was one reason she'd found it easy to forge a bond with Tad, and the primary reason both were eager to escape the station's boundaries for a few hours, at least.

Emily knew that if she didn't get away from Cutter's jibes and Mrs. Clark's suspicions for a few hours she might scream. Cutter was gone for a few hours, and she had the chance to leave. She would not let Mrs. Clark spoil that for her—or Tad.

"You are indeed a child, and children should be seen and not heard," Mrs. Clark scolded, the wild glint in her eyes highlighting her own fear. Emily knew the older woman had not ventured beyond the station gates since the trip from Fort Boonesborough, even though Cutter and Mack had both assured her it was safe.

After his grandmother's sharp words, Tad subsided into a sullen quiet that Emily knew from experience would take forever to coax him out of. She knew that if she didn't convince Mrs. Clark to let them go that Tad would be impossible all day, and she would not be in too pleasant a mood either. She needed to get away for a while.

"The boy has a point, Mrs. Clark," Mack finally put in. "He's a might big for even a b'ar to be carrying him off, and he's probably too scrawny for the Indians to bother with him."

Mack gave Tad a teasing grin that won a halfhearted smile from the boy.

"It does not matter," Mrs. Clark said firmly, frowning at Mack's clowning. "I will not have it."

"We do not plan to go far, just somewhere where I can practice my marksmanship," Emily continued as if the other woman hadn't spoken. "It is a shame to waste this fine weather and stay inside when we can get so much more out of a botanical lesson outside."

"I do not care about botanical lessons," Mrs. Clark said irritably. "You should concentrate your efforts on the languages and mathematics."

"Tad needs a well-rounded education, which includes the sciences," Emily answered quickly. She did not add that she also needed to begin Tad's shooting lessons or the boy would become impossible to work with, despite their increasing camaraderie. "As his teacher, I believe he needs some practical lessons. Not everything can be learned from a book or a lecture.''

"I will not put Tad at risk like that. It is bad enough that we have to live in Kentucky, where we face danger every day. I will not allow anything to touch my boy." Mrs. Clark laid her hand on Tad's shoulder, as if to reassure herself that he was safe, but Tad shrugged her hand away with a mutinous look on his face.

"If'n it would make you feel better, ma'am, I could go with the lady and the boy," Mack said, giving Emily a wink. "It just might be I could learn something from a botanical lesson. If I'm gone Cutter can't set me to hoeing a cornfield or milking a cow."

"Well, I don't know. It might be safer with a man along," Mrs. Clark said thoughtfully, giving Emily and Mack an appraising look.

Both her words and the obvious direction of her thoughts irritated Emily. Why they would be safer with Mack along Emily didn't know. Sure, the man was a good shot and woodsman, but she knew he would spend most of the time wooing her rather than watching the woods for danger.

That, of course, was the main attraction for Mrs. Clark. She was sure that Emily was chasing after her son, even after Emily had tried to assure she wanted nothing to do with the woman's infuriating son.

Emily was almost amused by the woman's obvious dilemma. On the one hand she did not want to risk her beloved grandson, but on the other hand she hoped Emily would eventually agree to marry Mack. Emily might have laughed if it weren't so very aggravating. She didn't want to marry either Cutter or Mack.

It seemed that everything wore on her nerves lately, Emily thought as she waited for Mrs. Clark to make a decision. Even though Cutter had been out of the station every day for the past week and they'd scarcely even seen each other in passing, let alone exchanged words, she still felt on edge.

That was why she was desperate to get away. Every day she stayed within the station walls Emily felt more trapped. She'd hoped this unreasoning attraction to Stephen Cutright would pass like a cold or chill, but it hadn't. If anything it was worse than before. That knowledge left her feeling more trapped than ever. Spending her days with Tad, who felt the same way, did not help matters at all.

Finally Mrs. Clark sighed and touched her grandson's cheek. "All right, you can go, but only for a few hours, and Mack must go with you. I want you to stay within sight of the fort."

"Grandma, if we stay in sight of the fort what's the point in even goin'?" Tad asked and groaned dramatically.

"Don't worry, ma'am. I'll see they don't come to any harm," Mack said.

"I know you will." Mrs. Clark smiled approvingly at Mack before turning her gaze on Emily. There was no smile for Emily. "I have your word this is strictly for lessons?"

"Of course. I have several important things to teach Tad." Emily smiled broadly at the other woman. She was glad she'd agreed to teach Tad, even if some of her reasons were selfish. She would especially enjoy teaching him to shoot, in direct opposition to his grandmother's and father's wishes. She would enjoy pulling one over on Cutter and Mrs. Clark.

Once free of the station walls, Emily immediately felt as if a great weight had lifted from her shoulders. For the next hours she would not have to guard her tongue around Cutter or avoid Mrs. Clark's sharp-eyed gaze. For the morning, anyway, she could do as she pleased with only Mack and Tad for company, and both seemed preoccupied with their own thoughts.

As they moved into the forest, Emily's spirits rose and she began to truly appreciate the wild beauty of the place she wanted to call home. Her only other chance to appreciate the splendors of Kentucky had been during her trip to Fort Boonesborough from Virginia, and then she had been nearly overwhelmed by the grief of losing her father. Now that she had come to terms with that loss, and was determined to make a place for herself here, everything she saw seemed to justify that decision.

Walking along the leaf-carpeted paths, Emily felt more at home than she ever had back in the safety of Virginia. It felt so untouched, as if no one had been here before her, and that intrigued her.

Strangely, she did not feel afraid, as Mrs. Clark and Ruth did. She knew there was danger here, but on this tranquil morning it felt distant and only added a slight spice to the peace she now enjoyed. Maybe people like Mrs. Clark looked forward to the day when the Indians would be driven back and the land settled, but Emily thought something valuable would be lost when this land was filled with cabins and crops.

They walked along the creek that eventually emptied into the Licking River. They discovered wildflowers in bloom and a variety of trees and plants. Emily and Mack tested Tad's knowledge of botany, sometimes teasing him by making up silly names for common plants.

Their walk was as much a lesson for Emily as it was for Tad. Mack pointed out tall cherry and walnut trees, groves of huge oak, ash, and beech, undergrown with the smaller dogwood, redbud, and tulip poplars. Sweetbrier tangled beneath the nodding heads of giant sunflowers. Lacy ferns and green mosses grew along the banks of the creek.

Some plants she knew by sight and others from their description, but there were many new and different ones. Tad enjoyed seeing his teacher stumped for an answer upon occasion, and soon all three of them were teasing and laughing together.

When they sat on great flat rocks that edged out into the creek, Emily raised her face to the sun and listened to the gentle sound of the water against the rocks. She felt completely at peace for the first time since her move to Cutright's Station. She turned to smile at Tad, but he was watching the way the light played on the surface of the rippling water and did not return her smile. Then Emily caught sight of Mack's thoughtful expression and she felt her smile slip away.

His look reminded her that Mack was not along on this jaunt for the pure enjoyment of it. He wanted her to marry him. He was a good man and she enjoyed his friendship, but it would never be more than that. In fact, she was sure his feelings ran no deeper than hers. So why did he want to marry her, and when would he learn to accept her answer?

"Tad, stay here while Mack and I walk along the creekbank for a moment," Emily said quietly, and Mack nodded as she carefully stepped off her rock.

They walked silently away from the boy, stopping when Tad was still in sight but where he would not be able to overhear them.

"Mack, why on earth do you want to marry me?" Emily asked in exasperation. She'd seen the way the young girls at Fort Boonesborough threw themselves at him. Heaven alone knew why he wanted a plain spinster woman like herself for a wife. "I have refused you often enough. Why pursue me when there are a number of women who would welcome your attention?"

"Maybe I enjoy a challenge." He cocked one eyebrow at her.

"That I can believe," Emily said crossly, but she searched his face to make sure she was right. She truly liked Mack and would miss his friendship, but if need be she would break his heart. She would not bind herself to any man, no matter how easygoing and pleasant. "I am glad to hear you do not tell me you are in love with me."

"Oh, but I am."

Emily felt a flush of guilt until she caught the twinkle in his eye.

"You are in love with me as much as you are with all women." Emily shook her head.

The handsome man gave her a long, slow grin that only made her feel guiltier for her stubborn refusal. Emily told herself she should not feel guilty. She'd been nothing but honest with the man.

"The question is, Emily, why will you not marry me?" The amusement was gone from his voice, and she saw he meant this question seriously.

"You know very well why. I'm not going to tie myself to some fool of a man, especially one as lighthearted as you." Her voice sounded shrill in her own ears.

"Have you not enjoyed my company today?" he asked.

"Yes, but that is not the point. I enjoy Tad's company as well," Emily pointed out. "That hardly means I should marry either one of you."

"Emily, you know you cannot make your own way here; it is too risky."

Emily bristled in anger at that, but Mack only shook his head.

"You know it is true, Emily. I admit you are as capable and intelligent as any man to set foot in Kentucky, but this is a dangerous time here. Any man, or woman, is a fool to brave it alone, and you are no fool."

"Your friend Stephen Cutright certainly thinks so." As soon as the words were out of her mouth Emily wished them back, especially when she saw the look of interest on Mack's face.

"Does his opinion matter so much to you, Emily?" Mack asked softly.

"Of course not," Emily said and turned away from him under the pretense of checking on Tad. It made her uncomfortable to lie to him. He and Ruth were the only friends she'd made in Kentucky. It didn't make her feel better to tell herself that Cutter's opinion really didn't matter to her. "Why would I care what he thinks?"

"Oh, I don't know," Mack said with a low chuckle and walked around Emily so he could study her face. "But it is obvious to me that he sparks something in you that I never could."

"I don't know what you're talking about," Emily said stiffly.

Mack tilted her chin up with his finger and took a step closer. "I think you do, Emily."

He gave her a gentle kiss with lips that were surprisingly cool on hers. The fleeting caress did nothing for Emily but give her a faint feeling of regret. It would be simpler if she could care for Mack, but she didn't.

When Mack released her he nodded as if he'd found the answer he sought.

"I saw you kiss Cutter, Emily, and only you can tell the difference, but you will be glad to know you finally convinced me that we will not suit."

She'd finally convinced him, but only because he too now believed she was chasing after Stephen Cutright, Emily thought irritably. Of all the pigheaded men in the world, he would be the last one she'd ever choose!

"Silas McGee, you will hold it right there," Emily said in a growl and strode quickly after him. "I don't know what you've got going on inside that thick head of yours, but I can assure you that you are mistaken."

"Am I?" Mack said as he turned around. "I know we are nothing more than friends. That was why I wanted to marry you, because I happen to believe passion will wear thin in time, while friendship is more enduring. However,

I will not step between you and Cutter, if that is the way of things.''

"It is not the way of things,'' Emily said through gritted teeth.

"Emily, now you are indeed being foolish,'' Mack said with a shake of his head. "I am not certain you and Cutter would ever be right together, but I saw you in his arms, and I know a willing woman when I see her.''

"Stephen Cutright is an insufferable cad. I did not welcome his advances, then or in the future.''

"If you say so,'' Mack said with a shrug that indicated that he did not believe her.

"How can I convince you?'' Emily asked in exasperation.

"You could kiss me like that,'' Mack said with a wide grin.

Emily narrowed her eyes at him. "I thought you just told me you did not take me for a fool.''

Mack threw back his head and laughed. "I do not, Emily, I assure you, but you cannot blame a man for trying, now, can you?''

Emily had to smile at his teasing. "I suppose I cannot hold that against you. It is in your nature, I suppose.''

"Yes, I am in the habit of chasing after skirts.'' His grin widened. "What of it?''

"I know, and that is one of the reasons I would not marry you, Mack,'' Emily told him honestly. "If I ever do marry, I do not want to worry about finding my husband in another woman's bed.''

"Well, that is one thing you won't have to worry about with Cutter; he is the most loyal of men.''

"Mack, it makes no difference to me what kind of husband Stephen Cutright would make, since he will never be mine,'' Emily told him loftily. "Just to prove to you how little I care for his opinion, I will now teach Tad how to shoot. You know very well his father would not approve of that.''

* * *

Cutter was waiting for them when they returned to the fort. The expression on his face was positively thunderous. Emily watched the happy, relaxed mood Tad had been enjoying slide away when he caught sight of his father. She touched the boy on the shoulder to reassure him, but knew she was no consolation to the boy, not when the father he worshiped did not even greet him properly. Emily frowned at Cutter, who returned her scowl in full measure.

"Go help Reuben with the firewood, Tad. I would have a word with Miss Keating alone."

"You would, would you?" Emily said coolly.

"Yes, I would. If you will excuse us, Mack." Cutter's gaze never left her face as he spoke.

Emily felt an urge to squirm beneath his piercing gaze, but she held firm and matched his glare with one of her own. She would not allow him to intimidate her as he did his son, and if she had her way she would make him pay for taking all the pleasure out of the day. Just because he so obviously suffered from a cursed childhood there was no reason to force it on his son.

"I will not," Mack's deep voice said just behind Emily, surprising her. She'd been so intent on Cutter that she'd thought Mack already gone.

"What?" Cutter turned his penetrating look to his friend, his frown deepening.

"I will not excuse you," Mack said with a grin and leaned casually against the log that served as a gatepost.

"I wish to have words with Miss Keating." Cutter's soft voice held just a hint of steel.

"I know you do. That is why I will stay."

Mack's casual shrug visibly irritated Cutter, and Emily hid a smile. Anything that caused Cutter displeasure was a delight to her.

"This is none of your affair." Cutter's voice seemed to rumble in his chest.

"I disagree."

"What?" The word sounded more like a challenge than a question. Cutter took a step toward his friend. Some men might have reacted to that aggression, but Mack only grinned.

"I believe you are going to take her to task for spending the morning in the woods, and that is as much, or maybe more, my fault than hers."

"Whatever I have to say to Miss Keating is between us."

Emily was irritated that the two of them were talking about her as if she weren't there, but she was also amused to see someone else break Stephen Cutright's control.

"No, that's where you're wrong," Mack said with a shake of his head. "You see, Emily and I came to an understanding today, and I think this is very much my affair."

Emily gasped in outrage. "Mack—"

"That's all right; I know you don't want to talk about it with Cutter. I just wanted him to know." Mack squeezed her shoulders and leaned in close to whisper in her ear, "Don't worry, darling; I know what I'm doing."

Emily wasn't sure what Mack thought he was doing, but his words had such a strange effect on Cutter that she wasn't in a hurry to contradict him.

Cutter's face seemed to have turned to stone, and he looked between them with hard eyes that left his expression unreadable.

"I see," he said at last. "That is very well for you, then, isn't it, Mack? You've finally gotten what you wanted. I would just ask that in the future when you choose to do your spooning in the woods you not drag my son along and put him in danger."

With that, he brushed past them and disappeared into the woods. Emily stared at the space between the tree where Cutter had disappeared until her eyes started to ache and she finally remembered to blink.

"Don't worry; he'll come back."

Emily whirled on Mack and smacked his broad chest with the flat of her hand. "What did you do that for, you big ox?"

"Why, I did it for you," he said, and gave her a look of childlike innocence that Emily didn't trust any farther than she could throw him.

"I do not need protection from Stephen Cutright. I can more than hold my own with him."

"I know that," Mack said, and gave her a wide grin. "But now we both know exactly how he feels about you, don't we?"

"Do we?" Emily said in exasperation. "I've known all along that the man despises me."

"No, that's just what he would like to think, but if it's true then why did he seem so put out by the fact that we're getting married?" Mack seemed to think his logic was obvious, but Emily was not convinced.

"We are not getting married," Emily said irritably. The man was making her head spin.

"I know that, and you know that, but why don't we just leave it be and see what happens? I like to see Cutter stew."

"Why would he stew over that?" she asked in confusion.

"Why, you silly girl, simply because the man is half-daft over you and too much the fool to admit it."

"I'll give you that the man's daft and a fool," Emily grumbled. "But I won't believe he has any interest in me other than to see me wed you."

"If it makes you feel better to think so. I do declare, I never saw such a pair of perfectly matched fools," Mack said in lofty tones that made Emily itch to knock the grin off his face with her fist.

"I don't have any interest in Stephen Cutright, and he is certainly not in love with me."

"If you say so." Mack shrugged, but as he walked away he started to sing softly to himself. " 'As I walked out, one winter's night . . . a'drinkin' of sweet wine . . . conversing with a handsome lad . . . who stole this heart of mine . . .' "

"Mack . . ." Emily called after him, putting a note of warning in her voice.

"It is just a song, Emily, my dear, just a song."

Chapter 9

It was just falling dark when Cutter returned to the station. He didn't know why he'd felt the need to walk the quiet paths surrounding the station. For some reason the fact that Mack and Emily had finally resolved their differences and agreed to marry disturbed him more than it should have.

For years he'd carefully avoided caring too deeply about anyone. He'd protected the soft core within that still ached whenever he thought about his wife, but today Mack and Emily had cracked his protective shell. How, why, he didn't know.

Hell, who was he fooling? Cutter thought as he sank down on one of the rough benches in the dogtrot and ran his fingers through his hair in frustration. It felt as if that shell had cracked all the way to the center of his being.

How could he have missed what was happening to him?

Emily disturbed him as no one else had been able to in a long time. He'd thought he was past it, past caring about anyone. Then Emily Keating destroyed years of building his defensive walls in less than a week.

Emily.

Days of avoiding her, hours of walking, nothing had rid him of wanting her. Whenever he closed his eyes at night, no matter how tired he was, it was her face that filled his dreams. Just allowing himself to think of her left the taste of her on his lips and the feel of her skin beneath his fingertips.

She raised something in him he hadn't felt since his wife died. After Caroline had died, Cutter hadn't wanted anything to do with women, or with anyone, for that matter. He'd left his newborn son to his mother's care and left to explore the wilderness on the far reaches of America's frontiers.

He'd risked his life time and time again, and somehow, against his will, he'd lived on. He'd grown to love Kentucky, but he guarded that love jealously and would allow no person to touch him as the land did. He'd carefully built protective walls around himself to make sure he would never be hurt again, yet Emily Keating broke through those boundaries.

She made him feel again, and he didn't like it.

Like it or not, the feelings were there, and so was Emily.

He did not know what it was she made him feel. He doubted it was love. He wasn't sure he could love another person anymore; that had died with Caroline. He cared for his son and his mother, but that was wrapped in responsibility and duty.

Whatever it was that Emily made him feel, it was apart from that. It was something he craved now more than food or sleep. Somehow when he was around her he felt more alive. He felt *more*.

For her, because of her, he'd even considered changing his solitary life. Not seriously—after all, they were barely able to exchange a civil word to each other—but some-

thing about Emily Keating made him want things he'd
thought he'd given up long ago.

Cutter shrugged. It wouldn't mean that great a change,
after all. It wasn't as if he didn't already have the responsibility of his son and mother. What was one more dependent?

Now Emily had agreed to be his friend's wife, and she
was forever beyond his touch. His chest ached in the place
where his heart used to be.

It was typical for him to realize how much Emily meant
to him only after she was already lost to him, Cutter thought
bitterly. It had been the same with his wife. That should
have been a lesson to him.

He was meant to be alone.

For years solitude had been his refuge and his greatest
solace. Suddenly Cutter didn't want to be alone anymore.
He wanted Emily.

Her laugh floated out through the open kitchen door
and, unable to help himself, Cutter stepped closer to the
door. He stood just outside the spill of light, feasting his
eyes on the sight within.

Emily sat at the rough wooden table in the center of the
kitchen. She was throwing kernels of popcorn at Tad and
Mack, who were attempting to catch the tidbits with their
open mouths. The floor was littered with the evidence of
their misses. Ruth and Reuben sat cozily by the fire as
they laughed at Mack's comical complaints about Emily's
throwing technique.

"You have to put more arc into it," Tad protested after
he missed a kernel that bounced off his nose.

"And you thought geometry had no place in your life,"
Emily heckled him. "See, you're already putting it to good
use."

"Well, if you made all your lessons as much fun as the
ones we had today maybe I wouldn't mind so much,

Teacher," Tad teased back. "Come on. Teach me some more about geometry."

When the boy grinned at Emily, Cutter suddenly realized it had been a long time since he had seen the boy smile. Tad's smile was so like his mother's that Cutter felt his gut twist at the memory.

Thinking of Caroline brought back memories of the pain, but also of the love they'd shared before she died. He hadn't wanted to feel that pain again, but now he knew he missed the love as well. He'd cut himself off from his son, his mother, and nearly anyone who might care about him.

Including Emily.

He didn't love Emily, Cutter reminded himself. He simply desired her; he craved her company and enjoyed their sparring. It was nothing more.

He did not love her.

He could not love her.

"Come on, Emily. Let's show the boy how it's done," Mack called out, giving Emily a conspiratorial wink. Her answering smile was warm and directed only at Mack. That smile left Cutter with a chill feeling in his core.

Cutter reminded himself that just because Emily had somehow changed his way of thinking did not mean he had a similar effect on her. She'd proven that by agreeing to be Mack's wife.

Cutter closed his eyes against the pain that knowledge brought, but instead he saw Emily's face, glowing with passion after he kissed her. She was going to marry Mack, Cutter reminded himself. Even knowing that, he couldn't move away from the sight of them together, from the sight of Emily.

Suddenly Cutter felt alone. For the first time in years there was no comfort there. He could go in the kitchen and join them, but he knew that if he did there would be no more laughter.

It was the life he'd chosen.

Soon his mother and son would go back east, and Mack and Emily would leave to make their own home. Then he would be alone again, and things would be right again in his world.

It would be the way he wanted it.

He didn't belong with other people; he didn't need other people. Soon he would forget about Emily Keating.

That was the way it should be.

Turning away from the light and warmth and laughter within, Cutter had never felt so lonely in his life.

It was full dark when Mack found him in the stables grooming the horses.

"I see you came back," the big, blond man said and leaned against the half wall of the stall.

"I came back." Cutter kept brushing, not even bothering to look up. It was easier to deal with animals. Their needs were few and simple.

"I missed you," Mack said, obviously seeking an explanation for Cutter's strange behavior. Cutter didn't have one—for himself or for Mack.

"I figured you'd be celebrating with your future bride," Cutter finally said into the lengthening silence between them. He'd never found silence awkward before, but the things left unsaid between them weighed heavy on his heart.

"I figured my best friend would want to celebrate with me."

That cut deep.

Cutter heard the questioning note behind Mack's words and didn't know what to say. He valued Mack's friendship, but until Cutter learned to deal with Emily, that friendship would be strained. Another reason why he'd made few friends. It was too much bother.

"Sorry," Cutter said with a shrug, unable to turn and even look Mack in the eye when he lied to him. He wasn't sorry at all.

Cutter didn't want to see Emily and Mack together anymore. He didn't want to see her smile at the other man, or touch him. Each smile, each caress, was like a blow to his gut, and Cutter didn't need that. If Cutter had his way he'd be hunting or surveying far from Fort Boonesborough on the day Mack married Emily. Maybe by the time they'd had their first child he would be over her.

"Not to worry," Mack said and slapped him on the back, startling the horse, who'd been half-asleep from Cutter's grooming. "I've got a jug of corn whiskey stashed in the grain bin. We can celebrate properly now that the women have gone to bed."

"No, I can't drink with you now that you're going to be a married man," Cutter said with a small grin, unable to resist Mack's exuberance. "It wouldn't be proper."

Cutter's smile slipped away when he realized he'd imitated Emily's favorite expression. The sooner that woman was married and away from him, the better.

"To hell with proper. I'm not married yet. Come help me celebrate my few remaining nights of freedom." Mack went to rummage in the corn bin for his hidden jug.

"I thought this was what you wanted," Cutter couldn't stop himself from saying.

"It is, it is." Suddenly Mack held up the jug in triumph. "Come on. Let's celebrate. After all, who wouldn't want to marry Emily Keating?"

Mack's eyes searched Cutter's face for something. Cutter was suddenly afraid his friend would read the envy in his heart.

He forced a hearty laugh and reached for the jug. "That's right, you got what you wanted, but remember what my mother always says: Be careful what you wish for; you just may get it."

"And what do you wish for, my friend?" Mack asked seriously just as Cutter took a deep swallow of the rough whiskey. The unexpected question made Cutter choke on the fiery liquid, and sent him into a coughing fit that brought tears to his eyes and made the horses look at him curiously.

"If I'd known you couldn't handle your drink I wouldn't'a have wasted a drop on you," Mack teased him as he pounded Cutter on the back.

"I'm just not used to such a fine vintage," Cutter gasped when he at last caught his breath.

"Ah, yes, made just last month, I believe." Mack smacked his lips after taking another swallow. "But enough about the whiskey; you have not answered my question."

"What makes you the philosopher this evening?" Cutter asked curiously, hoping to avoid answering. "It is not like you to look beyond a full jug of whiskey."

"Oh, I'm not overlooking the whiskey," Mack said with a chuckle. "But I guess planning my future with Emily makes me look deeper than usual."

"I think you just wish every man to suffer your same unhappy fate."

"Why would you think me unhappy?" Mack pressed him.

"Why not? You're marrying the most famous nag in all of Kentucky," Cutter said, and fortified himself with another swig from the jug. "Who would not be sorry to marry Emily the shrew?"

"Ah, but why dwell overmuch on her faults when it is her many gifts that will make her the ideal wife?" Mack said as he settled back against a pile of straw. "Why, I could love her for her beauty alone, but then there is her sharp wit, her quick mind, and her high spirits."

"Then there is her sharp tongue, her quick temper, and her high moral standards," Cutter reminded Mack—and himself. "Emily is no paragon of womanhood."

"If she is not, then would I know who is?" Mack said indignantly. "She is the very embodiment of womanhood, and you have only to look at her figure to know it. Why, Cutter, have you not noticed the way her skirts accentuate that narrow waist? And when she wears those buckskins, I declare there never was a more rounded—"

"Mack, I don't think it is appropriate to discuss your future wife's attributes," Cutter said disapprovingly.

"Don't tell me you haven't noticed?" Mack said in disbelief.

Cutter took another large swallow of whiskey to hide his unease. He shifted his body to ease the discomfort caused by the sudden tightening of his own buckskins just thinking about it. Yes, he had noticed exactly where Emily's body curved and rounded, but he was damned if he'd discuss that with Mack.

"I thought we were going to celebrate your few remaining nights of freedom," Cutter reminded him. "It's hardly a celebration of freedom if you spend the night talking about your bride."

"You are so right," Mack said and shook his head, taking the jug from Cutter. "I'm just so happy, I think I might burst if I don't tell someone. You are happy for me, aren't you, Cutter?"

"You're drunk," Cutter said, realizing that he too felt a comfortable warmth in the pit of his stomach, and even thinking about Emily didn't hurt quite so much anymore.

"Yes," Mack said with a grin. "So what? I think you're getting a bit fuzzy-headed yourself."

The moon was full and high in the night sky before the jug was empty. It had taken most of the jug to finally get Mack drunk enough to stop extolling Emily's virtues. Unfortunately, by that time Cutter was far from sober, and his mind was filled uncomfortably with Emily.

Mack was curled up in the hay, snoring happily with a silly smile still pasted on his face. Cutter couldn't blame him. The man should be happy; he had everything he wanted.

He had Emily.

Trying to force her out of his mind, Cutter staggered to his feet and realized he was drunker than he'd thought, but even so he was determined to sleep in his own bed and not wake up smelling as if he'd slept with the cows and horses. He didn't mind sleeping in the woods, but he was damned if he'd sleep in the barn when there was a perfectly good bed waiting in the loft above the kitchen.

After failing to wake Mack, Cutter shrugged and blew out the lantern. He doubted Mack would wake before dawn, and he didn't want to risk a fire in the barn. It seemed fitting to him that Mack would sleep in the barn tonight, for all too soon he would be spending every night in a comfortable bed.

With Emily.

He wasn't in love with her, Cutter thought as he made his way out of the stable. He sat down on the chopping block outside the door to rest before making the rest of the way to his bed.

No, he most definitely was not in love with Miss Emily Keating, but he wanted her very badly. It was desire, pure and simple. Not love.

Well, he'd learned to deny his body's cravings for food, water, and rest when on a long hunting trip, and he would be able to put that hard-learned lesson to good use. He knew wanting Emily Keating was a dangerous desire, even if she weren't going to marry his best friend.

Feeling slightly light-headed, Cutter leaned back against the rough log wall of the stable and closed his eyes. Hearing a sound that didn't fit with the station's normal nighttime noises, Cutter was suddenly alert. The sliver of ice-cold fear that sliced through his heart sobered him instantly. He cursed the devil that made him drink overmuch. He knew that if the station was attacked now he and Mack would put up a poor defense.

He listened intently for the source of the noise and peered through the darkness. As his eyes adjusted to the darkness outside the stable, Cutter caught a flutter of movement near the door of his mother's cabin.

Emily, wearing nothing but that damned white nightdress that taunted him in his dreams. Convinced it was only the whiskey playing tricks on his mind, Cutter closed his eyes tight, took in a deep breath, and then opened his eyes again.

She was still there.

He saw her head for the smaller wooden door cut into the wide station gate. He watched as she struggled for a moment with the heavy bar holding it shut. Then she opened the door and slipped out into the darkness.

Unable to believe what he'd just seen, Cutter stared at the door she'd shut so carefully behind her. "What the hell?" he muttered to himself and stumbled toward the door. Cutter had the wrought-iron latch in his hand before he realized he meant to go after her.

"I should just bar it again and let her spend the night outside the safety of the walls," he told the door bitterly. "That might teach her to respect the dangers out there."

Cutter knew he wouldn't sleep a wink knowing Emily was out there alone, facing God knew what dangers. He swore beneath his breath as he stalked back to claim his long rifle.

In the stable, Mack slept on, blissfully unaware of the danger his future wife had walked into. Cutter pulled his foot back, meaning to kick Mack awake and send him after Emily, but something held him back.

"I'll let him sleep," Cutter said to himself. "He has a lifetime before him of getting the woman out of trouble. I'll take care of it this once."

That was what Cutter told himself, but he knew it was a lie.

Rifle in hand, Cutter slipped out the door as Emily had done. He paused just outside the door, searching the cleared area for Emily, and was rewarded with a flash of white on the path along the river.

"Only a fool woman would go out for a stroll in the middle of the night," Cutter said in a growl and strode quickly down the path after her.

Emily wasn't really strolling. She set a quick pace, and although Cutter had sobered he still had difficulty negotiating the narrow path in the darkness. He stumbled several times and forced himself to slow down so he would not make enough noise to warn Emily that he followed. He wanted to know where she was going before he revealed his presence.

He wondered why she wasn't sleeping. He wondered why she hadn't gone looking for Mack if she wanted a moonlight stroll in the woods. He wondered if her sleeplessness was caused by her regret for agreeing to marry Mack.

Suddenly Cutter realized he hadn't seen any sign of Emily for several minutes, and his heart beat painfully in his chest. Where was she?

Then he heard her, somewhere off the path, close to the river. He heard her making some sound so soft he couldn't make out exactly what it was. Was she crying? Was she in pain?

Cutter found himself moving through the underbrush toward that sound. His need to get to Emily, to make sure she was all right, nearly overwhelmed his innate caution. He forced himself to move quietly. If she was in trouble he might need the element of surprise. Stopping to listen again, Cutter finally identified the sound she was making. She was humming.

He knew the song she was humming, a popular love

song that was almost always sung at gatherings at Fort Boonesborough. The fact that she was idly wandering through the woods at night, humming, no less, without any heed for her own safety infuriated Cutter. He couldn't believe she was so willing to risk herself.

Ready to confront her, Cutter stepped around the bushes that hid her from view. Then he saw her. Cutter stopped cold in his tracks.

Chapter 10

Emily stepped onto a large, flat rock jutting out into the stream. Curling her toes around the edge of the rock, she raised her arms above her head and closed her eyes. She felt the caress of the cool breeze as it lifted her hair back away from her face. Fingers of wind skimmed across the bare skin of her throat and arms.

Wearing nothing but a shift, and that made only of thin cotton, Emily felt naked and free.

She was free of the safety and confines of the station walls. She was free of bulky, voluminous skirts. She was free of society's dictates. This was what Kentucky meant to her.

At last Emily understood the fascination the frontier held for her father. She felt regret that he would never know the freedom and excitement of Kentucky, but vowed she would taste it fully in his place.

In a moment she would get down to her purpose in coming here, but for now she wanted only to bask in the feeling. The scent of pine and water washed over her. She was surrounded by the sounds of the forest: the quiet babble of the water, the gentle rustling of the leaves overhead, and the soft call of a night bird. Emily took it all in until it filled her soul. Then she looked down at the rushing water at her feet with a sigh.

After sitting by the stream earlier today, all Emily had been able to think about was coming here to wash. Since leaving Virginia she had never been able to fully immerse herself and wash all over. Bathtubs were few and far between in the Kentucky wilderness.

Although she'd managed to wash her hair and bathe out of a bowl, it wasn't the same. Sitting in the frigid water of a running stream would not be the same thing as a hot bath either, but Emily thought it more appropriate to Kentucky.

Cutter wouldn't like it that she was out here, but Cutter be damned, Emily thought with a smile. He was free to come and go as he pleased, and she would settle for nothing less for herself.

She would be free. No man would hold her back. Not even Cutter.

Mack's words came back to her. Could it be true that Cutter fancied her? Emily closed her eyes and gently touched her lips, remembering the way it felt when Cutter had kissed her. She slid her hands down her neck and then her slim frame, remembering the way it felt when his body had pressed against hers.

He'd wanted her then. Emily knew that as surely as she knew she was a woman. She also knew that that type of wanting went away. Except it hadn't for her. What did it mean? As intelligent as Emily was, she knew little of men, and what little she knew was not good.

Tilting her face up to the full moon that hung so low in the sky she could almost reach up and touch it, Emily sighed deeply. Stephen Cutright infuriated her and annoyed her, but one look from those green eyes and something inside her melted. He'd shown her passion, yet he was such a cold, distant man most of the time.

Emily wondered what would make a man that way. She wondered what would make a man change. She wondered if she could make him warm and gentle, if she could tame him with her kiss.

Closing her eyes, Emily wasn't so sure she wanted him to be warm and gentle. Mack's gentle kiss had not stirred her at all, yet Cutter's burning caress could even now make her skin tingle and her breasts swell when all she did was think of it. Just thinking of him could fill her with longing.

Cutter.

Strong arms suddenly snaked around her waist and pulled her back against a hard, male body. Emily gasped and then opened her mouth to scream, but a rough hand clamped over her mouth.

Struggling against the iron bands that seemed to hold her effortlessly, Emily soon realized her struggles were fruitless. Unwilling to give up without a fight, she bit down on the meaty part of the hand over her mouth.

"Damn it, Emily, you don't have to bite," Cutter swore behind her, releasing her as suddenly as he'd seized her.

Emily staggered back and might have fallen off the rock if Cutter hadn't pulled her back again. Once steady on her feet again, she shook off his hand.

"I don't have to bite?" she snapped at him, angry at him for scaring her half to death, angry at herself for being caught dreaming about him. She'd been wrong to think this man had any softness in him at all. "You didn't have to frighten me like that either. As far as I'm concerned you got what you deserved."

"As far as I'm concerned you got what you deserved," Cutter said, looking up from his study of his superficial wound to give her a disapproving look. "What if I had been an Indian or some frontiersman eager for the taste of a white woman?"

"What are the odds of either being out here in the middle of the night?" Emily asked scornfully.

"Have you learned nothing since you've been in Kentucky?" Cutter waved up at the full moon. "Do you know why they call this the hunter's moon?"

"I can take care of myself," Emily said and lifted her chin defiantly.

She knew Cutter was right, that she'd taken a great risk, but she would do it again. It was her right to do so. Just living in Kentucky was a great risk. She would not cower behind walls while life passed her by outside them.

"Not dressed like that you can't. You're just daring a man to . . ."

"To what?" Emily couldn't help asking.

That familiar dark, brooding expression was on his face. Emily felt a thrill of anticipation race down her spine at the sight of it. It was a hungry look that created an answering hunger in Emily that she'd never known before she'd met him.

"This."

He crossed the space between them in a heartbeat and pulled her roughly against him. His lips were hard on hers, punishing and cruel, demanding more of her than he ever had before.

It should have been more than she was willing to give, yet Emily willingly opened her lips to accept the probing caress of his tongue. She wound her fingers into his hair and pressed herself against him with a wanton abandon she knew she would regret later, but now all she wanted was this man, and the way he made her feel.

He tasted of corn whiskey. Just the trace of the intoxicating liquor made her feel light-headed. When his lips left hers Emily couldn't stop the small cry of regret that turned into a moan when his lips found a sensitive spot on her neck and then moved to tease her ear.

His hands were hot on her skin through the thin cotton

of her shift. They moved down her back to cup her buttocks and push her against him.

Emily felt his hard shaft pressed against the place where she was most vulnerable. Suddenly she ached for him to touch her with nothing between them. This was what she craved at night when she lay sleepless thinking of him, Emily thought in wonder. She'd never known what it was between a man and a woman. Now she knew just enough to create a tantalizing ache in that tender place.

Emily rolled her hips, rubbing her body against the hard length of him. The sensation felt delicious. Cutter growled deep in his throat. He reclaimed her mouth with a driving passion, making Emily mindless with each thrust and parry of his tongue.

A sweet ache in places she'd never known existed made Emily grow bold. A pressure built inside her, pushing her on. She ran her hands across his broad chest, slipping them inside the loose buckskin shirt. She felt the taut muscles quiver slightly at her touch as she smoothed her hands across his skin. Her questing fingers discovered a ridge of scar tissue just above his left nipple that made her wince. Then she found a trail of fine hair that led down his flat belly.

Cutter caught her hands at his waistband and pulled away from her. Emily barely caught the sigh of regret that formed in her throat. She raised her face to his, seeking some reason in his eyes, but he bent his head to hers and claimed her lips again. Pulling her close to him, he cradled her head against his chest. She could feel the beating of his heart beneath her.

"You cannot marry Mack, Emily," he whispered into her hair.

Emily smiled to herself.

It was that easy to tame the wildness in the man. She raised her face to his, soft words on her lips, but there was no answering softness in his eyes. She felt vulnerable and uncertain, where moments before she'd known exactly what she wanted.

He captured her chin in one firm hand and held her gaze steady on his. "Promise me you will not marry Mack."

It was not a request. It was a demand.

"Why?" she asked softly, barely stopping herself from begging for the answer she craved. She needed some hint from him before she could decide what she was feeling herself.

"Is this not reason enough?" he said, and ran a finger across the whisker-burn on her chin and gently touching her kiss-bruised lips. "Would you shame him before you are even wed?"

"What we have done will not shame Mack," Emily said. She would have no lies between them. Not now. "We are not going to be married. That was the understanding we reached today. Mack just let you believe otherwise to tease you."

"And you, Emily? What reason did you have to let me believe it?" His voice was deceptively soft, but Emily heard the hint of iron behind it.

"I was curious," she said, and lifted her chin in determination.

It was the truth, if not all of it. She met his hard gaze and knew she had not tamed him at all. She was beginning to doubt it was possible, and could not ignore the bitter taste of regret that filled her mouth.

"Curious?" he said, and arched one eyebrow at her.

Emily tried to pull away from him, but his arms still circled her waist and held her in an intimate embrace. It was unbearable that he could have such a hold on her while he broke her heart. Emily pushed that surprising thought to the back of her mind to explore later, when she was alone and Cutter was not there to disturb her with his presence.

"Mack thinks you have an interest in me," she said at last. "I wanted to see if it was true."

Cutter smiled. "Yes, it's true, but you already knew that." And his mouth found hers again.

This time his kiss was hot and deep. It left her breathless and dizzy and almost unable to remember what they had been talking about.

Almost.

"I think you are just as *interested* in me," he said, and gave her a wolfish grin that sent a chill down her spine.

She still did not know what she felt for him, but it was intolerable that he might feel nothing at all. "Why do you wish to kiss me when you do not like me much?"

Cutter sighed. "What we have between us has little to do with what is in our heads or hearts."

"I beg to differ." Emily stiffened.

It was unthinkable that she would feel this attraction for a man she found insufferable. Yet it was so hard to think when the touch of their bodies made her want only to feel. She tried—and failed—to separate the feelings from her thoughts.

"How old are you, Emily?"

"Old enough to know better than to fall for the tale you're spinning," she said haughtily. She knew enough of men to know they would say what they would to get a woman to tumble them.

"Assuredly, but tell me how many men have made you feel this way?" He rubbed his knuckles across her cheek and smiled at Emily's shivering reaction to his touch.

"I could tell you dozens," she said, and lifted her chin defiantly.

"Yes, you could, but I would not believe you. I would guess you may have been kissed a few times, but no one has taken the liberties I have." He looked so satisfied with himself that Emily longed to lie to him, but she couldn't.

"That is because you are no gentleman."

He chuckled. "I will agree with you there, but you do not give yourself enough credit, Emily. You let me."

Emily's face burned with embarrassment, and she would have wriggled out of his embrace, but still he would not let her go. Grudgingly she admitted she did not try very hard to move away.

"Don't worry about it so. I know you are no light-skirt, but that does not mean we cannot enjoy what we have." There was a rough edge to his voice. He was growing impatient, and God help her, so was she.

"Yes, it does." Emily struggled to keep her voice firm. She prayed he did not hear how weak she truly was, how much she longed for whatever he would give her. "I will not give myself lightly. If I ever join with a man it will be for love and respect."

"Come on, Emily. Admit you need a man; admit you need me," he whispered softly. "That is all that matters. Love and respect have nothing to do with what happens between a man and woman."

"I need no man." Conscious of every inch of his body that touched her, Emily knew she lied.

"Yes, you do. You need me; you need me right now." He bent his head and nibbled at her neck and earlobe until a reluctant whimper escaped her lips. "Admit it, Emily."

"No." Her voice came out in a hoarse whisper.

He shook his head. "You are a stubborn one."

"I could say the same of you," she said firmly, finally thinking of something that might win her time to regain control. "Why not admit you need me?"

"Oh, I will admit that, all right," he said and kissed her again, before whispering against her lips, "I need you, Emily."

She turned her head away from him, though it cost her every ounce of control she had. "No, not for that."

"That is what we have between us, Emily; don't fight

it." He slid his hand up her back, brushing the side of her breast with the tips of his fingers.

"There's more—I know it," she protested, frantically hoping she was right. She would not be ruled by her body. She was too clever for that, but Emily feared she could be ruled by her heart.

"You don't know; you haven't lived enough. This is all there is."

"It can't be!" she said in desperation, unable to fight the sensations his wandering hands and lips were creating in her body. They were incredible and new, yet somehow awakened a primal recognition that was almost impossible to combat.

"Trust me, Emily; I know." His voice was rough with desire, and that more than his touch nearly pushed her over the edge.

"Why won't you trust me?" It was a cry fueled by desperation. "Maybe you are wrong, and I am right."

"Will you believe me if I prove it?"

It was such a seductive promise, Emily couldn't find the will to argue against it. She was willing to believe there might be a way. It was an intellectual challenge that comforted her for the betrayal of her body. "How can you prove it?"

"Trust me."

Emily did not know what to say. It was rare for her to be at a loss for words, but that seemed to be the effect this strange, enigmatic man had on her. One of the effects. Her only consolation was that she'd broken that famous control of Cutter's. She'd always heard he was a soft-spoken man of few words. Well, not around her he wasn't.

She'd unlocked the passion in him as surely as he'd unlocked it in her.

"How?" she whispered. "How will you prove it?"

His answer was to slide his hands down her hips and thighs, leaving a trail of heat behind. Kissing her fervidly, he pulled up the skirt of her shift. The cool night breeze fanned across her fevered skin as he pulled her to the rock.

For one brief moment Cutter's chiseled visage stood out in sharp relief against the bright yellow glow of the moon. He searched her eyes for something; Emily did not know what. Unable to put a question or answer to words, Emily touched his cheek gently and guided his head to hers.

One muscular arm cradled her head against the rough rock beneath them, but Emily was scarcely aware of the cold surface when the hard body pressed against her created such heat. Cutter tenderly traced a path down her neck and the valley between her breasts.

He cupped one breast and rolled the nipple between his fingers until it swelled to a point. Then he bent over her and kissed her breathless again. This time when his mouth left hers it traced the path his finger had followed down her throat. When his hot lips closed over her breast, laving her nipple through the cotton of her shift, Emily closed her eyes and allowed the strange, overwhelming sensations to sweep over her.

She felt his hand gently sweep over her belly, past the bunched cloth of her shift around her waist, and cup the quivering mound between her legs. She didn't resist when he gently pushed her legs apart; she had already made all the protest she was going to make. She gasped in shock when one probing finger found the center of her being and sent an eddy of sensation, radiating from that spot, that threatened to overtake her.

Emily cried out but he covered her mouth with his. This time each exploration of his tongue was matched with the exploration of that other, more private place. By the time his mouth left hers to pay equal homage to her breasts, Emily's breath came in quick, short pants. An unfamiliar pressure was building inside her. She knew Cutter was the only one who could help her now.

"Cutter?" She whimpered into his neck. She clung to him, afraid that if she let go she might spin out of control and never return.

"Trust me."

Cutter kissed her deeply again, then suckled on her earlobe, somehow intensifying the sensations his fingers were creating below.

"Look at me, Emily," he commanded, and she did.

His eyes were dark and lonely, but there was tenderness there, and a hunger Emily knew well now. Yes, she knew that hunger, the desperate craving to end the unbearable pressure building inside her. She raised her hips to meet each movement of his hand.

Suddenly a series of tremors rocked her, every muscle seemingly quaking in response to an inner explosion that left Emily shaken and panting in Cutter's arms when it was through.

He smoothed back the damp hair from her face and kissed her gently. Emily reached up one trembling hand to caress his cheek. He captured her fingers and raised them to his lips, suckling on each fingertip. She'd thought herself beyond the ability to react to him, yet that simple action stirred her again.

"I did not know," Emily said, and she sensed rather than saw his smile against her fingers.

"I know," he said, and slid a possessive hand down her hip. "There is much I would teach you."

"Cutter, there is so much good in you; I know I could find the tender side to you, given time."

"No! Make no mistake; there is no tenderness left in me."

Her hand shook as she reached out to touch his cheek, moving her hand to follow when he turned away from her. "You are wrong, you know."

Emily knew it was true. She knew it in her heart, in her soul. A man without tenderness would not have done as

Cutter did. He would have taken her there on the cold rock; he would not have concerned himself with her pleasure, only his own. Then he would have left her. He would not stay to argue with her.

He would not have put her pleasure before his.

That was when Emily recognized the fact that she'd fallen in love with Stephen Cutright. He was right; she needed him, but she also knew that he needed her. "You are a good man."

"No!"

Emily heard the pain in his voice, and it spoke to her heart more than his words ever could have. That was when she knew it would take more than her words to prove to him she was right. Once she could prove it to him she would reap the greatest reward of all. She only hoped it would not cost her more than she was willing to give.

Chapter 11

"Trust me," Emily whispered against his lips.

Cutter groaned in frustration. She tasted so sweet, she felt so right in his arms, he wanted to trust her. He wanted to believe, as she so obviously did, that there was something good in him. He wanted to believe that somewhere, beneath the aloof manner and the cold cynicism he'd spent years perfecting, he could still care.

However much he wanted to believe, Cutter knew it wasn't true. He'd lost the capacity to care when he'd banished Stephen Cutright the man and become Cutter the frontiersman.

He didn't care for her, but he wanted her.

God help him, he wanted her more than he'd ever wanted another woman. Even the woman he'd loved and married, and mourned for twelve years. Oh, yes, he wanted Emily Keating in the most basic of ways.

The permanent ache settled between his legs was testament to that fact. He'd wanted her before, when all he'd known was the honey of her lips and the sweet scent of lavender on her skin. Even when she made him furious with her foolish risks and stubborn determination he'd wanted her. Now that he'd tested the depth of her passion, Cutter thought he might die if he didn't bury himself deep inside her.

It was the whiskey; it had gone to his head. There was no other explanation for what he'd done tonight.

He held back, even while he told himself he was crazy not to take her and make love to her until they both forgot themselves. Maybe for those brief moments he would forget the kind of man he was, forget the kind of life he was doomed to live. Maybe in Emily's arms he could pretend to believe.

Still he held back because Emily did believe and he wouldn't—couldn't—take advantage of that. He should never allow himself to forget what kind of man he was, no matter how badly he wanted a woman.

This woman.

"Cutter, love me," Emily said softly, touching a gentle hand to his cheek and sending a shiver of passion coursing through his body.

He knew she didn't mean for him to declare his love to her. He'd won that argument with her, but couldn't celebrate the victory because she had won everything else.

Her eager lips and the reaction of her body to his touch told him very clearly that she wanted him to make love to her, but Cutter did not want there to be any recriminations afterward. He wanted to be sure they were both ready to offer the same terms.

He wanted Emily.

She wanted him.

It was as simple as that. They would make love and there would be nothing between them.

Nothing.

"That is what you want?" He avidly studied her eyes, just

to make sure her expression matched her words. "There is only tonight. We won't have any tomorrows."

"I know you cannot promise me anything more than tonight," she said in that husky voice that sent a rush of blood straight to the source of his discomfort. Her hand traced a pattern down his belly until she touched his waistband.

Cutter ached for her touch, there and everywhere, but first he wanted her reassurance. He would not risk letting down his guard until he could be sure. He knew he should not let that guard down at all, but he wanted her so badly he was willing to take that risk. "You are certain?"

"I am certain," she said, and leaned up to kiss him, teasing his mouth with her tongue.

Driven to the limits of his control by that erotic gesture he had taught her, Cutter could hold back no more. He laid her back down on the rock.

Carefully he lifted her shift up past her hips and over her head. Then her soft skin was exposed to his touch, and Cutter moved away so the beams of moonlight would show him her body in all its glory. She was as beautiful as he knew she would be.

Her skin was creamy pale and smooth to the touch. Her breasts full and perfect, her nipples firm as ripe berries begging for him to taste. Her soft belly was slightly rounded and utterly feminine, filling the palm of his hand as he smoothed it over her. Her hips flared out from her slender waist, and her legs were long and shapely. Just thinking about those legs wrapped around him made Cutter groan with impatience.

But if there would be only one night with Emily, he would make it last. He would make it last a lifetime.

"Cutter, I want to see you."

Her voice was shy, but the way her hands touched him was not, and Cutter eagerly shed the last of his clothing.

Emily gasped when she saw his hard length, and Cutter quickly moved to lie beside her once more.

He longed to enter her and ease the ache she'd created, but he wanted her passion unlocked first. The look of wonder on her face when he'd taught her the first lesson drove him on to see it again.

"It is all right; you will see," he said, kissing her gently. "Trust me."

And she did.

This time when he laved her nipples and stroked her thighs Emily not only responded more quickly but initiated some explorations of her own. Her hesitant touch nearly drove Cutter to lose his control. He sighed with relief to discover she was wet and eager for him when he parted the petals of her womanhood and rubbed the nub he found hidden there.

When he heard her moan her own impatience, Cutter knew he could wait no longer and moved to lie between her knees. He probed her entrance with just the tip of his length, teasing her. Emily lifted her hips in unspoken invitation.

Unable to withstand that temptation, Cutter thrust deeply into her, ripping through the proof of her virginity with one violent, glorious motion. He felt her wince of pain and bent to kiss her again.

Losing himself in the sweet taste and feel of her mouth, Cutter slowly began to move within her. She was so tight and hot around him, he thought he might not be able to maintain his control for long.

Emily soon discovered the ancient rhythm that men and women had shared since time began. Her eager rise to meet each thrust pushed Cutter to the limits of his control. Then she cried out his name and Cutter felt her body clench around him. Unable to hold out anymore, he buried himself deep within her and let the sensations take over.

When it was over and Cutter lay beside Emily, their legs still tangled together, he had to smile at Emily's sigh of contentment.

"Do you understand now?" he asked, tracing the curve of her jaw with his finger.

He had been right. For the moment he was at peace with himself. Emily was to thank for that, and he was glad she had pleasure of their joining too. He allowed that peace to fill his being because he knew well enough it would not last.

"I can understand now why some women allow themselves to be enslaved by a man," Emily said, stroking his chest.

Cutter followed the arch of her waist and hip with his hand, noting with surprising pride the blood drying on her thigh. She was his only for this night, but she would always remember that he was her first. He had that much.

He pushed away the feeling of regret that soon they would part. There was no room in Cutter's life for regrets. Stephen Cutright had regrets, but not Cutter. Cutter moved forward and never looked back.

"Sometimes it works the other way; the man is enslaved by the woman."

Cutter knew it was true. It was extraordinary; this bluestocking, whom he'd thought plain and bitter, might have been able to enslave him when he'd been another man in another life. But that had been in another life. In that life they would never have met, let alone become lovers. It was too late now—for both of them.

All they had was tonight.

"Maybe," Emily said with a dismissive wave of her hand. "Maybe for some women, but not for me. If I marry at all it will be on equal terms with a man who respects me for who I am, not some fool who worships me for beauty that will fade."

"Ah, but Emily, your beauty will never fade," Cutter said and nuzzled her neck.

He was hungry for her again but knew there would be no more loving between them. He should leave her now before she made demands on him, but these moments of peace were so few he wanted to make this one last.

She lifted her face to kiss him, a sweet kiss that tasted of regrets, and sighed. "You do not need to flatter me, Cutter. You already have everything I can give."

"Emily, I do not flatter you," Cutter said seriously. He could not love her and marry her, but she deserved a man who could, a man who would treasure the gifts she had to give. "You are beautiful."

He smiled as she shook her head in disbelief.

"Your eyes are your greatest beauty, and they will never fade," Cutter said, and gently kissed each eyelid. "Your wonderful high cheekbones that make your face so distinctive will outlast the creamy skin of youth." Cutter kissed each cheek. "And the sweet curve of your lips will outlast the bloom of youth on your skin."

That kiss lasted longer than the others. "You are an intelligent, warm, and passionate woman. All these things make you desirable. Believe it, Emily."

"I thought men preferred their women to be demure," she teased.

"I don't know any man who would not want you in his bed if he knew what I do," he said, lying back and pulling her down to sprawl across him.

"What do you know?" Her generous mouth curved into a smile. She obviously did not believe him.

"Kiss me," he commanded.

She did. The woman who defied him every time he set a rule kissed him when he asked. She kissed him using every trick he'd shown her that night, and Cutter felt himself stir in reaction.

She nipped at his neck and then at his earlobe, teasing

his ear with her tongue, until Cutter grew hard from wanting her. He could not resist nudging the soft divide between her thighs, even though he knew it would only make his torture worse.

"Cutter, can we do it again?" she whispered against his neck.

"You know very well that I can." He chuckled. "I am sure you noticed my reaction to your newfound talents, but I am not so sure you would find it comfortable again so soon."

"Oh." Her disappointment was clear on her face and in her voice. She pressed her teeth into her lower lip in a tantalizing gesture that only made Cutter more aware of his discomfort. He'd never wanted a woman as he wanted Emily Keating. That was dangerous—for him and for her.

"Why did you come out here, Emily?" he asked softly, needing a distraction from the need she provoked in him.

"To take a bath. I think I need one even more now," she said with a wry smile.

"Then let us take a bath."

"Together?" she said in a shocked voice.

"Together. I hardly think bathing is as intimate an activity as what we just did," he said with a smile at her disapproval.

"I suppose you are right," Emily said, and moved away from him.

Cutter was surprised at the empty feeling she left behind. "I know I am."

"Does that hurt?" Emily said, staring openly at him and his erection with wide eyes. She reached out a tentative hand to touch it.

When he groaned at her touch, she pulled her hand back with a quick apology. "I did not mean to hurt you."

"You did not hurt me, Emily," Cutter said, and tilted her chin up to kiss her. The need to kiss her came so often now that Cutter did not know how he would resist when their night was over. "It was pleasure, but the longer I resist the more painful it will become."

"More painful than I am sore?" she asked in confusion. "Then why do you resist? I would like to do it again."

"I know, I know, and so would I. That is what I was telling you, Emily. You are a woman of deep passions. The man who finally gets you will be a lucky one. But take my word for it; you would not enjoy it as much. I would not have this memory marred by discomfort and pain. Now come. Let us take that bath. I don't suppose you brought any soap with you?"

"But of course, and even a towel. It is over there with my nightgown." Emily stepped away from him and then turned back. She looked so achingly beautiful, standing naked in the Kentucky wilderness, that Cutter thought he might choke on his desire for her. "Cutter . . . is it like that all the time?" The nervous downward movement of her eyes left him in no doubt about what she meant.

"No, Emily, only around you."

She gave him a wide grin in answer and a saucy swing of her hips as she moved to pick up her soap and towel. Cutter nearly groaned out loud from frustration. He hoped the water was very cold; he would need it.

As Emily started to wade slowly out into the water, she winced with pain at each step on the sharp stones of the streambed.

"Allow me, my lady," Cutter said and waded in after her. He swung her up into his arms and carried her out to a deep pool created by the rocks. It was deep enough to swim but there were no strong currents to threaten uncertain swimmers. Still, Cutter did not let go of her. Her arms twined around his neck and her breasts pressed against his chest. He could feel her hard nipples teasing against him.

Steeling himself, Cutter lowered her legs into the water. Emily still clung to his neck and raised her face up to his for a kiss. He could not resist. Their lips clung together as their tongues teased, tangled, and tasted freely.

As Emily rubbed her soft belly against him and locked her legs around him, Cutter felt himself grow hard despite the cold water. The temptation of her warm body rubbing against him was greater than the discomfort of the water and provided a contrast that only made his desire grow.

When her hot hand closed around the length of him and gently rubbed the sensitive tip, Cutter knew he was lost. He shifted her body and entered with a slow movement that made Emily squirm to speed his entry.

Cutter held her still against him, cupping her firm buttocks with his hand. As he gradually found his seat within her, he let his fingers trail between her legs and stroked her thighs. Emily moaned and rubbed her cheek against his.

"Please, Cutter."

Her breath was ragged and hot against his ear. Cutter felt himself swell within her. He thought he might burst and die from the effort of keeping his movements slow. Emily did not seem concerned about discomfort as he felt her strain against him.

"No, darling. This time we will take it slowly."

And they did, but still it was over far too quickly for Cutter. Emily laughed at him when he tenderly soaped her thighs and washed away the stain of her virginity. He pushed her away when she would have washed him too. He knew that would surpass the limits of his endurance.

Finally, when they were both clean, Cutter carried her back to the rock where they had first made love and kissed her long and hard before setting her down again.

He reached up to touch her cheek one last time and was surprised to find dampness on her cheek. Those tears wrenched at his heart.

"Why do you cry?" His voice was rough, but Cutter couldn't help that. Those tears brought home to him that he should never have let himself touch Emily Keating. He should never have let her touch him.

She was already too close.

She threatened his peace.

She was dangerous.

"I do not want it to be over," she said, so softly he could barely hear, but each word was like a knife to his heart.

"It is over," he said harshly.

Now he needed to drive her away before he allowed his emotions to get involved. Tonight there had been only passion, but if there was more than tonight . . . Cutter pushed that thought away. He needed to get away from Emily.

"But why?" It was a plaintive cry.

Before he could stop himself Cutter put a comforting hand on her shoulder. Unwilling to weaken now, he shook her slightly to disguise his mistake. "You knew it would end before it began. Do not try to sway me with your tears now. They do not touch me."

If only that were true. Cutter turned his back on her to pull on his buckskins. He heard her choke back a sob.

"Cutter, don't do this."

Emily, who was so proud and so strong, was begging him. Cutter closed his eyes, seeking the strength he needed to protect himself.

"Do what?" He deliberately kept his voice cold and did not even turn to look at her. "I have done nothing to you that you did not welcome."

"Do not turn your back on me."

She touched him, lightly, as if afraid. Her fingers were cold on his arm and she trembled slightly—from cold or emotion, he could not tell. He could not afford to care. He was already afraid this night would cost him far more dearly than he intended.

"This is the way it has to be." Cutter shook off her hand and turned to glare at her. "Now leave me be."

She winced at the anger he directed at her, but did not back down. She stood still, looking like a ghost in her white nightgown.

He did not care for her. She did not care for him. Women must naturally lay more importance on the loss of their virginity than it deserved. "Leave me be."

"I will not. It does not have to be this way. You cannot shut yourself away from all people for the rest of your life."

"I cannot? I have done well enough these past twelve years." Cutter reminded himself that he would be at peace as soon as Emily was gone.

"Have you? Is that why you have friends like Mack, who would give up their own happiness for you? Is that why your mother and son risked their lives to travel out to live with you?" Emily shook her head. "No, Cutter, you are not so alone as you would think. Why can there not be room in your life for me as well?"

"You know nothing about me," he said, and clenched his jaw to maintain control.

"I know everything there is to know." She would have touched his cheek but Cutter took a step away. He was thankful she did not pursue it. He was afraid he could not resist the lure of her touch for long. He needed to get away from her, but first he needed to make her understand. There would be nothing else between them.

"You know nothing."

"I know about your wife. I know that you cannot blame yourself for her death. You have suffered enough. You have paid enough."

This time it was Cutter who touched her. He grabbed her by the shoulders and held her gaze with the sheer force of his anger. "You know about my wife? Did you know that after Tad was born, in a frontier cabin miles from any doctor or even another woman, she bled to death? There was nothing I could do to stop it.

"Did you know that Tad was so small and frail when he

was born that I did not think he would live through the night? I took him to an Indian woman to nurse, and then when he was a few months old I took him to his grandmother. Then I disappeared into the frontier for years. My mother thought me dead."

"I know." Her eyes were luminous with unshed tears. Her voice was soft with love.

Cutter had faced Indian attacks. He'd fought the French. He'd even killed a wounded bear with his knife. None of those things scared him as did Emily Keating and the way she made him feel. He could not afford to feel like that.

"I know how you feel." Her voice was heavy with emotion.

"That is where you are wrong." Cutter forced out a laugh. "I do not feel at all."

"That's not true. I know it."

He'd hurt her. He heard her pain in her voice. Cutter told himself he was glad. Soon she would leave him alone. That was what he wanted.

"Go back to the fort. I don't want you here anymore."

"Cutter—"

"Go," he repeated in a loud voice.

"No." Her fingers clutched the bodice of her nightgown. Her eyes were huge.

Cutter felt as if something heavy were sitting on his chest. It was hard to breathe. Emily was smothering him. He needed to be alone.

"Don't you understand? I never took you for stupid before. It's this simple: I don't want you. You served your purpose. Now go."

Chapter 12

Emily lay on the rock and let her hand trail through the cool water of the stream. The dank breath of the wet limestone kept the heat of the day at bay here. The gurgle of fast water running over rocks filled her ears.

Leaning back she stared up at the clear blue sky overhead. The sun was dipping low in the west. Soon she would have to head back to the station, but she wasn't in any hurry. There was nothing back at the station for her. Cutter was gone.

After he'd driven her away the night they'd made love, Emily had returned to the station to weep silently into her cornhusk mattress. She'd been devastated by the pain of his rejection, following so closely on the magic they'd shared.

She'd cried herself out and stared dry-eyed at the rafters above her, waiting for morning to come and praying desperately for him to change his mind. She'd raged at herself for being the weak woman he'd called her. She'd fought against the growing certainty that something linked her to Cutter more closely than their physical bodies.

Then she lay exhausted, drained of emotion, and her mind frantically sought the truth, no matter how uncomfortable it made her feel. No matter the fear she felt at that loss of control, loss of herself. She hadn't mourned the loss of her virginity, but the feelings she had for Cutter changed her very identity.

When the morning light crept in through the ventilation slits built into the loft, it brought with it a revelation that sent a wave of energy through her. Emily realized that Cutter was afraid, too. That was the reason he'd sent her away.

The contrast between the gentle lover and the man who pushed her away had been what had tortured her through those long, dark hours before dawn. She knew the man who touched her so gently, the man who loved her so thoroughly, had to feel something for her. Now she was sure of it.

Despite the stiff feeling in her muscles, Emily stretched luxuriously in her bed. He did care. She knew, as surely as she knew that he'd somehow captured her heart, that Cutter felt something for her. That was why he'd driven her away. She'd touched him deeply, but the man who spent twelve years closely guarding his heart would not give in so easily.

She could understand his hesitancy.

Just feeling her life spinning out of her control made Emily more afraid than she'd been in her life. Not even facing her father's death or an Indian attack frightened her as much as falling in love. She had only Nelson's betrayal to overcome, and she knew Cutter was nothing like that. He'd already proven that to her. Yet Cutter had the loss of his wife and twelve years of shutting himself off to overcome.

She had hoped that giving herself to him would bridge the gap between them. Her heart ached to think about the love Cutter needed to heal the torment he'd suffered.

She wanted to give him that love.

She *would* give him that love.

It would not be easy, but Emily Keating never backed down from a challenge. In her heart she wanted him. Emily thought that after years of never finding a man who touched her as this one did, she would be a fool to throw it away without finding where it led.

Emily was no fool. She hoped.

When she descended from the loft Emily discovered it would not be as easy as she thought to tame Cutter. He'd ridden out early that morning, telling Reuben before he left that he'd be gone for days, or maybe weeks. That escape seemed to confirm Emily's belief. She must have touched him. There was no other reason for him to run away except the fear that she would undermine his determined solitude.

Emily had been able to hold on to the joy she had experienced that night with Cutter for days. She'd even been able to convince herself that he would come back for her.

As she mooned about the station, Emily suddenly realized that she had become what she always despised: a lovesick woman allowing a man to control her happiness.

That was when Emily had forced herself to reason out the situation with logic, not to rely on emotion. That was a woman's greatest weakness, she knew, and she feared that Cutter had used it against her for his own benefit.

She remembered that since the day they met he'd been determined to prove to her that she needed a man. He had achieved his goal.

Maybe Emily had no need for just any man, but each night when she lay alone in her bed thoughts of Cutter kept her awake. She dreamed of his hands caressing her, his lips tasting her, his body claiming her, and Emily knew she would no longer be content to live a solitary life.

She'd always known the life Cutter chose for himself was

not for her, but she'd thought she'd be content with close friendships. She'd thought that someday she might find a man willing to make her his partner in life with a relationship based on mutual respect.

Now she knew that was not true. She wanted a lover. She wanted Cutter.

Emily was glad that Cutter was gone. He'd saved her from making a fool of herself. He'd saved her from trying to win something she wasn't sure she wanted.

She'd never wanted a husband, as other women did, but even here in the Kentucky wilderness Emily knew they could not live as lovers. They might steal a few months or even a year, but all too soon there would be more settlers here. There would be preachers and churches, and they would be expected to live up to those standards.

Did she want Cutter enough to build a lasting bond? Was he the kind of man she wanted to spend the rest of her life with? Would she willingly subject herself to marriage?

Her heart cried out, *Yes, yes.* Her body craved him. Emily forced her mind to think. It was her only defense.

Cutter had married once before. He'd loved his wife. He took good care of his mother and son. He was not a drunk. He did not abuse his dependents. He was held in high esteem by all.

By all those counts he would make a good husband.

He was a loner who allowed no one close to him. He thought women less capable than children. He belittled her and neglected his son. He did not deal well with people. He did not trust easily.

All those qualities told her Cutter would make a terrible husband.

She loved him.

He said he could love no one.

Emily rested her head on her arm. Even intellectually she could not resist the challenge that Cutter offered. He said he would never love again, that he could not love. In her heart Emily knew he was wrong, and she longed to prove it.

Could she take that risk with herself? Did she have a choice?

The longer Cutter was away from her the more Emily struggled with that question. Was she willing to risk herself for love?

Rough hands seized her shoulders and hauled her to her feet. Emily turned and the greeting on her lips died as she caught sight of her captor. It was not Cutter.

Piercing black eyes seemed to reach into her soul and hold her paralyzed. The Indian's copper skin gleamed with bear grease. His scalp was plucked clean except for a thick black scalp lock decorated with beads and feathers.

Emily started to scream but he clamped a hard hand over her mouth and quickly slipped a foul-tasting gag over her head. Ignoring her struggles, he tied her hands together with a length of rope and used it to pull her along after him.

Terror tightened her chest until she could barely breathe. She was sure her captor could hear the thunderous pounding of her heart. All she could hear was the rushing of her blood in her ears as she stumbled after him.

They didn't move far down the river before three other braves moved out to greet him silently. They quickly bundled her into the bottom of a canoe and moved out into the swift-moving current.

A small pool of water in the bottom of the boat soaked the sleeve of Emily's dress, and she was helpless to move away. That was when the terrifying truth of her situation finally sank in.

Emily choked on the gag as sobs heaved her chest. She'd been captured. There was no hope of rescue. No one knew where she was, and by the time she was missed she would be long gone.

Worse, even if they wanted to follow there was no one who could. Mack could not very well leave the station defenseless with Cutter gone.

Cutter. She would never see him again.

On the heels of that came memories of every story she'd heard about Indian captives. Rape, torture, slavery. Death was the only option, and that would come only after hours, maybe days, of pain and suffering. The best she could hope for was to be kept captive and somehow survive years of drudgery and abuse.

Emily took a deep breath and forced herself not to panic. She needed to think. She remembered the talks that Colonel Calloway and Daniel Boone shared over firelight at night. The Indians respected strength and courage. If she was brave they might allow her a merciful death. Emily dug her nails into her palms and prayed for courage.

She wasn't sure how long she lay facedown in the canoe, but the rocking motion of the boat made her nauseous without being able to see. Finally they came to a stop and she was hauled up and thrown to the shore.

Then she got a look at her captors for the first time. Naked to the waist, they were clad in breechclouts and leggings. Now, faced with them as a group, Emily could not even pick out the one who'd captured her.

Just looking at them filled her mouth with the sour taste of fear. Emily forced herself to remember they were just men with weaknesses like everyone else. She told herself she had killed one Indian and would do it again, given the chance.

She would survive.

One brave held up a large knife and tested the blade with his thumb. He stared at her and Emily felt her gorge rise up in her throat. He stepped toward her and stopped so close she could smell the rancid bear grease he'd spread on his body. Emily used every ounce of strength she possessed not to flinch as he reached for her. Daniel Boone said that to show fear was a fatal mistake.

The Indian removed the gag from her mouth and tossed it aside as if it did not matter now if she screamed. Emily did not try because she knew they were too far from the station for it to do any good, and she did not want to give them the satisfaction.

Do not show your fear.

The Indian shoved her toward the water's edge and gestured for her to drink. Emily's mouth was dry and she couldn't be sure when she would next get the chance to drink, so she obeyed. Before she drank her fill, he pulled her up by her hair. Emily gave him a defiant look and spit a mouthful of water at him.

It missed his face but dribbled down his forearm, and his expressionless face was suddenly filled with anger. He raised a hand to strike her, but one of the other braves put a hand on his shoulder and stepped between them.

This Indian was older than the others, Emily noticed. He seemed to wear more decorations; silver bracelets gleamed at his wrists, and feathers hung from his scalp lock. She guess that he must be the leader of their group. Something about his manner made Emily relax. She sensed he meant her no harm. After delivering a long message to the other Indians, who jumped to obey his orders, the older man turned to her and grinned.

Emily's mouth curved in response before she caught herself and steeled her expression to one of disdain. The Indian threw back his head and laughed. The unexpected sound drew the attention of the others, but the leader waved them away again.

He carefully helped Emily to her feet and led her away from the water. "Cutter's woman has spirit. I can see why he chose you."

Emily stared at him in astonishment. He could speak English. He thought she was Cutter's wife. She did not know what to say. Should she tell him he was wrong? She knew Cutter was respected by the Indians. They might not harm her if they thought Cutter might retaliate. Or would it make her more valuable as a captive?

"You surprise to hear me make white man's talk," he said with a nod. "I learn from Cutter. I speak good?"

"Yes," Emily said slowly, unsure what to do. Why would this man, who obviously knew Cutter well, kidnap the woman he thought to be Cutter's wife?

"I am known as Silver Fish." He smacked his chest proudly and stared at Emily expectantly.

Biting her lip in confusion, Emily hesitated. She did not know what the protocol was in this kind of situation, but she thought it best to play along for now. Maybe he would let her go. "I am Emily."

"Come walk with me, Cutter's woman."

"Where are we going?"

He gave her a disapproving look and then stared ahead thoughtfully. Taking advantage of her newfound calm, Emily looked around her to locate the other Indians. She noticed they'd fallen into a line with one brave ahead of them and one following. She did not know where the third was, but she assumed he was scouting the terrain ahead.

Despite the number of people in their group, Emily was disconcerted to notice how silent their progress was. It also disturbed her to note the sound of the river fading behind them. She bit her lip nervously and looked again at the Indian walking beside her.

Once they were away from the river she would never be able to find her way back, even if she did manage to escape. Then she would depend on rescue, and Emily knew there was no way she could count on that. Many settlers had disappeared from Kentucky into the Indian lands and never been heard from again.

She closed her eyes and prayed for the courage to face

this challenge and survive. She would not give up without a fight.

They made their way through the low brush. The pace they set seemed easy enough for the men, but soon Emily was struggling to keep up. Yet keep up she did, because she feared what would happen if she fell or caused them trouble. Silver Fish was tolerant of her struggles now, but she could not depend on that tolerance. She would make no difficulty until the time was right.

She must keep her wits about her, Emily thought, even as she noticed her breath was coming harder and her chest hurt slightly from the effort. She tried to take slow, even breaths. Concentrating on her breathing helped soothe her nerves.

The terrain was rough, thick with trees and underbrush, yet the leader seemed to know exactly where they were going. Emily realized she could no longer hear the water behind them and she panicked for a moment, thinking herself lost already. She forced herself to calm down and think.

She needed to know what direction they were going so that if she got free she could find her way back. Looking over her shoulder, she noted that the sun was slightly past her left shoulder. She could barely see it over the treetops as it dipped low in the sky.

It would be night soon and then she could rest. Surely they would not travel at night. Then that comforting thought was replaced with the realization that they were heading northeast, which could only mean they were headed for the Warrior's Path. The Indians' ancient trail crossed Kentucky and went straight over the Ohio. Once past the river and into the Indian lands there would be no return.

Emily shivered, and she knew it was not from the cool breeze that picked up as they entered the forest again. It was from fear.

When they finally stopped, Emily collapsed to the ground and lay gasping for breath, willing her quivering muscles to relax. After the worst had subsided she struggled to a sitting position. She was so tired and frightened she desperately wanted to cry, but one look at the Indians convinced her differently.

Although Silver Fish seemed inclined to be kind to her and protect her, the mean one, Evil Eye, as she dubbed him, continued to watch her closely. Even now when he caught her watching them talk he scowled at her.

Determined not to cry, Emily raised her chin and scowled right back. She willed herself to adopt the same expressionless face the Indians fronted.

After a while, Silver Fish sent one of the younger braves over to give her a gourd full of water and a handful of dried corn. Though so tired she wanted only to curl up into a ball of misery, Emily dutifully took both. She knew she would need her strength. She needed to survive.

Emily found it encouraging that they did not light a fire that night but simply lay down on beds of pine needles and leaves. She hoped it was because they still feared pursuit. There was a chance, if only a slim one, that she would be rescued.

As it grew full dark, Emily lay tethered to a tree some distance from the men, but she knew she would not escape that night. From time to time she caught the glint of Evil Eye's knife in the dark as he fidgeted with it. She knew he was watching her, if no one else was. Afraid of what he might do to her when the others slept, Emily was afraid to close her eyes, but eventually her exhaustion was too much and she slept.

The next day was more of the same except now Emily was exhausted and sore from sleeping on the ground. With each step she felt the weight of despair pulling her down, for each step took her farther and farther from escape, from rescue, from hope.

Again Silver Fish fell into step beside her, but today he seemed kinder to her. He did not talk to her but sometimes took her arm when she stumbled and guided her around obstacles she was too tired to note herself.

That night they made camp beside a spring. A big willow tree's gnarled roots bulged out right over the spring. The constant shade and delicate green ferns growing around the spring kept the place pleasant. As the others set a fire Silver Fish took off her tether. "I will untie you if you promise not to run."

Emily met his gaze straight on. She thought about lying to him, but something in his eyes stopped her and she shook her head. "I cannot promise that."

He grinned, as if pleased with her answer, but he still untied her hands. "I know, but if you run I will send that one after you. I do not think you will like it if he catches you."

Silver Fish pointed at Evil Eye, and Emily couldn't stop the shiver of fear that crept down her back. Silver Fish was right. She had been treated well so far, but she knew that if Evil Eye was given his chance things would be very different.

"Do not worry, Cutter's woman. Your man will come for you," he said agreeably and nodded his emphasis.

Emily did not know how he could be so sure that Cutter would come, but she couldn't stop the swell of hope in her chest at that knowledge. She wouldn't allow herself to think about the fact that he might not come.

Then she realized that if he did come, the Indians who had kidnapped her would scarcely give her up without a fight. "What will happen?"

"We will talk. My English fathers have asked me to send a message to the white man known as Cutter. We will give him this message and he will go with me to Detroit to give my English fathers the answer they seek."

"What if he will not go with you?" Emily asked, her mouth dry with fear. She could not imagine Cutter going anywhere tamely, but especially not to the English stronghold.

"We fight." His mouth made a grim line. "I not want to kill Cutter, but I will."

Emily couldn't help glancing at Evil Eye, who stared at her malevolently, as usual. Silver Fish noticed her look.

"Do not worry, Cutter's woman. You, I will not kill. I will take you home with me. Cutter's woman will fetch a good price, many furs."

Emily found no consolation, although the chief's expression told her he meant to comfort her.

They spent the next days at the campsite near the spring. A young brave would take her into the woods to collect firewood and allowed her some freedom, but she was never far from someone's watchful gaze. She always knew when Evil Eye was watching her, because it made her skin crawl just to have him near. Still, no one touched her, and for that she was grateful.

But each day she saw Silver Fish study her more carefully. At night when they thought she was asleep she heard them talking, and she knew it was about her.

After three days a fourth brave joined them and was greeted with pleasure by the other Indians. He was young, barely on the threshold of manhood, and from his marked resemblance to Silver Fish she thought he might be his son.

After he delivered his message, the young Indian studied her with open curiosity that only made Emily more nervous. With each passing day it became increasingly obvious to her that there would be no rescue. Cutter was not going to come. What were the Indians going to do about it?

Evil Eye was frustrated and angry; she knew if her fate was left up to him it would not be a pleasant one, but even

Silver Fish's kinder plans were not the life she wanted for herself.

Trying to move away from the young Indian's avid gaze, Emily edged closer to the other Indians and suddenly realized they were arguing. It was clear they were not happy about the message the boy delivered, and somehow it affected her.

Making a sound of disgust, Evil Eye turned away from Silver Fish and advanced on Emily so quickly she did not have time to move away. Sick with fear, Emily swallowed the hot bile that rose in her throat and stood her ground. She gripped her skirt with shaking hands and hoped he did not see her fear.

He raised his fist and she heard Silver Fish cry out in protest. Then there was an explosion of light as his fist collided with her head in a flash of brilliant pain. The taste of blood filled her mouth as she fell, and Emily's last thought was that she hadn't begged.

Chapter 13

Cutter knelt to study the human tracks following the trace. His knees crunched into the dry soil. It was not much of a path, barely more than a space that animals used between the trees, but Cutter could tell that more than animals had passed through here in recent days. The markings were faint, but he could read all the information he needed there.

Emily.

Three, maybe four Indians had passed this way, taking with them an American wearing shoes. A woman.

Emily.

As he traced the footprint she'd left behind, Cutter tried to tamp down the fear he felt for her, the fear that had grown stronger with each moment since he heard of her capture, stronger with each day that passed that he did not find her. He needed to harness that fear and use it to push him on, but he would not let it rule him. He needed to think, to be strong, to be constantly alert.

Cutter skimmed his hand across the loose-packed dirt.

They were taking her to the Warrior's Path. That fact made him the most fearful of all.

Once they crossed the river and lost themselves among the thousands of Indian villages to the north, there would be nothing he could do to bring her back. He had no idea which tribe these warriors belonged to, let alone what region they called home. He could spend a lifetime searching and still not find her. If he lived through it at all.

A breeze ruffled his hair and made the leaves overhead rustle noisily. Cutter lifted his face to the wind as if he could catch Emily's scent. There was nothing there for him but the damp promise of rain.

Cutter rose to his feet and glared at the trees before him, but the forest held on to its secrets. It had been days since they passed this way. Anything could have happened to her.

He had to believe she was alive. Until now he had found no sign of a fire, no sign of torture, but he knew there were ways to make her suffer that did not require torture. There were things a man could do to a woman he held captive.

Cutter gripped the bone handle of his knife in his hand and knew he would kill any man who had touched Emily. If they dared to hurt her then he would make their deaths slow and painful. Cutter had learned much from the Indians, and he would use all his knowledge to save Emily. If he was too late, then he would use that knowledge to make them pay.

"I will find you, Emily; I swear it," he promised the wind and started once again to run with the ground-covering lope he'd learned from the Indians.

As he ran, Cutter did not ask himself why he was so determined to rescue the woman who by turns infuriated him and captivated him. He'd gone away to be alone in the woods, to find the inner peace he'd worked so hard to create—the peace Emily had destroyed in one night. He had not found it.

He'd returned because he needed to see her again. He knew there was no future for them, but he could not let her suffer this fate either. Guilt suffused him every time he thought about her capture. He knew why she had been by the river that day, alone.

When Mack took him to the place where she'd been captured, the wave of guilt he'd suffered nearly brought him to his knees. The spot was where he had found her standing in the moonlight like an ancient goddess, nearly naked, holding her face up to accept the moon's caress— the rock where he'd made love to her and learned he was not so impregnable as he had once thought.

Memories of Emily that night filled his brain and kept him moving long after his feet ached and his muscles cramped. Another man might have stopped, but Cutter knew that guilt would allow him no rest.

Emily was always on his mind.

Emily's hair fanned out around her face as he bent to kiss her. Emily's cry of passion as he entered her. Emily's arms around his neck as he carried her. Emily's plea for him to love her.

He knew what drew her back to that place. It was the same thing that kept him there for hours after she left him alone that night. The thing that drove him away from her the next day. The thing that brought him back to the station to see her. The thing that made him willing to follow her to the very gates of hell if necessary to save her.

Cutter knew that if she died because of his neglect, part of him would die with her. The guilt would destroy any hope of his escape, any hope of peace. This time it would be worse than it was with Caroline. He did not dare question why, but he knew it as he knew the damp in the air meant rain.

It did not mean that he loved her.

She was his responsibility. It was that simple, and that complicated. After Mack told him that Emily was taken, Cutter had ignored Mack's offer to go after her. It was Cutter's fault she'd been taken, and it was up to Cutter to bring her back. He had ignored his mother's pleas to stay at the station and protect them. She seemed convinced that the wild red men were determined to get her. Tad's assurance that he would protect her only sent her into hysterics.

Cutter simply sent Ruth to console his mother and continued with his preparations. There was no time to deal with her. All his energy was devoted to Emily.

He took the time only to refill his budget—the leather pouch he wore over his clothing Indian-style—with dried corn and restock his supply of powder and shot before Mack took him to the point on the opposite shore of the river where the war party had landed its canoe.

Mack clasped Cutter's arm between his hands and wished him Godspeed.

"I will find her," Cutter promised him, knowing that the days that had already passed might mean that was impossible, but he had to say the words just the same.

Mack did not remind him of that fact but simply nodded. "I know if anyone can, you will."

"I will," Cutter said and walked into the forest.

Three days later, Cutter still had not found her.

Glancing up at the darkening sky, Cutter knew it would soon be too dark to continue. He could find his way through the forest at night, but he might miss an important sign or, worse, walk into a trap. If he was captured then Emily had no hope at all.

The wind was picking up, whipping branches into his face, and occasionally huge drops of rain penetrated the leaves overhead. The air was thick and musty from the coming storm. Still Cutter pressed on. He would not stop until he could no longer read sign. Emily had been missing for nearly three days when he set out to find her, and this was the third day of his search. He knew he had to find her soon.

Emily.

Just the thought of her pushed him forward despite his exhaustion. He barely stopped for rest or meals, he drank when he passed running water, and he ate dried corn on the run as the Indians did. Still he had not caught up with the party that took Emily. A prickling sensation at the base of his neck made Cutter think that he had to be close. During his years on the frontier he'd learned to trust that feeling.

A lash of lightning across the dark sky suddenly lit the forest, and a crash of thunder sounded ominously close. Soon he would have to stop for the night. Cutter had rarely hunted this far north. He had met with some of his Indian friends at a spring near here before the Americans and English had clashed in war and forced the Indians to choose sides. He would head for the spring to spend the night. Surely they had passed this way. There might be fresh sign there for him to follow in the morning.

It was full dark by the time Cutter reached the clearing that surrounded the spring. He stopped just outside the ring of trees and surveyed the clearing for some sign of other humans. His neck still prickled with warning, but as he searched the clearing he found nothing.

Then as another flash of light illuminated the sky, something caught his eye. A huddle of something lay to one side of the clearing, not far from the spring and the huge, sprawling willow beside it.

Something dark. Unmoving. Cutter waited impatiently for another flash of lightning. It was still there. He wasn't sure what it was, but he doubted it was some animal. It did not look like fur.

Another quick study of the clearing satisfied Cutter that this was not a trap. He was alone. He took advantage of the next flash and stepped out into the lashing rain. Dropping to his knee beside the still form, Cutter saw that he had been right. This was not fur, and it was not an animal.

It was a woman.

Emily.

When he brushed back her hair from her face, Cutter knew he'd found her. A smear of blood on her forehead and her cold skin almost made Cutter's heart stop, but when he slipped his hand beneath her he found warmth. She was still alive.

Alive and breathing, but even when he scooped her up she did not respond. She had not been heavy before, but now she felt as light as a feather. It was as if there were nothing left of her.

Just the thought of coming so close to saving her, and arriving only in time to watch her die, made Cutter clutch her more tightly to his chest. Emily cried out in pain and then she called his name. Her voice was barely more than a whisper, but it echoed in Cutter's mind long after she'd silenced again.

He would not let her die. He would die with her first.

Cutter pressed his lips to her cool forehead and sought desperately for a plan. Emily needed to be dry and warm. He could not tend her properly in the center of a thunderstorm. As if to drive that point home another boom crashed overhead, and he heard a crack in the distance as a bolt of lightning struck a tree.

Cutter staggered to his feet with Emily in his arms. There was a cave. It was not close by, and it would take a long time to get there, but it was their only chance. Emily's only chance.

He did not know how long it took him to find the cave, or locate some dry wood to start a fire. It was full dark and they were both soaked to the skin. Emily still didn't rouse, even when he kissed her. Her lips were cold to the touch and sent a shiver of fear through Cutter.

He would not let her die.

He stripped off her wet clothing and wiped the blood off her face. There was a bruise and a knot from the blow she'd suffered on her left temple, but he could find no other signs of injury. It must have been a fierce blow, though, to have knocked her out for this long.

She was still so cold. Cutter rubbed her skin, massaging her hands and feet, and still she was cold. Her skin was warmer to the touch now, but occasionally a shiver would rack her body.

He didn't know what else to do, so Cutter stripped off his own wet clothing and lay with her on the nest of leaves he made for her. He pulled her into his arms and warmed her with his body. Holding her, even when she lay so still, eased the ache in his heart.

He stroked her hair and talked to her until the storm finally subsided outside the cave. The fire gradually died, but Cutter did not want to leave Emily to seek out more wood, and he let it die. She was warm enough now. Finally he must have fallen asleep himself, because it was just daybreak when Emily's voice woke him.

"Cutter!" Her husky voice came out as a bare croak, but it was the sweetest sound Cutter had ever heard.

"Shhh, don't talk now," he said soothingly. "You are safe. Rest while I go fetch some water."

"Don't leave me." She clutched at his arm and sat up. She suddenly realized they were both as naked as the day they were born and her eyes widened.

"I won't go far, Emily; do not worry." He gently kissed her forehead, and that must have reassured her, because she dutifully lay back again and closed her eyes.

"You came for me," she whispered as she fell asleep.

Content that she would be all right once she'd rested, Cutter pulled her back into his arms and slept as well.

When Cutter woke next it was near night again. He was immediately conscious of the soft warmth cradled against him. It had been years since he had slept with a woman, but he knew instantly that it was Emily he held in his arms. Soon he would need to rise and take her back to the station, but for now she was all his. He savored the moment. He hoped she did not hate him.

As he lay still, willing this moment to last forever, Cutter felt Emily's hands skim across his chest and her soft lips graze his chin.

"It is time for you to wake up, Cutter. I have let you sleep long enough."

Cutter couldn't stop the smile that curved his lips. It felt strange; it was a long time since he had last smiled. It was a pleasant sensation.

"You have, have you? Maybe it was I who was letting you sleep."

She shook her head impatiently. "I have been awake for such a long time now, waiting for you."

"What have you been waiting for?"

"This." Emily kissed him softly at first, then slid her tongue between his lips to tease him.

"Where are my clothes, Cutter?"

"They are drying by the fire. You were so cold and wet. I needed to warm you."

"I'm not cold anymore," Emily whispered into his ear as she rubbed herself against him.

Cutter nearly groaned in frustration. When he'd been caring for Emily, desperate to warm her and save her life, he had not been aroused by her naked body, but now that she was awake . . . "Emily, stop."

His words were strangled in his throat as her hot hand slid along his hip and she trailed her fingers down his thigh.

"Yes, Cutter." Emily smiled at him provocatively, arching one eyebrow. "What is it I can do for you?"

"Don't," he said in a hoarse voice he scarcely recognized as his own.

"I don't think that's what you want, not really," Emily said against his lips and lightly scraped her nails along his inner thigh. "Tell me what you want, Cutter."

"You had a blow to your head, Emily. We shouldn't . . ." Cutter moaned and forgot anything he meant to say as Emily trailed her lips down his throat, then followed the fine line of hair from his chest to his stomach and below.

"I'm fine, Cutter; I feel just fine. You seem to be better for your rest as well." She gave him a wicked smile, then ran her finger along the length of him with tantalizing deliberation.

Cutter thought he was going to explode. He pulled her tight against his chest. It was the only thing he could think of to make her stop torturing him so. "You might have a fever."

"I think you are right about that," Emily said and kissed him again. "I have a fever."

Even though he held her pinned against his chest, that did not stop her from wiggling her hips and straddling him until her soft heat pressed against him. Having the source of his torment so close was enough to drive a man insane, Cutter thought, and prayed for the strength to resist.

"You need to take care; I must get you back to the station. . . ."

"You are right; we need to take care." Emily drew back from him and gave him a fierce glare. "We could be killed this very day. I could die of a fever tomorrow. Those are all truths, but we are not dead now. Right now we are alive and together. Can you not understand that I want to celebrate that? I am alive. Let this be my celebration."

She tossed back her hair and her face was in profile against the setting sun outside the cave. She was the most beautiful thing he'd ever seen.

"Emily." This time when he said her name it meant surrender, and she knew it.

* * *

When it was over he lay cradled against Emily's breasts as she caressed his hair and stroked his back. He would have moved off her but she held him with her arms and legs and begged him to stay. As she touched him, tracing his body, cradling him against her, and pressing her lips to the top of his head, Cutter felt something give way inside him. He felt something he thought long dead and buried come to life in his chest.

He felt the need to be loved. To be cherished. To be needed, not for what he could do, but for who he was.

It was tempting. The love he felt from Emily beckoned him to walk toward her, toward the light, and it took a tremendous effort of will simply to remain as he was and not give himself up to that light. Even as he fought he found himself asking why.

The light was so seductive, he wanted nothing more than to bury himself in Emily until he drowned and there was nothing left of himself without her.

That was a dangerous thought. He'd destroyed Stephen Cutright. If he lost Cutter, what would be left? Even as he floated on the haven she represented he knew the darkness beckoned.

It always beckoned. For so long darkness was all he knew of love and life. Cutter knew it would not give up so easily. It was a jealous master. As tempted as he was to stay with Emily, he knew it could not be.

Still, knowing full well he would pay the price for this later, he did not leave her. He could not leave her. It frightened him beyond words that he did not have the will to move away from her. How would he ever find the courage to leave her again?

And leave her he must.

"I thought you would hate me," he said softly into the

darkness. It shouldn't matter so much what Emily thought of him, but it did.

"I could not hate you." She touched his cheek, but he did not turn his head to look at her as he knew she wanted.

"Don't say that." When Cutter pulled away from her he felt as if he'd ripped off a part of his body, or his soul, and thrown it away. "You will hate me in time."

"No, Cutter, you are wrong," she said in a gentle voice so filled with love he could not help but turn to look at her.

She lay where he had left her, her body still shiny with the dew of their loving. She smiled at him. "I cannot hate you because I love you."

Emily's body ached.

She had never been so tired in all her life. She felt every inch of every muscle. She felt every step she'd taken these past days. Her stomach was so hollow she thought she might never be full again. Her mouth was dry. Her hair was in tangles. Her clothing was torn.

She felt wonderful.

Cutter loved her.

He would not admit it. She could see him struggle with himself during their long trek back to the station. Since they had made love in the cave he had spoken only a half dozen words to her. He touched her only when he thought she needed help to cross a stream or negotiate a particularly rocky stretch of ground. Once past it he would loose her arm as if her touch burned him. They slept apart each night.

And still, she knew as a woman knows these things that he loved her. She'd seen it in his eyes when she told him that she loved him. She felt it in the way he touched her.

Cutter loved her. He knew it too, and that was the war he waged within himself.

She was content to let him fight that battle, because she knew that ultimately she would be the winner. She had to be. He had no choice. He made that choice the day he followed her into the wilderness to rescue her. Cutter loved her and there was nothing he could do about it.

There was only one thing that troubled her: that she could remember nothing of the days when she was taken from that spot on the river by the station until the moment when she woke in Cutter's arms. There were hazy memories of dark-skinned men and a shiny knife, but that was all she could remember.

Yet there was something, just beyond the blackness, that she knew she needed to remember. Something she needed to tell Cutter. Something urgent.

When she strained to remember it brought on blinding headaches that made it impossible for her to walk. During those times Cutter would cradle her head in his lap and rub her forehead until it went away. He would show her the tenderness he did not dare show her when she was well.

He too wanted to know what had happened during those days, but would not question her after he saw the results of her struggle with her memory. It was yet another sign that he cared, even if he struggled to present a distant facade. She knew better.

Emily let him continue his charade that he did not care, because she knew the truth. She no longer allowed her forgotten memories to frustrate her, either. She would remember soon enough. There was time for her memory to return. There was time for Cutter to admit his love for her. In time, anything was possible.

Suddenly Cutter stopped and turned to face her. She could not stop the smile of greeting that rose to her lips just at the sight of him. His expression was stern. She had not seen him smile since that day in the cave, but it was the face of the man she loved, and she welcomed it.

He scowled at her. "We are only a few hours from home now. Can you make it that far or should we stop to rest?"

"Can we afford to stop just for a few moments? I think a brief rest would help a little, but I do not want to be traveling after dark."

"We can spare a few moments," he said in a rough voice, but his gaze studied her intently.

Emily sank down onto a half-rotted log with a sigh and stretched her legs out in front of her. She massaged her calves to ease the twitching muscles. After her breathing slowed to normal again, Emily rose with a sigh.

"We can rest longer."

Emily almost smiled at the care he took to appear unconcerned about her.

"No, I would rather see this journey end and then rest."

"As you wish."

Tad must have been watching for them, because it was his cry that roused the station. By the time they reached the edge of the field, everyone was standing in the gate and raised a ragged cheer to greet them.

Mack was the first to reach them. He took one look at Emily's pale face and swept her up into his arms. He grinned at Cutter's dark look and shrugged.

"Emily, it is good to see you well and whole," Mack said to her. "But I am not sure who rescued who."

Emily just smiled. She'd never expected Cutright's Station to feel like home, but after being away for more than a week, it felt like a homecoming indeed. Even more so when Tad reached them and squeezed Emily's hand.

"I have been studying," he said eagerly. "I knew you would come back. I knew my father would get you back."

"I knew he would too," Emily said, and gave Cutter a quick glance. He avoided meeting her gaze, but she did not let it bother her. She knew how he felt.

"Oh, miss, I am so glad to have you back," Ruth said with a genuine smile of greeting.

"It's good to be back."

Once inside the gates, Mack lowered her to her feet, and Emily's knees nearly buckled beneath her at the loss of his support. With a cry of rage, Cutter stepped forward and caught her.

"Has she not been through enough without you dropping her?" he said to his friend with a snarl and carried Emily into his mother's cabin and laid her gently on the bed. He turned on his heel and left without so much as a good night, but for now his tender touch was reassurance enough for Emily.

She was right.

Cutter loved her.

As she let her eyelids close and she drowsed on the comfortable bed, Emily heard him bark out a series of orders: telling Ruth to go in and see to her, instructing his mother to sleep in the loft, ordering Mack to secure the gates, commanding Tad to get something for her to eat.

She was hungry, but now that she finally lay down on a bed and was safe, the only thing Emily wanted to do was sleep. Cutter's voice was the last thing she heard.

Chapter 14

When Mrs. Clark found her, Emily was eating breakfast. She was dutifully eating all her corn mush under Ruth's watchful eye as Tad questioned her endlessly about her capture. Imogene Clark brought an immediate chill into the cozy room with her, and all talk and laughter ceased.

"You look well enough for having suffered such an ordeal." The older woman pinched her lips together and gave Emily a look fraught with disapproval. "I trust you expect to assume your duties now that you have returned to us."

Emily's mouth twitched at that. The other woman made it sound as if Emily had been enjoying a pleasure jaunt rather than surviving a nightmare. Sooner or later she and Mrs. Clark were going to have a serious disagreement— about Tad, but especially about Cutter.

It was only a matter of time, and from the look on her employer's face, Emily thought that time had come. She looked longingly at the unfinished bowl of corn mush. She doubted she would ever be full again, but if Mrs. Clark wanted to talk to her, then talk they would. From Emily's viewpoint, better to get it over with. "Yes, Tad and I were just discussing his lessons."

"Were you? I thought I heard him asking if you'd been tortured." Mrs. Clark's tone implied that she would not be sorry to hear that Emily had been tortured. "I did not realize that was a part of your curriculum."

"I thought it best to satisfy his curiosity now so that when it is time to get to work he won't have any distractions."

"Well, you would know all about distractions, now, wouldn't you, Miss Keating?" Mrs. Clark laid a hand on Tad's shoulder but never turned her gaze away from Emily. "Tad, why don't you go lay your books out and review your Latin grammar?"

"Aw, Grandma—"

"Now, Tad." Mrs. Clark's voice was soft, but Tad must have heard the anger beneath it, and he left without further protest.

"Leave us, Ruth." Her cold stare remained on Emily.

Ruth followed Tad out the door after giving Emily a sympathetic look.

"I doubt this talk is going to be about Tad's lessons," Emily said and laid down her spoon.

She knew Mrs. Clark would not be happy about her relationship with Cutter. However, unhappy or not, the older woman would just have to learn to live with, Emily thought, and lifted her chin to match Mrs. Clark's determined look.

"That will do to start. There will be no more lessons. I do not want a woman like you teaching my grandson. I want him to be a gentleman above all, and I doubt he can learn any of the qualities necessary from a woman such as you." Her lip curled into a sneer when she finished.

"What kind of woman am I, Mrs. Clark?" Emily asked with genuine care. It would be interesting to know just what Mrs. Clark had guessed about Emily's relationship with Cutter.

"You are a woman of low morals." Mrs. Clark's voice rose with her indignation. "You seduced my son, encouraged Mack, and the good Lord only knows what you did with those heathens."

Emily had expected the accusations about Cutter and Mack, but the other was a surprise. The heavy smell of grease from Ruth's frying pan turned her stomach. "You act as if I asked to be carried off!"

"For all I know you may have," Mrs. Clark said, her chin now trembling with her rage. "You! I know how you are, sneaking out and staying out half the night. Always going off on your own. Carrying on first with Mack and then with Stephen. Given time, no doubt you would seduce my darling Tad. Well, I won't have it. If you are well enough to be up and about, then you are well enough to leave."

"Now?" Gripping the rough edge of the wooden table, Emily wondered if the woman expected her to make it to the fort on her own. Maybe she hoped that Emily would be captured again.

"No, Mack will escort you to the fort tomorrow. I will not allow my son to risk himself on your behalf again. He only went after you this time because he felt a responsibility to you. As far as I am concerned that responsibility has been fulfilled."

"Mother, I will decide when and where my responsibilities are fulfilled, not you."

Cutter's quiet voice startled both women into silence as he entered the kitchen.

"This has nothing to do with you," Mrs. Clark said firmly. "I hired the girl. Now I am dispensing with her services."

"I thought Emily was the answer to your prayers, Mother."

Emily heard a hint of amusement in Cutter's voice. She suspected Mrs. Clark heard it too, because the older woman's mouth tightened as she obviously struggled for an answer.

"I was wrong."

"Do you still intend for Tad to go to university?" His voice was conversational.

Mrs. Clark straightened her spine before she spit out her answer. "I do."

"Is she not arguably one of the best-educated persons in Kentucky, and the only one available to tutor Tad?"

"Yes." She glared at Emily.

"Then I do not understand what the problem is," Cutter said smoothly.

"I do not believe she is a suitable person to spend so much unsupervised time with Tad."

Cutter crossed his arms across his chest and studied his mother for a moment. "What has led you to that judgment, Mother?"

Mrs. Clark worked her lips before answering. "I know very well she has been carrying on with you, Mack, and any other man she can find. I can only believe she left Virginia originally to avoid scandal because she carried on like this there. She is a woman of loose morals. She is not fit to be near my grandson."

"You do realize, Mother, that sooner or later Tad will probably associate with women of far looser morals than Emily? You cannot keep him tied to your skirts forever."

"So you admit she is of loose morals!"

"I admit no such thing." Cutter turned to look at Emily for the first time since he entered the kitchen. She blushed guiltily under his surveillance. "I was about to disagree entirely with you."

"Stephen, I know the two of you were outside the station together for most of a night. Something happened that night. Why else did you leave so suddenly if not to avoid her?"

"You are right, Mother," Cutter said in an even voice,

still looking at Emily. "Something did happen that night, but it was not something illicit and shocking, as you seem to imply."

"Then what happened, Stephen? What exactly happened between you?"

"Exactly, Mother, I do not know." Cutter shook his head. "I will not share the details with you. That is between Emily and me."

"Stephen—"

"My name is Cutter!" he shouted and then seemed surprised at his outburst and half smiled in apology. "Will you learn not to call me that other, please? That is in my past. I no longer go by that name. Now leave us, Mother; I would talk with Emily."

"I want her to leave the station today," Mrs. Clark said, stubbornly standing her ground.

"She will not, unless she chooses to go," Cutter said. "Do you choose, Emily?"

"No." Emily was still dazed that Cutter had actually defended her to his mother. He had come close to admitting to care for her. Almost. It was not enough, but enough to give her hope.

"There, that matter is settled. Now leave us, please, Mother."

"Cutter, no . . ." Mrs. Clark reached out a hand to her son. She hesitated, and then let her hand drop without touching him. Instead she turned on her heel and left the room. Emily could not help thinking that things might have gone better for Cutter if his mother knew how to touch him.

For a long moment the only sound in the room was the quiet crackle of the fire and the thumping of Emily's heart in her chest. Had Cutter finally come to accept what was between them?

He cleared his throat with a nervous gesture that touched her heart and gave her hope.

"My mother was wrong about something very important."

"What was that?"

"I have not disposed of my obligation to you."

The heavy note in his voice tied Emily's stomach into knots. He did not want to talk of love; he wanted to talk of obligations.

"There are no obligations between us, Cutter," she said hesitantly, searching for just the right words. She wanted Cutter, but she would not have him because he felt he owed her something. She would have him because he was hers, as she was his. "Everything we shared was freely given and freely taken. How can you talk about obligations in connection to what we shared?"

"You may be carrying my child. Have you thought of that, Emily?"

His voice was harsh, and his refusal to soften even a little toward her hurt Emily more than she cared to admit. She had not thought about the fact that she might be carrying Cutter's child. If she was, Emily would consider it a blessing, but she would not let Cutter use it to push her away.

"What if I am?" she tossed back at him angrily. "What is that to you?"

"That makes you my obligation."

Emily was beginning to hate that word.

"Why?"

That made him pause for a moment.

"I made you pregnant."

"We do not know that yet."

"No, we do not, but it does not change the fact that I took your innocence and you may be carrying my child."

"Cutter, you took nothing."

"You were a virgin. There is no denying that."

"Yes, I was a virgin, but you did not take my innocence. You made love to me because I asked you to."

Emily's throat felt tight. He loved her. What would she have to do to prove it to him?

"It was my choice. It was my action. It is my duty to be responsible for the consequences."

"What about my choice, my actions?" Emily protested. "You do not make the world spin, Cutter. If I am indeed pregnant then it is as much my doing as yours."

"Maybe so, but we will bear the penalty together."

"We will not."

"Damn it, Emily, you will marry me!" He seized her by the shoulders and shook her slightly.

Emily's heart twisted in her chest. She'd thought those were the words she wanted to hear, but not this way. She knew he did not ask her because he loved her. He asked her because he felt an obligation to her. *Obligation.* Emily hated that word.

"Do you love me?" she challenged him, daring him to answer with her glare.

"Do not expect me to love you, Emily. Love has nothing to do with me or how I lead my life." His voice was flat, emotionless, as if he truly felt nothing for her.

"Then I will not marry you." Emily lifted her chin and glared at him defiantly. "I will not marry without love."

"You will if you carry my child," he said sternly. "Would you have your child carry the burden of shame?"

"Would you have your child live without love?" The picture of Tad's face as he anxiously waited for some sign of affection from his father filled her mind. She would not subject herself, or her child, to begging for scraps of affection from Cutter. There would be no commitment between them without love. She had time to convince him of that.

"What does marriage have to do with love, Emily? Many people marry without it." His expression was as coldly logical as his voice. Emily might have hated him if she thought that was all there was to him.

"Then I might as well marry Mack," Emily countered with a smile, just to needle him.

Cutter's eyes flashed at her. "You will not marry Mack."

"Cutter, why will you not admit you love me?"

"Because I do not."

His voice was discouraging, striking at Emily's heart, even though she knew he lied. He had to be lying.

"Then I will not marry you." Emily said firmly.

"If that is your wish, I must abide by it, but you will not leave Cutright's Station until I am satisfied that you are not carrying my child."

Cutter strode from the kitchen, slamming the door so hard it shook the small building.

"Cutter, there's a rider coming," Mack said. "Looks like one of the scouts from Boonesborough. Maybe Daniel's sending you a message."

Cutter slammed his fist against the log wall of the cabin one last time, leaving his knuckles raw and throbbing. He hoped Boone had sent him a message, maybe even needed to send him out to scout. Cutter needed to get away from the station, even though he had not yet been back a whole day. He needed to get away from Emily.

"Don't you look cheerful this morning," Mack observed when he and Cutter opened the gate to admit the rider from the fort. "Lover's quarrel?"

"Shut up," Cutter said in a growl and went to greet the scout he recognized as Will Smith. "Welcome to Cutright's Station, Will. What brings you out so far?"

"Heard you had a bit of Indian trouble."

"Just a bit, but nothing I couldn't handle," Cutter said tersely.

"That is exactly what Boone thought you'd say." Will laughed and slapped his thigh. "There've been attacks all over Kentucky. I've come to tell you to expect more where that came from."

"Boone taken to foretelling the future now, has he?" Mack quipped.

"You don't need much of that after you read this." Will handed Cutter a printed handbill.

" 'To all Kentuckians,' " Cutter read aloud, " 'Join the Canadian forces. If you will, you may have pardon, lands, equal rank, and equal pay. If you will, these Indian attacks will cease.' It is signed by Sir Guy Carleton."

Mack gave a long whistle. "No less than the commander in chief of Canada is fit to deal with us, boyos. Where did you come by this, Will?"

"A man was left dead, scalped, outside the gate of Logan's fort. This message was found with him. Boone, George Rogers Clark, and Benjamin Logan received personal invitations to go to Detroit and treat with General Hamilton himself."

"Why are we so important to the English?" Mack shook his head in amazement.

"Because if we fall there is no one to guard the colonies' backs against an English and Indian invasion," Cutter said softly. "I've heard some talk of it but did not think it would come to this."

"It has. No mistake of that. Daniel believes they will make a concentrated effort to drive us from Kentucky one way or another." Will's expression was stern. "Boone's sending me to all the outlying stations. You'd best get your family to the fort, and fast. No telling when the next attack will be. I have to warn one other family before I get back there myself."

"I'm damned if I'm going to sign any private treaty with the English, and I'm damned if I'm going to let them drive me from my home." Cutter kept a tight rein on his anger and fear. He didn't fear for himself, but for his family, the people who depended on him. He feared for them.

"Well, if that is your attitude, then you may well be damned, Cutter. I wish you luck and God's goodwill. You will need both," Will said, and rode out of the gate.

"Cutter, I am no weakling, but even I can see that it is

foolhardy to risk ourselves," Mack said softly. "It is well and good for you and me to make the decision to fight and stay, but what of the women and the boy?"

"We will let them make their own decisions," Cutter said with a nod.

Mack was right. The thought of moving to the fort left him with a sick feeling in his gut, and Cutter doubted he could do it.

Then there was Emily.

He would not be alone with her once at the fort, and if she chose to push him away there was nothing he could do. Maybe it was for the best. He could not give her what she wanted. He could not give her anything at all.

When he had his small group of dependents gathered together in the dogtrot, Cutter felt a heavy weight descend on him. Each one of these people depended on him to protect them, and the danger seemed to grow each day. He could barely protect himself. Maybe Mack was right and going to the fort was the only answer.

Looking at them, he felt a noose closing around his neck, and the walls seemed to hem him in more with each breath he took. Emily was right about one thing: for someone trying to avoid commitment, he had far too many.

"I cannot believe you would consider staying." His mother's sharp voice grated on Cutter's nerves. "Do you not care about the lives of your mother and son at all?"

He frowned at her. "I do, but there are no certainties. What if we are attacked before we reach the safety of the fort? We will not be able to travel very fast because there are not enough horses for everyone to ride. The trip itself would be a great risk."

"I am willing to take the risk." Imogene Clark pressed her lips together in a firm line that Cutter knew meant her mind was made up. "I would rather go back to Virginia but since you seem determined to make your home in this heathen land then at least let us enjoy the safety of the fort."

Mack shook his head. "The fort may not be the safe haven you think it is. What if we are in the fort and it falls?"

Mrs. Clark gave him a disapproving look. "Pish-posh. That will not happen. Daniel Boone and Colonel Calloway will not allow it."

"There is a good chance it might," Cutter said. "I think the British will make the fort a primary target. You heard what the notice said, and it mentioned Daniel by name. The British know that if they can take the fort then Kentucky will fall."

Ruth gave a low moan of fear and hid her face in Reuben's shirt. Tad's face was pale but his eyes danced with excitement.

"We will not let the British take us," Tad said quickly. "We will fight them, won't we Pa?"

Cutter smiled sadly at the boy. "We won't make it easy for them anyway."

"Look on the bright side," Mack said in an effort to break the tension. "The English must be afraid they can't beat General Washington. Why else would they need to go in the back door, so to speak? This means we're winning the war."

Imogene Clark did not find Mack's statement amusing, Cutter noticed. His mother suddenly looked old to Cutter. She'd always been a handsome, strong-willed woman determined to make her life to suit her.

"We can't stay here, and we can't go to Fort Boonesborough. Is there nowhere safe in all of Kentucky?" She twisted her hands helplessly in her lap and stared at her beloved grandson with tear-filled eyes. "Where can we go?"

"I don't know if there is a safe place in Kentucky," Cutter said slowly. "But there is always Detroit."

"What?" his mother said in surprise.

"If we give our allegiance to England we might convince the Indians that their English fathers want them to leave us alone," Cutter said, angry that there were no good options for him to protect his people. He would not swear allegiance to the English, and he would not give in to the Indians.

Emily suddenly cried out. When Cutter turned to her, she was pressing her hands to her head and suddenly becoming pale. Cutter reached out for her and barely caught her before she fell.

"What is wrong with that girl?" Imogene Clark cried out in annoyance. "We have no time for hysterics now. We need to pack and get to the fort."

"Mrs. Clark, I am not sure the fort is the right answer," Mack said with a shake of his head. "The more I think of it, the less certain I am."

"Nonsense, we need to leave today," Imogene said indignantly.

"We will not be going anywhere today," Cutter snapped and swept Emily up into his arms. Cradling her next to his heart with her head on his shoulder, Cutter suddenly felt more calm than he had since Will rode in with his news. This at least felt right. It was a relief to have the decision taken out of his hands.

"What are you talking about?" his mother asked impatiently. "She will come around soon enough."

"These headaches of hers are getting worse. I will not risk Emily by forcing her to travel with one. That is my final decision."

Cutter carried Emily into the cabin she shared with his mother without waiting for anyone to disagree with him.

Chapter 15

Her headache was gone. For days the pain came in turns, aching, throbbing and threatening to crush her brain. Now it was gone. Emily reveled in the sensation, the freedom from pain.

There was pressure on her head though. A soft pressure. Someone gently rubbing her temples. Their touch soothing and tender. Emily recognized that touch.

Cutter.

"Emily, you have to wake up. Things won't be the same without your sharp tongue to keep us all dancing. Someone needs to stand up to me. Someone needs to talk back to my mother. Emily, wake up, please."

It was the please that touched her.

Cutter demanded. Cutter took. Cutter did as he wanted. Cutter never said please. She would never expect him to say please with that soft, pleading note in his voice. It would take a stronger woman than Emily to resist that pleading, and where Cutter was concerned, Emily had no resistance left.

She opened her eyes and smiled up at him. He was so handsome, so strong, so unexpectedly tender. Emily was filled with the wonder that this man could love her.

Then she remembered.

"Cutter!" she gasped, her body tensing as she tried to rise, suddenly afraid for the man she loved. "You're in danger."

"No more than I have been," he said soothingly and pushed her back down on the bed. "Don't worry about me. Now you rest. You need to take care of yourself."

"No, Cutter. It is you who needs to take care." Emily struggled against the strong hands that held her down but Cutter was immovable.

"Hush. Just lie back now."

"Cutter, I remember."

He released her as if he'd been burned. His expression hardened. A cold shutter closed over his eyes, closing her out. The tender lover was gone, as if he'd never existed. This was the fierce frontiersman, the wild man who cared about no one, the man who kept her at a distance.

"What do you remember?"

His voice was so harsh Emily winced. Something flashed in his eyes, but she couldn't be sure what it was before it was gone.

"Your head?"

Emily shook her head. "It doesn't hurt. I feel fine. The headache's gone."

It is you that hurts me, she wanted to tell him, but she knew this wasn't the right time. There were more important things to talk about. Like his life.

"You're in danger."

Emily made the mistake of touching his arm, trying to convey her urgency. For a moment he tolerated her touch, but then he shook it off and rose from the bed to pace.

Emily smoothed her hand across the rough wool blanket, touching the spot where he'd been. She missed the warmth of having his body near. She felt so cold without him. The chill seemed to spread to the very core of her being.

Watching him prowl the room, Emily was reminded of a caged mountain lion she'd seen in Virginia. The animal was thin and ill-kempt, but its natural grace and the wild gleam in its eye were the same as Cutter's. They'd killed the animal a few days later, Emily remembered with a shudder, after it attacked its keeper. She did not want to think about that anymore.

"Cutter, please listen to me. You are in danger."

"You said that before, Emily." He waved his hand in an impatient gesture. "It is scarcely news. We are all in danger. The Indians are on the warpath, thanks to the English."

"It is more than that. If you would just listen to me—" Emily swung her feet out of bed.

"Stay in bed!" Cutter jerked around as soon as her feet hit the floor. "I will listen."

"At least look at me while we talk."

When he turned his fierce look on her, Emily was almost sorry for her request, but she needed to see his face, to judge his expression. Two long strides closed the distance between them. He loomed over her, pinning her to the bed with a single look.

"What do you remember?"

"Everything," she whispered.

Everything about the way he loved her, cared for her, rescued her, all the reasons she loved him, but that wasn't what he wanted to hear. Emily laced her fingers together to resist the impulse to touch him. She knew he would only pull away.

"We need to get to Fort Boonesborough. You need to get to the fort." Emily bit her lip nervously. She didn't know how much to tell him. What did he need to know to protect himself? How much would jeopardize any chance they had of finding peace for themselves?

"Why me especially?" His voice was soft, but every line

of his body demonstrated his tension. Like the mountain lion, he was coiled to spring.

Emily wondered if he saw her as another bar on his cage, another obligation caging him in.

"You are in danger. The English want you just as badly as they want Daniel Boone and Benjamin Logan. That's why they took me. I was just bait for the trap."

"Trap?"

He frowned at her but Emily didn't care. At least he was listening. She didn't like the reckless streak in him. He took care of others, but he never took care for himself. It was as if he placed no value on his own life.

"For you. Silver Fish waited to give you a message from General Hamilton."

"Silver Fish!" Cutter was still looking at her, but his eyes looked right through her as he pondered the meaning of what she told him. "Hamilton. The hairbuyer. What would he have to say to me?"

"I don't know, but Silver Fish said his instructions were to take you to Detroit. One way or another." Just saying those words sent a chill down her spine. "He said his English fathers wanted to talk to you. Why, Cutter, why do they want to talk to you?"

"You know why, Emily. The same reason they want Boone and Logan. Without leaders they believe Kentucky will fall into their hands easily, leaving the rebel colonies vulnerable to attack from both sides. I am just surprised they are that interested in me." Cutter turned away from her and leaned his forehead against the rough-hewn log wall.

Emily longed to go to him, to comfort him. She wanted to tell him that she loved him, but she knew he would only look at that as another burden. He did not need another burden. When would she finally prove to him that love was a gift, a support, not a burden?

Emily drew in a ragged breath. "I'm sorry, Cutter."

"For what?" His words were soft as a sigh. "It is not your doing."

Emily twisted the rough-woven blanket with her hands.

"Silver Fish seemed to know you well. He said you taught him English."

Cutter laughed, but there was no humor in it. "Yes. I taught him English and this is how he repays me."

"He said you were friends."

If only she could make him talk. He kept so much bottled up inside him. He needed to let it out. If she could only reach him. If only he would let her love him.

"We were blood brothers. Do you know what that means?" Cutter didn't wait for an answer. He stalked to the bed, reaching for her with such a violent expression on his face that Emily flinched back without thinking. When she saw the pained look on his face she wished she could take it back. It was too late.

"We were blood brothers," he said softly, touching the bruise on her temple with a gentle hand that made her want to weep for him, "and this is how he repays me."

"Silver Fish never hurt me," Emily said, glad she could give him that much.

"Then who did this, Emily? You were in his care." Only the tic of a muscle on Cutter's jaw betrayed his tension. He stood so still, intent on her words.

"It wasn't Silver Fish." She didn't know why it was so important to her for Cutter to know that his friend's betrayal did not include this, but she knew it was important to Cutter. "Evil Eye hit me."

"Evil Eye?" The corners of his mouth twitched, almost as if he wanted to smile. "I never knew an Indian who would tolerate that name."

"That was not his name; that is what I called him. The way he stared at me . . ." Emily shivered, remembering. "He wanted to hurt me, but Silver Fish wouldn't let him."

"What happened, Emily?"

His hand was still on her hair. Emily did not dare move, hardly dared breathe, for fear he would remember and move away.

"Silver Fish was sure that you would come." Emily looked down at her hands, gripping the blanket in her lap. "He thought I was your wife. That is why they took me. He wanted you to come. So we waited for three days."

"Silver Fish, Evil Eye, how many others?"

"Two more, younger. They did what Silver Fish said. Only Evil Eye dared argue with him."

"Why did they stop waiting?"

"There was a messenger. Maybe Silver Fish's son, I thought. They didn't like the news he brought. Then they argued. Evil Eye was so angry. He didn't like what Silver Fish said. He stared at me. Silver Fish tried to stop him, but Evil Eye got to me first. That is all I remember."

"They went away?" he said to himself.

"They will be back. I'm sure of it," Emily said urgently, afraid he would not heed her warning.

"Don't worry, Emily. I believe they will too."

His hand moved across her head, his fingers barely caressing the curve of her cheek. The touch was a mere whisper, and then he moved away. Emily thought she might have imagined it if her skin weren't still tingling from his touch. He stood, staring at his hands, and Emily's heart ached for him. He was so alone.

"Will we go to the fort now?"

"Yes, we will go the fort." He sighed. "Tomorrow. It is too late now, but we will leave at first light. I have things to see to before we go. Get some rest."

He moved briskly to the door, not looking at her again.

"Cutter."

He paused at the door, but Emily hesitated before speaking, wetting her dry lips, trying to find the right thing to say.

"What?" His tone was impatient, his hand already on the door latch, but he waited.

"Thank you." *I love you,* her heart told him.

"For what?" *Don't love me,* his tone said.

"For taking care of me. It was good of you." *Don't push me away,* she begged him.

Cutter laughed harshly. "When are you going to learn, Emily? I'm not good."

Emily lay back against the feather pillows with a sigh. He loved her. She knew it. There was no other explanation for his tenderness. Just when she was ready to give up on him, declare it useless, he would show her some sign of the man she knew was within. No matter what he said, there was good in him, but Emily was not about to spend her life fainting just to see some kindness from the man.

"Men!" she said in disgust and threw a pillow at the door just as it swung open again.

"What have you done with my grandson?" Imogene Clark's eyes were only narrow slits in her face as she advanced on Emily. Her carriage was so stiff and proud, Emily thought she might shatter if someone touched her. "Where is Tad?"

"I don't know."

Mrs. Clark clenched and unclenched her fists as she pursed her lips. Emily bit back the sharp reply she wanted to give the older woman; something in her eyes warned Emily that something was seriously wrong.

"When did you last see him?" Emily asked softly. She didn't give two bits about Mrs. Clark's feelings, but Emily did care about Tad.

"When we were all together. Just after you fainted." The other woman's lips were tight as she spoke, but her chin trembled slightly.

"He is not in the kitchen or the loft?" Even as she asked, Emily knew Mrs. Clark had already looked in those places,

KENTUCKY KISSES   183

and any other possibilities within the limited confines of
the station.

"I looked everywhere. I thought perhaps he was in here
with you. . . ." This time when she met Emily's eyes there
was no anger in them, no arrogance, simply fear.

Almost against her will Emily felt herself caring, if only
a little bit, about Imogene Clark. "I'm sure there's a simple
explanation."

Glancing at the hearth Emily noted the empty brackets
above the mantelpiece. "Where is Mack?"

"Cutter sent him out to scout around the station to look
for any signs of trouble."

"Did Tad go with him?"

"He might have. There was so much going on. I didn't
see him leave," Mrs. Clark said doubtfully. "I know Mack
took him with him several times while Cutter was gone.
Against my wishes."

"Mack will take care of him," Emily said, to reassure
Mrs. Clark and herself. "Tad's just fine, I'm sure."

Catching her lower lip between her teeth, Emily couldn't
be so sure.

After Mrs. Clark left her, Emily could not stay in bed
any longer. Whatever Cutter said, she felt fine, and the
sense of unease sitting on her was growing with each passing minute. It would be better to busy herself with the
other women and prepare for their journey to the fort.
Anything was better than sitting still and waiting, with nothing to do but think.

When Cutter passed Emily in the yard, where she was
airing bedding before it was packed away, he gave her a
baleful glare. Still, he didn't order her back to bed as she
half expected. It was just as well. She wouldn't have obeyed
in any case.

As she worked, Emily thought more about Cutter and

what to do about him. What to do about the feelings she had for him. Watching him work with Reuben as they packed for their journey and secured things at the station, Emily was struck anew by Cutter's separateness. Despite being surrounded by people, he was alone. She reminded herself that it was his choosing. Still, her heart ached for him.

"Emily."

She started, nearly crying out in fear when Mack laid a hand on her arm. She'd been so intent on Cutter she hadn't noticed the other man approaching her.

"Have you reached an understanding with him yet?"

Mack's expression was sympathetic. Emily wished she could have fallen in love with him. It would have been simpler—for all of them.

"You could say that." Emily laughed bitterly. "We understand each other very well. He understands that I love him and I understand that he will never admit that he loves me."

"He cares for you." Mack nodded toward Cutter. "He is a stubborn man, but then I know you are a stubborn woman."

"I know." Emily smiled a little. "I thought to give him time, sure that eventually he would discover he could not lock his feelings away, but now time has run out."

"You know as well as any of us the risks we face. We may not make it to the fort. I don't think you can afford to wait." A wicked gleam sparked in Mack's eyes and he grinned. "Of course, you can always change your mind and marry me. I'm much more even-tempered."

"Mack . . ."

"I know, Emily. Just don't wait too long."

Emily bit her lip as she watched Mack walk away. He was right. She'd thought there was time, but there was no time. Time just ran out. She could not wait. She would not wait.

"Cutter, I would talk with you."

He was checking the horses, picking up a hoof and looking at the shoe. Watching him run his hands along the animal's legs raised a primal instinct in Emily that made her all the more determined. She shivered at the memory of those hands running across her body. She could not bear it if he never touched her again.

"Cutter?"

He finally looked up at her and shrugged. A flicker of something flashed in his eyes. Worry? Fear? Anticipation? Emily couldn't be sure.

"So talk."

"You aren't going to make this easy on me." She laid a hand on the bay mare's neck, drawing energy from the warmth of the creature.

"You've never made things easy on me, now have you, Emily?"

A lock of dark hair tumbled into his eyes, and without thinking Emily reached down to brush it back. "Cutter, we need to settle this between us. I thought to give you time. I wanted to give you time, but there is no time."

"Does that mean you will marry me? We can have Squire Boone speak the words over us when we arrive at the fort tomorrow."

Cutter did not even meet her gaze as he spoke. She felt separate from him. He was building a wall between them she could never breach. He would marry her, but he would not commit to her.

Cutter was still speaking: "I think it best. You are right. We have no way of knowing the future. I will not leave you pregnant and alone. This way if I am killed you will at least be acknowledged as my wife."

"I am not talking about marriage." Emily scowled at him. "I am talking about love."

"As I said before, I don't know how to love. I am willing to give you my name. Is that not enough?"

Emily laughed; there was no joy in it, but it was either

laugh or cry. "Your name. The name you won't even claim yourself. That is some gift. I don't want your name. I want *you.*"

"That is something I can't give you."

He stood and shifted so his back was to her, but Emily would not let him end the conversation this way. The heat of anger slowly boiled through her until Emily thought she might explode from it.

Who was he to dictate what she would feel, who she would love?

Damn Cutter for being the pigheaded fool he was. She would not let him ruin his life this way—or hers. She would not let him break her heart.

"Don't you dare turn away from me, Stephen Cutright. I won't let you walk away."

He straightened slowly and turned to face her. With scarcely a hand's length between them he matched her glare for glare. "When will you learn, Emily? The only thing we have between us is this."

He seized her arms in a bone-breaking grip and pulled her hard against him. His lips punished hers until Emily couldn't breathe. She fought back the only way she knew how, kissing him harder and more violently than he kissed her.

She clung to him, her mouth wild and willing beneath his. Passion met passion. Hunger met hunger. Heat met heat.

It was over as suddenly as it began. They stood panting, staring at each other, still rocked by what passed between them.

Cutter's eyes glittered dangerously. "That is all there is, Emily. The same basic attraction that draws animals together. Nothing more."

Emily pointed her chin defiantly. "Some animals mate for life. You have chosen me and I have chosen you. We will be one, whether or not you choose to accept it."

"Emily—"

His mother's scream cut off Cutter's words. As he watched, his mother threw herself at Mack.

"Tad!" Staring in confusion at his mother, Cutter barely heard Emily's cry, but when she clutched his arm he turned to look at her again.

She'd gone pale. "We thought Tad was with Mack. I just talked to Mack and didn't make the connection. I was thinking about something else."

"I'll find that fool boy and teach him not to wander off again."

Cutter shook her hand off his arm and strode toward his mother.

Chapter 16

It was just after daybreak when Cutter stopped at the edge of the clearing that marked the beginning of his cornfield. A light mist whispered across the silky tops of the corn. He stared through the fog, searching for the gates of the station.

They stood closed tight, blank and accusing. A monument to his failure.

He'd built the walls to protect his family. Now his son was taken.

Unable to bear looking at the reminder of his failing, Cutter looked down at his hands. They'd been clenched into fists for so long his fingers were cramped. Slowly he forced his fingers to uncurl. He wiped his sweaty palms across his buckskins.

He rubbed the back of his hand across his eyes. They felt gritty and dry. His whole body ached from the effort of moving forward. He was exhausted, but there would be no rest for him.

No rest until he found Tad.

He'd searched for the boy through the remaining hours of daylight and then through the night. He'd found Tad's trail without much trouble and discovered the spot where the boy was taken captive. He'd seen the dead squirrels Tad had killed to bring home for supper. No bullets penetrated the furry bodies. The squirrels had been killed with a grazing shot, just as every other woodsman tried to do.

The boy was a good shot, Cutter thought with some pride before the guilt hit him.

They'd taken his son.

Captive.

There was no blood, no body. Tad was still alive. For now. He doubted they meant to hurt the boy or kill him. No, Tad was simply bait, as Emily had put it.

Bait for a trap.

A trap set for him.

If Hamilton wanted to see him, Cutter thought as he caressed the stock of his long rifle, then he would go see Hamilton. He would deal with the hairbuyer, and then he would bring his boy home.

Whatever it took.

Whatever they wanted.

Cutter started across the field. Before he could go after Tad there were things he needed to do. He had to tell his mother. He had to send Mack to take the others to the relative safety of Boonesborough.

Then he would go after his son.

When he reached the station walls the small door beside the gate opened and Emily slipped through it. She wore a wool shawl over her cotton nightdress. Her feet were bare and damp from the dew on the grass. She shivered slightly in the cool morning damp.

"You should be in bed," Cutter said roughly, but when she reached for him he went into her arms gladly.

She wrapped her arms around him and pressed her lips

to his. If ever he'd needed her before, that need was only a pale shadow of the need that possessed him now.

She knew. She didn't say a word. She simply opened her arms to him and gave.

Cutter would be sorry later for accepting this gift. She would be sorry later. Knowing that, he still went willingly into her embrace for the consolation he needed. He clung to her, drawing comfort from her warmth, from her vitality, from her. There would be time for regrets later.

A lifetime.

He couldn't look at her face. He didn't want to see the love in her eyes. He knew it was there, but somehow it would be worse to face it. It would only make it harder to walk away.

"They've taken him," he said at last and drew away from her. "I have to go after him."

"I know." Her voice was full of the love he needed but couldn't accept. The love he had to walk away from, for her sake, and for his own.

He couldn't look at her, but he could touch her. Closing his eyes, Cutter traced the curve of her face, ran his fingers through hair that coiled and tumbled like a living thing beneath his hands. He memorized it all, for the countless days and nights that would come without her.

She sighed his name, softer than a caress.

The pain from the aching, gaping hole in his chest seemed to ease. That wasn't right. He could not find ease, comfort, not when Tad was in danger because of him.

"I failed him," Cutter whispered into her hair because he needed to say it. "I failed Caroline. I promised her I would look after him. It was the only thing she asked of me. And my mother. God, somehow I have to tell my mother."

Emily touched his shoulder gently. "She's waiting for you."

Cutter went to find his mother.

Imogene sat in a rocking chair before the fire in her cabin. The fire blazed bright and hot. She was wrapped in a blanket, yet still she shivered.

She rocked and stared into the fire, not giving any sign that she heard the door open and close. When she spoke her voice was hoarse from crying. "You did not find him."

"No." Cutter nearly choked on the word.

"You will go after him." Her voice was flat, emotionless. It was as if she'd given all the emotion she had and now there was nothing left.

Cutter recognized that sound, that feeling. "Of course."

Imogene sighed and her shoulders shook. She never made a sound, but he knew she was crying again.

Helpless to comfort her, Cutter stepped closer to the fire. The heat in the room was suffocating. Cutter found it hard to breathe, or maybe it was just the tightness in his chest. There was no need of a fire during the warm Kentucky summer, but when he knelt beside her and touched her hands they were cold as ice. "I'm sorry, Mama."

Looking up at her face Cutter almost recoiled in shock. In the few hours he had been gone his mother had grown old. All her adult life Imogene Clark had fought a constant battle to keep her beauty, even in the wilderness. She'd enthralled two husbands and had scores of admirers back in Virginia. In Kentucky, Cutter had had more than one offer for her hand, one from a man considerably younger.

She'd always been an attractive woman who looked young for her years. Now wrinkles seemed etched into her face, but it was her eyes more than anything that had aged. Those green eyes, so like his own, had been brilliant with anger earlier today. Now they were faded and dim.

He didn't know what to say, what to do, to comfort her. He gently stroked her hands. "I'm so sorry."

She didn't acknowledge his touch, only crinkled her forehead and tightened her grip on the coat she held in her lap.

Tad's coat.

"So cold," she murmured so softly he had to lean closer to hear her. "It gets so cold at night. He didn't even have his coat. He'll catch a cold."

Cutter couldn't bear it anymore. He gently kissed the top of his mother's head and moved to the door. As he swung it closed his mother called after him.

"You'll bring my boy back to me, won't you, Cutter?"

Cutter shut the door without answering.

He was through making promises he couldn't keep.

Emily found him saddling the horses. His face was stony, his expression unreadable.

He was alone.

She knew he needed comfort. She knew he would take no more from her. She'd been surprised that he let her hold him when he returned. It was only for a few moments, but more than she'd expected. It was a moment of weakness he probably regretted. He would not let it happen again, she was sure.

Still, there were things that needed to be said. She had to try to reach him. It wasn't in Emily's nature to simply give up without trying. "It's not your fault."

"What do you know of it?" He would not even turn to look at her.

"I know that you took every care for his safety."

He laughed, a harsh, humorless laugh that sliced through her heart like a hot knife.

"Every care? I did not even know he was gone from the station."

Emily bit her lip as she searched for the right words, if there were any. "That does not make it your fault. He was not a baby to be watched every minute. He knew the risks just as I knew the risks."

"I'm his father. He was my responsibility."

Cutter lashed his words at her like a whip, but Emily refused to back down.

"I have told you before, Cutter, that the world does not spin because of you. Everything that happens is not your fault, and everyone who is hurt is not your responsibility."

"He is my son. That makes him my responsibility. He was taken because he is my son. That makes it my fault."

The pain etched on his face made Emily want to hold him again, kiss him, love him until he forgot to hurt, but she knew that he would not let her.

He was drawing back within himself. Once he'd disappeared into the blackness he found, there would be no way for her to reach him. No way for her to save him. She could not let that happen. There was only one way to reach Cutter now.

Emily reached deep inside herself, drawing on her anger—the anger she felt against fate, against Silver Fish, against the British, and, yes, against Cutter.

"Yes, this is your fault, but not for the reasons you think." Her words gained heat and momentum as they spilled out. "You failed Tad. You failed to show him a father's love. You failed to spend time with him. You were the reason he was out risking himself yesterday. He wanted to impress you. That was his reason for everything he did, and you never noticed. You were so full of yourself you couldn't spare your son one moment's notice."

"I noticed." His voice was soft, his anger tightly reined in. Still, he would not look at her.

"Then why could you not show him that you loved him?" Emily said with a snarl, prodding him, pouring salt into his wounds, anything to stir a reaction. "He worshiped you and what did it get him? Nothing but heartache."

"I cannot love." His voice was desolate. "There is nothing but heartache for anyone who imagines they love me. There is no room for love in my life."

He would not fight with her. That more than anything

else told Emily how heartsore he was. She didn't know
how to reach him, how to convince him that he was not
the monster he believed he was.

She felt him slipping away from her. She feared that
once he did she would never be able to reach him. He
would be lost to her forever.

Emily would not let that happen. She touched his arm,
felt his muscles quiver beneath her touch in response.
"No. You are wrong, Cutter. Your life is full of heartache
without love, not with it. You can love. I know you can.
You love Tad. You love your mother. You love me."

Cutter pulled away from her as if her touch burned him.
"Cease your harping, woman, and go get ready to go to
Fort Boonesborough. Mack will take you and the others.
I don't want to hear any more of your foolish talk."

Still he did not look at her.

"I am ready." Emily hesitated, knowing he would resent
her words. "It is not foolish talk."

"It is a waste of my time. I need to think on other
things."

"I wanted to make sure you are all right."

Cutter made a sound of disgust. "I am as all right as I
can be with my son captive."

The shutters were coming down again; the walls were
going up between them. He was blocking her off. He would
not look at her.

Emily dug her fingers into his arm. This time she would
not be shaken off. This time she would not let go until
she stirred a response in him.

"No. You are not all right. I will not walk away from
you, Cutter, and I will not let you drive me away. You need
me, Cutter."

"Go away, Emily."

Still he did not look at her.

"I love you, Cutter."

She touched his cheek with her free hand, barely skimming his skin before he caught her hand in a painful grip. He wrenched her away from him, but it was not the pain that made her cry out when he finally looked at her.

His eyes were fierce. Wolf's eyes, full of violence and stunning strength. The strength to walk away from her— if she let him.

"You do not love me. You are only a foolish woman who confuses the pleasures of the flesh with something more."

Emily pulled her hands out of his grasp and slapped him full across the face. The angry red imprint of her hand stood out in sharp contrast. She watched in fascination as his hands curled into fists at his side, and she thought for a moment he might hit her back.

Instead he simply lifted an eyebrow mockingly. "Do you feel better now?"

She wished he'd hit her.

"No, but I expect you do. I'm surprised you haven't taken to whipping yourself. Or do you just prefer your bruises on the inside?"

He laughed at her, and Emily felt something tear away inside her. She was powerless to help him. There seemed nothing she could do for him. She thought he cared for her.

She was wrong. So very wrong.

She couldn't stop herself from begging one last time. She hated him for it. She hated herself for it. "Why won't you let me help you?"

"If you really want to help me, Emily, then go make sure my mother is ready to leave for Boonesborough."

Then he turned away from her again. Not knowing what else to do, Emily did as he asked.

When Emily opened the cabin door she was struck by a wall of heat. Mrs. Clark sat huddled before the fire.

"Is that you, Cutter?" The voice was so feeble, so weak,

Emily could not believe it belonged to the virago who had cursed her only yesterday. Who would probably curse her today.

Emily braced herself. "No, it is Emily."

"Good. Come here, girl, so I can talk to you."

Surprised by the note of welcome in Mrs. Clark's voice, Emily seated herself on the stool beside her chair. The woman rocked, staring into the fire while her hands stroked Tad's coat with a rhythmic movement that mesmerized Emily. When the older woman reached for Emily's hand she was again taken by surprise. It was cold and frail, feeling like nothing more than skin and bones, but her grasp was still strong.

"I am so afraid, Emily. I don't want to lose my boy."

Against her will, Emily felt sorry for her. This woman was self-centered and tyrannical. She'd done her best to make Emily miserable and drive her away. Imogene Clark was all those things, but she'd also lost everyone who was important to her. Emily knew how that felt. She patted her hand with awkward reassurance.

"Cutter is going after Tad. He will bring him back as he brought me back."

Mrs. Clark shook her head and turned to look at Emily. Her eyes were filled with fear. "This is different. With you, he needed only the skills he knows well, tracking, hunting. This time he will be dealing with men of a different sort. It has been too long since he dealt with men who are not as honest as he is."

Mrs. Clark gripped her hand and leaned forward. "Promise me you won't let him go alone."

Emily didn't understand what the other woman was asking. Only yesterday Mrs. Clark had ordered her to stay away from her son, accused her of being little more than a whore.

"What?"

"He will need you," Mrs. Clark said simply.

Emily shook her head. She might not understand what Mrs. Clark wanted of her, but she knew very well what Cutter wanted. "Cutter does not need anyone."

"Do you love him?" Cutter's mother searched her eyes and seemed satisfied with what she found there. "You know he will let this destroy him. I think you are the only one who can stop him."

"I can't. I've tried." Tears stung her eyes. Failure and rejection lumped in her chest, making it hard to breathe.

"I've seen you together. You touch him. I think he might love you. Even if he doesn't, he lets you closer to him than anyone else."

Mrs. Clark choked back a sob, her voice heavy with regret. Emily's heart ached for her, for her son.

She blinked back her own tears as she admitted her failure to reach Cutter. "He shuts me out."

"He shuts everyone out. That is his way, but you slip under his guard, Emily. I have seen the way he looks at you."

The older woman gave her a pleading look. "Please help me, Emily. Help Cutter."

"I thought you hated me," Emily whispered.

"You are not the woman I would choose for him, but he has chosen you." Mrs. Clark sighed and let go of her hand.

"Has he?" Emily did not know whether to believe her or not.

"There is no one else, Emily. Please, I don't want to lose them both." Mrs. Clark's eyes filled with tears—the eyes that were so like her son's.

Emily's heart rose in her throat. The choice had already been made. She loved Cutter. She always would.

"I promise."

Chapter 17

Cutter woke with a start. His heart pounded painfully in his chest. The station was too quiet. His senses strained, seeking some sign of life. Then he remembered why there was none. He'd sent everyone away.

Tad was taken from him.

Emily had left him.

He swung his feet to the floor and ran his fingers through his hair while he tried to make sense of his inner turmoil. He'd always thought he wanted solitude, quiet. He wanted no one, needed no one. He'd struggled to find such peace for twelve years, and now he discovered it wasn't what he wanted after all.

The silence crushing in on him created the same pressure on his soul. The station was empty and so was his life. Empty without his family, without Emily. He was used to waking to the sound of Tad's chatter, Ruth's singing, Mack's whistling.

He wanted them back. He wanted Emily back. They were all gone. He was alone. Just as he would be alone for the rest of his life.

He couldn't stop the picture of Emily from forming in his mind any more than he could stop the guilt from eating at him. She loved him, and he'd driven her away.

It was no use telling himself that she was better off without him. They were all better off without him. That was the truth, but so was the fact that he wanted her. Her loss still made him ache inside, but there was no time to wallow in his misery.

It was time to go after Tad.

A quick glance out the door told Cutter it was past noon. He'd slept too long. He resented the delay. He wouldn't have rested at all if his mother hadn't nagged him into it.

He'd only lain down at all to ease the look of worry on her face. It was the least he could do, he'd thought at the time. After all, he'd failed her just as he'd failed every other person foolish enough to care for him.

Habit and exhaustion made him fall asleep quickly. The few hours of rest had not done anything to make him feel better. Cutter doubted anything would, until he saw his son safely reunited with his grandmother.

Cutter didn't really expect that even that would ease the ache in his chest. Not when he'd lost the most important thing in his life.

Emily.

Nothing, not even his son's safety, would make up for her loss, but Cutter would take this last chance to prove to his son that he cared for him. He couldn't love Emily and he couldn't love his son, but he would protect them. That was the only thing he could do for them. Then he would find a way to make it through the rest of his life.

Alone.

Cutter forced himself to his feet. There was no time to waste dwelling on his pain. There would be tomorrow and the day after to think about it, but every hour he wasted now meant Tad was taken farther away.

He'd slept in his clothes, so with a quick scrub of his

face he was out the door, giving his supplies a last look. Hefting his saddlebags over a shoulder, Cutter headed for the stable.

He paused in the barn door, taken aback by the sight of three horses inside. He'd told Mack to leave his black and a packhorse. He hadn't wanted to take even those, knowing his family should ride to make it safely to Fort Boonesborough. However, he needed speed to catch up with Tad's captors.

Stepping inside the barn, Cutter ran a hand over the bay mare's neck to soothe her. "What are you doing here?" he asked softly.

The mare's ears twitched in recognition.

"Waiting for you, just like I've been."

Emily's low voice struck him in the gut like a physical blow.

Cutter turned so fast the horse gave a snort of displeasure and sidestepped away from him.

Emily stood in the doorway. She was wearing the buckskin clothing that annoyed him so much. The clothing he'd forbidden her to wear. Her clothes didn't anger him nearly as much as her presence, even though he couldn't stop the sudden lift of his heart at the sight of her.

He growled to make up for the welcome he felt. "You should be on your way to Boonesborough. You'll be safe there."

She folded her arms across her chest and lifted her chin with a look of determination on her face he recognized well.

"My place is with you. Safety be damned."

Earlier it had taken all of Cutter's control to push her away. Now she'd caught him with his defenses down. He could no longer keep his fear for her bottled up inside.

Damn the woman for taking such risks with herself and damn him for caring. He couldn't afford to care about her, about anyone, not even himself.

"You will only be in the way. You will slow me down."

"I won't slow you down. The way I see it, you will not track; you will either head straight for Silver Fish's home or straight to Detroit. Either way you will be riding hard, but nothing I can't handle."

Her expression was defiant but her eyes held a softer emotion that shook him to the bone.

He didn't dare think about that now. Damn Emily Keating for slipping beneath his defenses and making him weak. He couldn't afford weakness now. Tad needed him.

"You are not going," Cutter said with a snarl and let loose a string of curses that would have made another woman clap her hands over her ears. Emily merely looked interested, as if recording them for future use.

When he finished she lifted her eyebrows questioningly. "Did you or did you not ask me to marry you?"

"I did, but—"

"Then I accept. I realize we won't have time for Squire Boone to marry us, but it might be better to wait until Detroit. Surely they will have a true minister there to do it right."

Cutter ground his teeth in frustration. "This is not a pleasure jaunt."

"I am fully aware of that," she said in a cool voice as she stepped past him and reached for a saddle. "That is why it is so important for me to go with you."

How could she be so calm when she was tying him up in knots? Cutter slammed his fist down on the saddle so she could not pick it up. "You are not going."

She turned back to face him. "You don't have much choice, now, do you? Mack is gone and you won't leave me here alone."

The fact that she was right only increased his anger and his frustration.

"I could kill you and blame it on the Indians. Then you would no longer pester me." Cutter forced his hands down to his sides. He wasn't sure if he meant to throttle her, shake her, or hold her. Either way he was damned if he did and damned if he didn't.

Her eyes widened but she did not back down as he hoped. He wasn't surprised. As hard as he tried to intimidate her, to frighten her away, Emily never backed down. It was his downfall, and hers.

"You will not hurt me, Cutter. I know that, even if you don't."

Her voice held a quiet confidence that Cutter wished he could echo. He knew better than anyone what happened to the people who loved him, who believed in him.

"I wouldn't count on that if I were you." Cutter took hold of her shoulders and shook her a little just to prove her wrong.

He had to release her quickly before he gave in to the need to hold her. That need frightened him more than the thought of traveling through the wilderness to rescue his son.

He scowled at her to cover his weakness. "Right now I am so angry I might just strangle you for the sheer relief it would give me."

She didn't spit fire back at him, as he'd come to expect. She didn't even scowl. She smiled, and then reached up to cup his cheek with her hand. "It's all right if you take your temper out on me. I understand."

The jolt of pure pleasure her touch sent coursing through his body was more than Cutter could bear. He pushed her hand away and stepped back. "Don't touch me."

"If that is the way you want it." She shrugged. "I love you, Cutter. I'll be here when you need me."

After delivering that enigmatic statement she tugged the saddle off the bar and heaved it onto the mare's back. Cutter glared at her and went to saddle the black.

"I won't need you," he muttered under his breath to the horse just to show her he was still in charge.

A week later, Cutter didn't feel in control. Not at all.

Yes, he chose the times when they mounted up in the morning and made camp at night. He selected where they would make camp. He even gave Emily orders that she obeyed. None of that mattered; as each day passed, Cutter felt less and less in control.

He scowled at Emily's back as he rode behind the bay mare. His black mood deepened when she leaned forward to pat the mare's neck and he watched the buckskins tighten around that round bottom he knew so well.

Damn her.

Emily should have been the perfect traveling companion. She never complained. She performed her share of the chores. She followed directions.

When he'd been silent so had she. When he lay down at night, so did she. The only difference was that when she slept, he didn't.

He lay awake staring at the stars overhead and wishing that he dared share her blanket with her, wishing that he dared share his life with her.

She'd been true to her word all this past week. She hadn't touched him. No matter that he ached for her touch. He lay awake at night, knowing she was so near he could hear her breathe, and did not touch her. His arms ached with the effort it took to keep from touching her.

The torture intensified during the day. From the moment he woke to watch her brush her hair, the sun picking out strands of gold among the brown curls, until she mounted up and he was forced to watch her firm behind bounce ahead of him all day, it was sheer torture.

He wanted her. The need to hold her, to draw comfort from her, to love her filled his every waking hour. Even when he finally managed to sleep there was no escape, for Emily haunted his dreams as well.

In his dreams there was one difference: that Emily touched him, and more. Sometimes he dreamed of the shy Emily he'd first loved on the banks of the river near his station. The Emily he had introduced to passion. The Emily who had taught him his heart was not as carefully protected as he thought.

More often he dreamed of the passionate woman who loved him in the cave. The woman who seduced and enchanted him in turns. The woman who demanded that he love her.

God help him, Cutter thought angrily, he did. This was the price he had to pay for allowing Caroline to die. This was the price he had to pay for putting Tad in danger. His penalty was to love Emily, to want her, to need her. His penance was to know she was within arm's length, and he could never have her.

This was hell.

He might have found relief if she would at least argue with him. Then he would be able to release some of his pent-up frustration. Yet no matter how many times he growled at her she would only smile sweetly. When he ignored her she would sing cheerfully to entertain herself.

Cutter knew Emily was not without flaws.

She was grouchy when she was hungry, and she didn't like to wash dishes. She flat-out refused to skin and clean any of the wild game he shot. Usually Emily lost her temper when he snarled at her, but not now. No matter how sharp his words, she would not fight back with him. He saw that control sometimes cost her and had been cheered to catch her throwing rocks at a tree one night while cursing him roundly.

No, Emily Keating was not perfect, but she was everything he wanted and couldn't have.

Cutter closed his eyes, knowing full well it wouldn't help.

Her image was forever burned into his brain. His other senses were too keen where Emily was concerned for him not to know when she was near.

He could hear her humming softly to herself. The scent of her, the taste of her, the feel of her still filled his senses. There was no escape.

Cutter groaned in frustration.

"Are you ill?" Emily called back to him, quickly reining in her horse and riding back to his side.

Opening his eyes, Cutter saw a pucker of worry form between her eyes as she brought her horse beside his. "Is something wrong?"

"Yes," Cutter snapped at her. "Something is wrong. The world is wrong. Now leave me alone."

The scent of lavender tickled his nose, irritating Cutter all the more. How could she smell like lavender after a week on the trail and bathing in cold streams? The woman was a witch. There was no other explanation for the hold she had on him.

Emily shook her head and reached out to press her palm against his forehead. "If you are sick—"

"Emily, get away from me," Cutter said in a growl. "You cannot help me."

"Nonsense. You are just being a baby, although I don't know why I expect different from a man," Emily said coolly, patting the neck of her horse to calm the mare. "If you will at least let me see if you have a fever—"

"Trust me, Emily. If you touch me, I will have a fever." Cutter urged his horse forward, desperate to get away from her.

"Cutter—"

"Just ride on, Emily. It is nothing that cannot wait. We will be stopping soon enough." He threw his words over his shoulder and prayed she would listen.

"If that's the way you want it," she said with a toss of her head and rode on.

Cutter hoped that would be the last of it. He did not know how much longer he could keep away from Emily. If she came so close to him again he might not be able to withstand the temptation.

The memory of his mother's face the morning after Tad had disappeared was the only thing that kept his resolve firm. Her misery mingled with Caroline's deathbed pleadings left Cutter with no choice.

Loving him always led to disaster, and he would not let that happen to Emily. He thought he could keep her safe by withholding his love, but that hadn't protected Tad. It certainly wouldn't protect Emily if he couldn't keep his distance from her.

Emily did not even look his way as he tended to the horses and she set up their meager camp for the night. Lulled by her apparent uninterest, Cutter paid her no attention when she moved around the fire to stand beside him. Before he had time to stop her she placed a cool hand on his forehead. Cutter jerked back from her and slapped her hand away.

"What are you doing?" he said with a snarl, his anger more for himself than for her. He needed to keep her at a distance. It was getting harder and harder to maintain that distance, especially when she stood so near her hair brushed his cheek. He took a step back, and then another just to be safe.

"I want to make sure you don't have a fever," Emily said calmly, folding her arms across her chest. "You are acting very strangely, Cutter."

"I told you not to touch me," Cutter said in frustration, unable to think with her so near.

Emily took a step closer to him as if she hadn't heard him speak. She stood so close Cutter could barely think.

He could smell a hint of lavender on her despite the fact that she'd been riding hard all day. That subtle scent, mixed in with the womanly smell of her, made Cutter's head spin with memories of the way she tasted. He could feel her heat radiating at him, and it took all his control not to crush her against him and never let go.

The want for her was so deep in him it sank into his bones, into his very soul. He wanted her. He wanted to pound himself inside of her until they were both lost to anything but each other.

Behind that want, that need, was fear.

Fear snapping like a wolf on his heels. He feared for her. He feared for himself. He feared what he knew, but most of all he feared what he didn't know. There was so much he didn't know, but he was certain it would mean Emily's doom to love her. It was not a risk he was willing to take.

"You have to stay away, Emily." His voice sounded hoarse to his ears. "I asked you to stay away."

Emily didn't look convinced. She raised an eyebrow and gave him a skeptical look. "Yes, you did. I abided by your wish, however idiotic I think it is, but I am not willing to take any chances with your health. Too much depends on you now."

Every nerve in Cutter's body screamed out a warning, but he couldn't resist the lure of those blue eyes, those full lips.

"Why do you care?" He meant to sound scornful, but his voice was too soft to convince even himself.

It certainly didn't convince Emily. "You know that I care, Cutter."

"But why?"

The anguish in Cutter's voice pulled at Emily's heart. He was suffering. He was in pain. She needed to comfort him. No matter what rules he thought to put between them, Emily would not stay away from her man when he needed her.

"Because I love you."

Emily lifted her face to his and smiled at him. She desper-

ately willed him to recognize that love. She almost begged
him to accept it, but what little pride she had left wouldn't
allow her to. She'd begged once before and it had gotten
her nothing but the bitter loneliness of empty arms.

When she saw the defeat on his face Emily almost cried.
Then he pulled her into his arms.

"Emily." He moaned into her hair. It was the cry of a
desperate man. "You will be the death of me yet."

"No, Cutter. No." She pulled back enough from him
so she could see his face, so he could see her eyes; it was
important for him to read the truth of what she said in
her gaze. "I am meant to be the life of you."

She kissed him fiercely. For the briefest instant he was
still beneath her lips. Then with an animal-like cry he
stopped fighting her.

He took her to the ground with the rush of his passion,
and her own erupted to meet his. She'd kept a tight lock
on her feelings for him for the past week, fighting her
needs, giving him space. Now she released that pent-up
emotion and was swept away by the frenzied feeling.

It was unexpected.

It was dangerous.

It was glorious.

There was the elemental smell of the earth mixed in
with the sharp scent of him. His grip on her was fierce,
painful, yet as his hands streaked across her, yanking at
her clothing, Emily reveled in the sensation and fought
just as hard to remove his. She barely heard his pants and
her moans above the rushing of her blood in her ears.

His lips were hot and hungry on her, ravishing her
mouth, sucking on her breasts, nipping at her neck.

Her hands fisted in his hair as his mouth plundered
hers. She crushed herself against him.

Emily knew he craved everything she had to give him,
and she was willing to give it to him. That and more.

He nipped at her shoulder and she cried out at the

deep, grinding, glorious pain, the aching need he created in her.

He covered her mouth with his and muffled her next cry.

Every nerve in her body was brought to exquisite attention. She was dimly aware of the hard ground beneath her, rocks digging into her flesh, but the feel of Cutter's hands on her bare skin, his hard body against hers, was enough to push everything else to the background.

It was a hot, frantic coupling, more intense than any they'd shared before.

When Cutter came to a shuddering climax he cried out her name and what sounded like a curse. His final, violent thrust set off tremors in Emily's center that rocked her until she wept.

After Cutter fell asleep Emily cradled him against her breasts like a baby. She smoothed his damp hair away from his face and whispered promises to him that she hoped he would let her keep.

Chapter 18

Emily woke slowly, feeling content and happy for the first time in days. The sky was the weak gray light that came just before dawn. Sometime during the night she'd changed positions with Cutter and curled up against his chest. Luckily the night had never grown chill and the air still lay thick and heavy, so they had no need of a blanket.

All they needed was each other.

Caressing his face, she listened to the twitters of the birds in the trees overhead and the crunching of the horses' hooves as they shifted in place on the far side of the clearing.

Cutter slept on.

She couldn't remember seeing him ever sleep this soundly. Soon, she knew, she would have to wake him, but surely they could afford a few minutes more. She knew he'd hardly slept since Tad was taken. He needed his rest, she thought, rubbing her cheek against his chest.

"You are like a cat." She felt the rumble of his voice in his chest beneath her head.

Emily raised her head to meet his amused eyes. "In what way?"

"My mother had a cat back in Virginia that would rub her head against you just so if you did not pet her."

"Then it is your fault," Emily said, and kissed him lightly. "You must not caress me often enough."

"Emily, my Emily, it is not for lack of wanting." He groaned and pulled her tight against him and kissed her long and hard. He released her with a sigh. "You know I care for you, Emily."

Emily saw the light go out of his eyes, and she knew she would not like what he had to say next.

"I know you love me," she corrected him, aching inside with the need to hear it. No matter that she knew it was true, Emily still wanted to know he believed it too.

Cutter traced the outline of her face with his hand in a gentle touch that rubbed her heart raw. "I gave up love when Tad's mother died. I have lived without it so long, I doubt it will ever come again."

"It has, Cutter; why won't you believe me?" Tears filled her eyes, frustrating Emily because she didn't want to cry. She needed to be strong for Cutter. She wouldn't sway him with tears.

"Maybe because I don't believe in it anymore."

Emily couldn't tell who he was trying to persuade, her or himself, but either way it was breaking her heart. She didn't know how long it would take to assure him that they had a fighting chance. She didn't know how long they had until everything fell apart. She had to keep trying.

"I believe, Cutter."

She could hear the sweet, delicate voice of a warbler in the bushes. Another answered from across the clearing. It seemed like a sign. As the bird sang to its mate, Emily prayed that Cutter would hear it too, and believe.

He sighed. She felt his sigh through the hand that rested

on his chest. It sent an echoing tremor of despair through her body.

"I can't give you what you want, Emily. What you need. I can't."

Emily blinked back her tears. She could either weep or rage. She thought anger would be more effective with Cutter than tears. She wanted more than comfort from him. She wanted a pledge. "How can you be so sure that you are not what I want?"

"I know."

The certainty in his voice shook her. She was sure that he loved her, but they could not both be right. She had to believe that she was right, but it was so difficult to listen to him and remain confident.

Emily sank her teeth into her lower lip as she sought some glimmer of hope in his eyes. Her only comfort was the fact that he still held her tenderly in his arms.

It was not enough.

"You always think you know best." Some of her bitterness leaked into her voice.

She wasn't sorry.

"And you do not?" He raised an eyebrow and gave her a half smile.

"Not always." Emily smiled back; even though her heart was breaking she could not resist his smile.

"But most of the time?" Cutter teased.

"I will not give you the satisfaction of answering." Emily didn't have the heart to banter with him.

"Then I will assume the answer is yes." Cutter's smile faded as he looked up at the brightening sky. "Now it is time for us to be on our way."

"Cutter, please do not turn me away from you again." Emily held her breath, waiting for his answer.

"I will not make any promises about our future." His voice was husky with emotion.

"I am not asking for one," Emily said softly. "Just do not turn me away."

"Emily, don't ask for promises I can never hope to keep. I don't want to lie to you. I won't hurt you that way." The pain in Cutter's voice was as raw as her own. Emily thought his suffering might be worse because he truly believed there was no hope.

At least she had hope. Emily choked back a sob.

"You won't hurt me." She pulled away from him, sitting so he could not see her eyes and the tears welling up there. "You can't hurt me any more than you already are. You hurt me every time you push me away. You said you would marry me. Was that a lie?"

"I will still marry you if you carry my child, but there will come a time when I have to leave."

She heard the cool tone of his voice. It hurt more than the words.

"Leave! Then what use is it for you to marry me?" Emily asked in outrage.

"You will have my name," Cutter said simply.

She did not understand how it could be so simple, how he could not see that she wanted only him.

"I don't want your name." Emily reached out to touch his hand, drawing comfort from his nearness, at least for the moment. "I want you, Cutter. That is all I want."

He drew his hand away from hers. Emily felt him pulling away emotionally as well.

"I can't stay."

"You won't stay," Emily challenged him. "There is a difference between *can't* and *won't*. This is your choice."

"None of this is my choice," Cutter blazed back. "It is not my choice to hurt inside every time I look at you."

That bruised Emily. She turned away, not able even to look him in the eye. How could she fight this demon inside him that tortured him so? How could she hope to win against something so terrible? She choked back a sob. "Is there nothing you can give me?"

"There is now. I can give you now."

Now, Cutter thought as he watched Emily ride before him on the trail. *Now, not tomorrow and certainly not next year.* There was only now. He'd thought himself dead inside for the past twelve years, and now he had learned that was a lie. His life was a lie.

He could remember a fierce Indian battle he had fought with Daniel Boone when he first came to Kentucky. As they tended a young man who'd been injured, scarcely more than a boy, the youth had cursed his pain. Daniel told the boy not to curse his pain, but rather to savor it, because the pain told him he was alive.

Cutter finally understood what Daniel meant. For years Cutter had believed himself dead inside. Now he knew he was alive because of the pain, but he could not relish it. Unlike the boy, whose wounds eventually healed, Cutter's wounds would never heal. They would spread and destroy him. He knew this as surely as he knew the sun would rise tomorrow, as surely as he knew he loved Emily.

She loved him, and he'd hurt her.

They hadn't talked about it again, and they made love each night, but now there was a bittersweet element to it. Each knew that this time might be the last. Emily did not reproach him. Neither did she beg him to reconsider, but when she thought he did not notice, the haunting looks she gave him tore at his heart in a way no words could have. He had hurt her, and Cutter was sorry for it.

Yet better she should suffer now than to allow that love to grow and watch him walk away from her. He'd seen the pain on Rebecca Boone's face every time Daniel left her.

Daniel had left for years at a time. Rebecca had survived that, as she had the loss of one son to the Indians and the near loss of a daughter.

Cutter had seen the handsome woman age before her time for the love of a man who could never settle down to be a husband and father. He'd even heard she took a lover when Boone was gone for those many years in Kentucky. Cutter couldn't bear for Emily to languish without him. He couldn't bear to see her love another.

Cutter knew the wildness was worse in him than it was in Boone. He'd been settled once, and it hadn't taken. He couldn't go back. Too much in him had changed, and not for the better. He could never become Stephen Cutright again, not even for Emily.

It was better for her to lose him now.

The devil of it was, even as he had her with him now, Cutter knew it was better for him to leave her. Worse, he didn't know if he would be able to find the strength to do it.

With each passing day it would be harder for him to leave. Every day he learned something about Emily, and about himself, that would make it that much more difficult to leave her. Every day she managed to find another crack in his armor and slip through it.

Every time he loved her he only wanted her more.

It was useless to think on it. The more he thought the more hopeless it looked. It was far easier to concentrate on the landscape and try to develop a plan for Tad's rescue.

They were making for Silver Fish's village in hopes that the war chief still had Tad. Surely they had not taken the boy on to Detroit. Cutter knew that the Shawnee would not have kept him long, but he would rather deal with the Shawnee than the British. He knew he could trust Silver Fish's word.

He had no such faith in the English.

They rode along the crumbling banks of an ancient riverbed. The sky was the achingly pure blue of Emily's eyes. Cutter knew that forever when he saw a sky like this he would remember the woman he loved.

There would be no forgetting Emily. He could only hope to go on without her. He didn't know how he would forget, how he would go on, but still they rode on into their future.

The air was humid and heavy, so moisture-laden it left the taste of mold in his mouth from breathing it. The only sound was the incessant buzz of locusts and sometimes the skitter of rocks breaking loose and sliding down the rock walls. The sun rose golden and hot in the sky, only a hazy glow through the thick air. His skin felt slippery from sweat. They stopped frequently to water the horses and drink eagerly themselves.

Ahead he could see Emily's head hanging as she sagged in the saddle. She was exhausted. He knew he was pushing her, pushing himself, to the limits of endurance, but too much time had passed.

Tad could be anywhere. God only knew what he had suffered.

Part of Cutter did not want this journey to end, because then he would have to part with Emily. Yet still he pushed forward, knowing his son's life depended on him. It was the same dilemma that tainted his life, his own happiness balanced against that of the people he loved.

The crack of a rifle echoed against the stone walls, and rock shattered overhead. Ducking to miss the flying rock shards, Cutter strained his eyes, searching for the source of the sound.

More rifles sounded. He felt a sharp, stinging pain in his left arm. Clapping his hand over it, Cutter discovered warm, sticky blood oozing from the wound. A bullet had grazed him. It hadn't penetrated his arm, but he knew that if he didn't tend to the wound soon he would lose a great deal of blood.

There were rocks on their right side and trees to their left. Somewhere in the trees their attackers lay in wait.

Another rifle shot and Emily's horse went down with a squeal of pain. He heard Emily cry out, and Cutter urged his horse forward.

"Emily!" He did not mean to cry out her name but couldn't help it any more than he could help hurtling to her side when she might be hurt.

Before he could reach her another bullet struck his right leg in the meaty part of his thigh. A red haze of pain clouded his eyes. He felt himself sliding off his horse. He clutched at the pommel. His hands were slick with blood and too weak to hold him in the saddle. It took forever for him to fall; then the ground rushed up at him with a bone-shaking crash. The last thing he heard was a Shawnee war whoop, and he knew he'd failed both Emily and Tad.

Somehow Emily rolled free of the shuddering body of her horse. She was shaken. Every bone in her body ached, but she was whole and well—unlike her horse, whose blood continued to gush from the terrible wound in her chest to cover Emily with gore. The mare's terrible squeals of pain echoed in her ears as Emily twisted around to reassure herself that Cutter was still alive and well.

Her heart stopped when she saw him recoil from a wound to his leg and then fall to the ground. She didn't even try to catch his horse as it thundered by her, still leading the packhorse. Her entire being was focused on Cutter.

When she knelt by his side she found him bleeding from the leg and arm. Exploring his injuries with trembling fingers Emily determined his arm was not badly hit and seemed only to ooze blood. His leg was much worse. The wound was deeper; blood had already soaked through his pant leg. She suspected the bullet was still lodged in his leg.

She had to find a way to stanch the blood somehow. Then she would have to think of a way to get the bullet out of his leg. Now she wished she'd spent more time with Ruth learning about healing. She wished she'd spent time learning about medicine rather than languages, but now was not the time for wishing.

She had to think.

She needed something to bind his arm and leg to stop the bleeding. Cloth. Barely registering that the shooting had stopped, she ran back to her horse. As she knelt beside the still-trembling animal, Emily wished there were something she could do to ease the mare's suffering, but if she was helpless to heal Cutter she had no hope of helping the horse.

Pulling a shirt from her saddlebag, Emily had started ripping it to shreds when she heard the rattle of stones behind her. She started to turn when naked, greasy, brown limbs moved around her, pinning her arms to her side.

A scream choked in her throat.

Emily yelled and struggled to free herself, kicking her legs and wriggling her body, but the Indian seized her hair and pulled her head back, leaving her neck stretched out with a cruel blade pressed against her throat.

"No," Emily whispered, knowing it would do no good. She couldn't be killed or captured now. Cutter needed her. Without her help he would die—if they hadn't killed him already.

Afraid for him, she tried to twist around to see Cutter, but the knife blade pricking her throat forced her to be still. Another Indian came running at her and let out a loud yip that made her cringe against the brave holding her captive.

Her wrists were bound tight with leather thongs. The

Indian holding her thrust her away so violently that she fell to her knees, ending up facedown in the dirt, unable to catch herself with her hands. When Emily raised her head she caught sight of her captor for the first time and knew her terror had just begun.

Chapter 19

Evil Eye.

Fear clenched tight in her chest.

He shouted at her, his black eyes flashing hate. She could not understand the language he spoke, but she understood his body language well enough.

He meant to kill her. Still kneeling in the dirt, Emily glared up at him defiantly. If she was going to die she would not give him the satisfaction of seeing her beg. There was no point to it. She already knew Evil Eye had no mercy.

He demonstrated that fact by seizing her hair in one large fist and pulling her head back until Emily thought her neck would snap under the strain. She couldn't stop the whimper of pain that escaped her. She heard him grunt in satisfaction. His satisfaction gave her the strength for courage.

The tip of his knife caressed the line of her throat, pricking the skin just under her chin until Emily fought back a scream of terror. She bit down on her lip until her mouth filled with the coppery taste of blood. The pungent odor of bear grease filled her nose. She could barely hear above the pounding of her blood in her ears.

She didn't want to die.

A loud command from another brave made Evil Eye move his blade from her throat, but he did not loosen his hold on her hair. Tears of pain and fear stung Emily's eyes. She desperately needed to see Cutter. She needed to know if he was alive. If he was dead there was no reason to fight for her life. If he was dead there was no reason to be brave.

She didn't want to die.

Evil Eye was shouting now. His grip tightened in her hair. His knife blade wavered dangerously close to her face. Emily closed her eyes. If she was going to die today she did not want to see the knife sink into her flesh.

The commanding voice was closer now, directly behind her. Emily could not understand what they were saying, but she heard Cutter's name used. She prayed that meant he was still alive.

She remembered that the last time she'd been captured by Evil Eye it was only Silver Fish who had kept her alive, but she knew she had not heard Silver Fish's voice here. She was sure that if Silver Fish was here, Cutter would not be wounded and Evil Eye would not dare to touch her like this.

The two men were still arguing about her. Even though she could not comprehend their language, Emily strained her ears to listen. Evil Eye was growing angrier, pulling back still harder on her hair until she was sure it would come loose in his hand. Emily bore the pain, telling herself that if Evil Eye was angry it could only be good news for her. She prayed it was true.

Evil Eye released his grip on her hair and dealt her violent, backhanded slap that knocked Emily i... ground. Gritty, sandy soil filled her mouth and st...

eyes. With her hands bound she could not even wipe her face. Emily lay still for a moment, waiting for his next attack, waiting for the knife to fall.

He seized her hair again and hauled her to her feet. Emily's head throbbed. Her knees were so weak she could barely stand. Evil Eye held her erect by his grip on her hair. The dirt in her eyes blinded her so she couldn't see. The commanding voice sounded again, and she felt the cool blade of Evil Eye's knife against her wrist.

Emily prayed.

Then her hands were free again.

Someone handed her a scrap of soft skin to wipe her face. When Emily could see again she slowly lifted her gaze, almost afraid of what she would see.

It was the young brave whose arrival at the spring had disturbed her captors so much. Just as his father had before him, he smiled at her. His smile was handsome and pleasant despite the parallel streaks of ocher paint across his nose and cheekbones. His teeth were straight and white in his russet face.

"Hello, Cutter's woman. Do not be afraid. I am Stands Firm. I will take care of you."

He was so young, Emily thought as she twisted her trembling hands together. How could her fate rest in the hands of someone so young?

"How is Cutter?" Emily would have moved around the young brave, but he put his hands on her shoulders and held her firmly in place.

"No, they are tending him now. You will only be in the way."

"I need to see him." This time Emily could not stop the tears that filled her eyes from running down her face and streaking grimy trails through the dust on her cheeks. Frustration and fear mingled together.

"He will live," the youth said, and firmly moved her

farther away from the spot where she sensed Cutter was struggling to live.

"Please." Emily would not beg for herself, not from a savage, but she would for Cutter. "Please do not hurt him."

"My father said he was not to be hurt. Do not worry, woman," he said in lofty tones, as if she should already have known this.

"If he was not to be hurt, then why is he?" Emily asked, brave in her worry for Cutter. "Why did you shoot at him?"

"That one hates the white man." Stands Firm waved his hand at Evil Eye. "He knew he would not kill and says he shot only to stop him so he would not fight us. Now you— you he would like to kill. I told him that would be for my father to decide."

A chill went down Emily's spine at that. Before, Silver Fish had guarded her well because she was important to him. Now he had Cutter and Tad. There was no reason to protect her anymore. She was not even Cutter's woman. He might kill her in anger if he discovered the truth.

The youth patted her awkwardly on the shoulder. "Do not worry, woman. My father will not want to listen to him. He will be very angry that his order was disobeyed. Cutter should not be hurt."

"Can I see Cutter, please?"

"No, woman. I said not. You will see him when we get to the village. Now we go."

"Why? Shouldn't it be my place as his woman to see to him?"

"Look." He took her by the shoulders and swung her around so she could see Cutter. Two braves were packing leaves around Cutter's wounds and then binding them. Evil Eye stood over them, watching Cutter as he'd watched her.

Hoping for the opportunity to kill.

"He leads this war party. If you push him he will kill you and your man."

"But you stopped him before."

"No. I tell him again my father's words. He is the leader. If he orders me to kill you, I would do it."

Stands Firm's expression hardened, and Emily was reminded of the young warrior she'd killed. These people were taught to kill, even this young. She and Cutter were still alive, but there was no safety here.

"Will you run away?" His obsidian eyes searched hers.

"I will not leave Cutter." Emily lifted her chin, determined not to show this boy her fear. She could not hide the tremble in her voice, but she still met his hard gaze with an equally resolute one of her own.

"That is what I thought. Now come."

Looking away from the young warrior, Emily saw a brave leading horses from the trees, including her mare and Cutter's mount. Several of the braves leaped onto their horses and raced around them. Stands Firm ignored them and led her to Cutter. As she watched, they lifted Cutter into the saddle of his horse. He slumped and wobbled, barely keeping upright by clinging to his saddle horn. Emily bit her lip so hard she tasted blood.

She turned to Stands Firm. "I am afraid he will fall if left alone. Let me ride behind him and hold him on."

When Stands Firm translated her request to Evil Eye, the older warrior's cold smile sent a chill down her spine.

"Cutter's woman will ride with Cutter," Stands Firm said, and then helped boost her up in the saddle. After he mounted he took the reins of Cutter's horse in his hand.

"Do not try to get away," he warned with a darting look at Evil Eye. "Our horses are faster and stronger than the one you ride. Your horse is tired and carries two. You would not go far. We will catch you. Then things would not go so good for you."

Emily tightened her grip around Cutter's waist, as if she could protect him. The blood on his torn clothing frightened her more than anything Stands Firm said. If Cutter was strong and well, she could face anything with him, but she didn't know if she was strong enough to be brave for both of them.

"Cutter, how badly are you hurt?" she whispered against his back.

"Not as badly as they think," Cutter said in a low voice. She could scarcely hear him above the sound of the horse. "It hurts like hell, but not as badly as my pride."

"They trapped us. How could you know?"

"I knew. I should have known better. I was stupid. A green kid would have been more careful than I was. I knew that once we got close to Silver Fish's village he would be on the lookout for us. I should have known he wouldn't let us just ride in. That would make him look foolish. Now I look like the fool."

Emily couldn't stand to hear the bitterness in his voice. "I'm sorry, Cutter. If I had not been along to distract you this would not have happened."

"It is not your fault, Emily. If you had not been along they might have killed me."

For all Cutter's brave words, Emily heard the pain in his voice and she worried. She wanted him to lie down and rest, but who knew when that would be allowed? Maybe they would both be dead by nightfall.

"No, Stands Firm said his father will not let that happen. Evil Eye wants to kill you, but Stands Firm reminded him of what Silver Fish wants."

She felt Cutter's shoulders shake as he gave a dry chuckle. "I should have guessed who your Evil Eye was. That, Emily, is the esteemed warrior Big Fist."

"It is not his fist I am so afraid of, but rather his sharp knife." Emily couldn't help but look again at the big warrior who controlled their fate. It was not a reassuring sight. Even with several horses between them, she could see the hate in his eyes, it burned so bright.

"Be afraid of both," Cutter said as Big Fist shouted at them. "We'd best stop talking; it makes Evil Eye nervous."

The smell of wood smoke on the breeze made Emily lift her head from Cutter's shoulder. Her eyes burned from exhaustion.

Yesterday they had ridden for hours and then spent the night in a cold camp. Cutter had slept, his wounds weakening him, but Emily hadn't dared sleep for fear they would be separated, or worse. Big Fist had kicked them awake and forced them onto the horse again before dawn so they could ride for hours more. She hoped the smoke meant they would be stopping soon.

The woods around them gave way to cleared fields separated by pole fences. Some of the fields were in corn; others full of pole frames were leafed over with climbing pea and bean vines. The neat rows of crops took her by surprise out here in the wilderness far from any settlement.

Any *white* settlement, she corrected herself.

The Indians urged their horses forward as they made their way on the narrow road that ran among the fields, but still there was no sign of the Indian village. Then, above the shaggy tassels of the corn, she saw curls of smoke drifting up faint against the backdrop of the forested bluff.

Emily's stomach clenched into a fist of fear.

The first dwelling she saw was unlike any building she'd ever seen. The size of a small cabin, it was dome shaped and covered with slabs of tree bark. An animal skin hung in its doorway. As she watched, a black-haired woman, naked except for a small deerskin apron and moccasins, pushed the skin aside and emerged from the hut.

The woman waved at the incoming riders, but her unblinking stare was fixed on Cutter and Emily. Her lack of emotion disturbed Emily more than hate would have.

Filled with apprehension, Emily tightened her grip around Cutter. He moved his hand to cover hers.

Now the Indians started yipping loudly, and as they rode around a curve in the road, Emily caught sight of their home for the first time. The road widened and led directly into a huge village of cone-shaped dwellings like the first one mixed in with long, low lodges almost as big as the houses she'd seen in Virginia as a girl.

Emily had not really thought about how the Indians lived. Once she thought they lived scattered throughout the vast forests of the wilderness, barely scraping by in shabby huts or unprotected by the elements. She'd pictured them as nomads with no homes, no ties to any particular place.

Even when Cutter talked of Silver Fish's village, she had never actually pictured a town like any the whites had built back east. Here the streets were clean, the children obviously well cared for, and friends called eagerly to each other as they lined the street to watch their group ride in. It was a village like any other, except the people here might kill her before the day was out.

Emily straightened her back and held her head up high. She knew it was important for her not to show her fear. She worried that when she was told to dismount, her shaking knees would give her away. She was sure they would not be able to hold her upright.

People kept crowding into the roadway, clapping and cheering, but they parted as the group made their way down the street. The Indians stepped back only far enough to allow the horses passage, and some reached out to touch warriors who were either friends or relatives, Emily supposed. Many poked, pinched, and prodded at Cutter and Emily until she was sure they would be covered with bruises.

The crowd closed in behind them and followed. Big Fist led his parade to the front of the biggest of the lodges, marked with elaborately carved poles at the entrance.

Silver Fish stepped out of the lodge. He did not turn his head to look at Cutter and Emily. He launched into a lengthy speech that obviously congratulated Big Fist, because the man's chest visibly swelled with pride as the crowd cheered. When he finished speaking, Silver Fish waved his hand and people slowly began to move away.

Silver Fish turned to look at them, his expression serious. "I am sorry you were hurt, Cutter, but if you came before I took your son we could have talked like friends."

"Does that mean we are now enemies?" Cutter asked.

"Are you my enemy, Cutter?" Silver Fish countered with a half smile.

"I do not want to be, but I think you want to be my enemy," Cutter said bluntly.

Silver Fish gave him a pained look. "This is not so. Who told you these lies?"

"Your own actions told me, Silver Fish. You took my woman and my son. This is not what friends do."

"I told your woman I wanted to talk to you. My English fathers want to talk to you. When you did not come, I must make you come."

"I am here, Silver Fish. Talk to me, or would you rather have your warriors shoot me again?"

Anger flashed in the chief's eyes, but his voice was calm when he spoke.

"They were not to hurt you, but they must defend themselves."

"I did not shoot your warriors."

Emily felt Cutter tremble slightly in her arms. She knew he was growing weaker and kept his voice strong only by an effort of will. She hoped his strength would last long enough.

"No. Big Fist says he caught you by surprise."

"I heard Big Fist crashing through the forest," Cutter's voice sneered. "I could have shot, but I did not want to hurt you or Stands Firm. I was sure one of you would be there. Why is it I have more care for your family than you do for mine, my friend?"

"I took care so your woman was returned to you and your son is well."

Unable to stand any more of this tension, Emily could not be still any longer. She could feel Cutter weakening and knew he could not stand much more. "I want to see Tad. I want to see that he is well with my own eyes."

Silver Fish gave her a disapproving look, but he nodded. "Come with me and see your son, Cutter."

Emily managed to dismount stiffly and helped Cutter without appearing to give him support. He stood erect, barely limping on his injured left leg, but Emily saw the beads of sweat on his upper lip and knew how much the effort cost him.

They ducked through the low, narrow doorway of the lodge. Emily paused to let her eyes adjust to the dim light within. There was a small fire burning in the center of the large room, but she was surprised to note that it was less smoky than most frontier cabins.

Then she noticed the large group of men seated to one side of the room equally divided around one ancient Indian so wrinkled and bent over that Emily could not tell if it was man or woman. The ancient one's hair was snow white and still lay thick with abundant beads and feathers to decorate it.

Tad was seated cross-legged beside the old one. He was dressed like an Indian, wearing only a breechcloth and leggings. His head was smooth except for a shaggy scalp lock running down the center. Emily scarcely recognized the boy as the youngster she'd tutored in preparation for going to William and Mary. Remembering a long-ago lesson, Emily thought he would have done better to learn Shawnee than Latin, as he'd said.

He looked well enough. He was thin, his ribs showing in his bony chest, but he'd never had much fat to spare in any case. His eyes lit up at the sight of his father and Emily. When she managed to give him a small smile he smiled back.

The men who had been so silent now disrupted into many voices, but Emily heard Big Fist's voice rise above the rest, and then the man stood before her. When he was done shouting a number of the Indians cheered and yipped in response. Then the old one spoke, directing his words to Silver Fish. Silver Fish took her elbow and led her to the door. Emily was nearly there before she realized that Cutter was still standing beside the fire.

"No, I will not leave them." Emily tried to shake free of Silver Fish's grip. "Cutter, tell them we are not to be separated."

"Go, Emily. This matter is between the men. You must go. It will be all right."

Silver Fish thrust her through the door. Emily stood blinking in the sunlight and thought that if Silver Fish did not kill Cutter, she might like to.

Chapter 20

Cutter watched Emily go, knowing full well it might be the last time he saw her. Knowing that angry glare she gave him might be his last memory of her face.

His heart beat painfully in his chest. He loved her. He wished now that he'd told her before they were separated. She should know.

Still, Cutter was glad she was angry with him. She would need that anger to see her through the next days. Maybe then she wouldn't blame herself for what he was about to do.

At a nod from Silver Fish, Cutter seated himself beside Tad. He squeezed his son's arm, reassuring himself the boy was well but not daring to show any more affection than that.

He'd already put Tad in enough danger. He was well aware of the dozen black stares glaring at him across the smoky room. Many of these men had reason to be suspicious of white men, and they would decide the fates of his son and the woman he loved.

Cutter knew his life was already forfeit.

Cutter turned his attention to He Who Walks with the Clouds, the shaman. The ancient would be the one who ultimately determined the fate of Cutter and his loved ones. His friendship with Silver Fish—and Big Fist's hate— would weight the scales along with the Shawnees' need to ally with the British.

Then the shaman would decide who lived and who died.

Once Thomas Jefferson had told Stephen Cutright he had a gilded tongue. The other lawyer had meant it as a compliment, but Cutter hadn't taken it as such at the time. Both then and now he did not like to win a war of words through trickery. Now he hoped that Jefferson had spoken truth.

Until today Cutter had had no need of smooth words and a quick tongue, but now he needed those talents more than he needed his skills as a hunter, tracker, and woodsman. He still did not want to resort to trickery, and would save that as a last resort. He knew it was only his brain and his skill as an orator that stood between death and his family.

He Who Walks with the Clouds inclined his head to acknowledge Cutter and offered his wrinkled palm to indicate that Cutter could speak.

"Why have you brought me here, Father?" Cutter asked the shaman in Shawnee, bowing his head slightly out of deference to the man's position with the People, as the Shawnee called themselves.

The shaman carefully loaded his pipe with tobacco and lit it. Each movement he made was measured and slow. He drew in a deep breath of smoke, held it, and exhaled before answering. Cutter felt his life ebbing away with each moment the shaman delayed his answer.

Cutter's back itched with impatience as he sensed Big Fist's glare burning into him, but he knew that his ability to wait patiently would also factor in the shaman's eventual decision. It would be easy for the Indian to sacrifice an alien Long Knife, not so easy to hurt a longtime friend who understood the People.

When the old one finally spoke his voice was low and rough, like the whisper of wind through cornhusks.

"You call me Father. You call Silver Fish friend. These things have been true. You have eaten at our fires. Slept in our village. Hunted with our warriors. You have lived with the People and been one with us. This is no longer true. How can you be one of the People and make war upon us?"

"I have not made war on your people," Cutter said, weighing his words carefully. "I have only shot at men who attack my home, just as the People do. I have only killed men who would kill me, just as the People do. I have always taken care not to harm the People. In my heart and through my actions I have remained your friend."

"You lie!" Big Fist stood up and pointed at Cutter with a hand trembling from his rage. "Long Knives killed my son."

Flecks of spit flew from his lips, and Tad cringed away from the angry man. Cutter put a comforting hand on his son's leg but did not back down, as the Indian obviously hoped he would. Big Fist pushed his way through the crowd to stand before Cutter, his body trembling with fury.

"I will take your son from you as my son was taken from me. Only then will I rest." Big Fist seized Tad by the arm, pulling him away from his father.

Tad cried out.

Seeing the terror on his son's face, Cutter uncoiled his body and lunged for the warrior. The need to protect his son was stronger than any other impulse. Before he could reach the other man, Silver Fish blocked Cutter's path. Several braves caught his arms behind his back, so he was forced to stand helpless and watch Big Fist drag Tad from the council lodge.

Cutter fought against the arms holding him back, but they were too many and too strong. Despite his injuries, it took five warriors to hold him down and pin him to the ground. Three of those were nursing injuries by the time he was through with them, Cutter observed with some satisfaction.

Silver Fish stood over him. His bronze arms folded over his bare chest. "He will not hurt the boy. He grieves for the loss of his son. I believe he would take this child to replace the other, who is in the spirit world."

"No," Cutter said through gritted teeth as he strained against his bondage. "I will not let him take my son from me."

"It is not for you to say, Long Knife," He Who Walks with the Clouds said as he moved slowly to stand beside Silver Fish. "Soon you will go to the big fort. You will not be able to take care of your son and your woman. We must decide what is to become of them."

A red mist descended over his mind, and Cutter fought against the hands holding him. They could not take Emily away from him. He would not let them hurt Tad. He felt the wounds on his arm and leg break open and the warm sting of blood. His wrists were rubbed raw. He barely heard the grunts and groans of the men holding him down.

"Enough!" The shaman's heavy voice rolled over their struggle like thunder, stilling white man and red men alike.

The sound rolled through Cutter's anger with a shudder that shook his body. He closed his eyes and slowly waged a battle within himself to control his rage. He could not win this battle. Nothing would be gained by violence now.

He knew his show of anger had alienated the shaman and the chief. It might prove to be a fatal mistake. He could not afford to force their hand. He needed to fight with his wits and not his hands. He needed to think. Willing himself to relax was the hardest thing Cutter had ever done.

Opening his eyes again, Cutter sought the shaman's gaze and was surprised at the sense of peace he felt staring into the old man's rheumy eyes. The peace he found there gave him the strength he needed to speak calmly.

"I am sorry I sought to do violence in your presence, my father, but just as Big Fist mourns the loss of his son, I feel the loss of my son—the son who was taken from me wrongly. I have come so far to protect him. It is a hard thing for a father to know he cannot protect his son."

"Will you sit and talk with us again, like men should?" the old man asked sternly, never taking his eyes off Cutter's face. "If you will behave like a beast then we must treat you like a beast."

Although Cutter feared for both Emily and Tad, he knew the only way to help them was to reason with the chief and the shaman. He did not think Big Fist would hurt either of them until the leaders of his tribe allowed it. He prayed he was right.

"I will behave like a man. You have my word."

The shaman stared into his eyes for a long moment before nodding for the warriors to set Cutter free.

When the braves holding him released his arms and legs it took every ounce of Cutter's control to sit calmly across the fire from Silver Fish and He Who Walks with the Clouds. The need to escape the lodge and see to Emily and Tad's safety was almost overwhelming. Cutter thought he might explode from the effort it took to keep that need locked inside him.

After he seemed satisfied that Cutter would not attack again, the shaman sat down as well.

"What you say is true. It was wrong to take your son from you, and before that your woman, but our reasons for doing those things were good."

"Does one right thing make the bad thing go away?" Cutter asked quietly. He had spent many a night talking with Silver Fish and He Who Walks with the Clouds in a more peaceful time that now seemed long past. Cutter knew how the shaman thought. He understood what mattered to the Indian—he hoped.

The shaman nodded at him, signaling his approval of the question. "No, it does not. Still, we need to weigh the greater good of the People against such things from time to time."

The shaman leaned back and puffed on his pipe, idly blowing smoke rings as he waited for Cutter to answer.

"Yes. So many wrong decisions are made, for what was thought to be the right reason," Cutter said, sighing to show his regret for that necessity.

"It was not a wrong decision," Silver Fish said quickly, looking at Cutter with narrowed eyes, obviously suspicious of his former friend. "I am sorry if you suffered pain and fear for your woman and your son, but I do what I must for my people."

"Are my woman and son such a threat to your people?" Cutter looked up at the chief, but Silver Fish looked away. "Have the People become so weak that they are afraid of a woman and a boy?"

"The People are not weak!" Silver Fish glared at Cutter. "We fear no one."

Cutter grinned, satisfied that he had pushed the Indian to lose his temper, just as the Indian had pushed him. Silver Fish bent his head slightly to admit that Cutter had scored a point.

The chief's voice was more controlled when he spoke again. "I would not hurt you, my friend, as you would not hurt me. Our English fathers want to talk with you, Cutter. This was the way I determined to bring you to me. And so you have come. Soon we must be on our way to Fort Detroit. There you will talk with my English fathers and all will be well."

"Why?" Cutter asked softly, moving his gaze from the shaman to the chief. He knew it was Silver Fish who dealt with the English. "Why do the English wish to speak to me so badly that you need to kidnap my son to bring me here?"

"You must convince the other Long Knives to leave our lands. You do not belong here."

The chief's gaze was hard, his expression unyielding. The brief accord they'd reached disappeared as quickly as the smoke rings the shaman was making.

"You once welcomed me to your lands, to your village." Cutter tried to keep his voice low, unthreatening. His life—more important, the lives of Emily and Tad—depended on his ability to convince Silver Fish that Cutter was still his friend. "What has changed?"

"It changed when your people came and built forts on our land. It changed when your people killed my people for walking across our land." Silver Fish leaned forward, his black eyes glinting in the firelight. "Your people have done these things and more."

"Do you deny this?" The shaman's rough voice broke through the silence where Silver Fish's words hung.

"People have done these things, but I have not done these things," Cutter said, and raised his eyes to meet the shaman's unwavering gaze. "You know this is true."

"This is true, my son." The shaman laid a hand on Silver Fish's shoulder and spoke in slow, measured words. "I know in my heart that you have not raised your hand to our people, but the other Long Knives have harmed our people. They must be stopped."

His last words raised a cheer from the warriors still seated around the fire, especially the young, hot-blooded warriors still seeking to prove themselves. Cutter knew they longed to fight the white men and prove their strength. He could not let that happen. Too many people he cared about would die, both white and red.

"The Shawnee are a brave people," Cutter said, and let his gaze sweep across the audience. Many of the braves nodded appreciatively. They wanted to fight the white man, but they would listen to him praise the People first.

"For countless moons the Shawnee have lived as the True God told them. They have killed only the animals they need for food and clothing. They have gone to war, fighting well and honorably, but only to protect their people and homes. Good fortune smiled on the Shawnee because they lived according to the ways of the People for more dawns than anyone can remember."

Cutter paused and let his gaze sweep over his attentive audience once more. Every muscle in his body ached from the effort to control his anger and his fear. He knew the Indians could see the emotions battling within him. They were more skilled at reading body language than most whites, but he knew they would respect the way he kept those emotions under control. He hoped they would listen. "The way of the Shawnee is good. You know that, for you are God's chosen people."

A murmur of agreement swept through the crowd. They knew their tribe was blessed by God. It was good that this white man knew also.

Cutter swallowed to ease the dryness of his mouth and breathed deeply. Now he must speak the difficult words, the words the Shawnee would not want to hear.

"I know all this because when I first came to hunt on Shawnee lands I was amazed by the beauty of the land and the grace of its people. Life was not always easy, but we know that God wants to challenge us to make us better people."

Cutter looked at He Who Walks with the Clouds and smiled. "A wise man taught me that. I did not believe it for a long time, but I am beginning to accept it."

The shaman inclined his head, accepting the praise Cutter offered.

"The Shawnee are facing more difficulties than ever before. Strange people have come to live in their land.

People with white faces who build homes and forts out of logs and hunt with rifles in place of the bow and arrow.''

A murmur of displeasure swept through his audience, and Cutter knew he must keep speaking. If he lost his audience now there would be no second chance. If this crowd lost control he would be dead. He did not doubt that Emily and Tad would not long survive him.

''In the beginning it was only a few people. Some red men and white men learned to become friends. Others killed each other. White men killed red men. Red men killed white men. This has been the way of things. If the English have their way it will continue to be the way of things.''

Cutter paused. Many of the warriors' eyes gleamed bright in the firelight, but a few, including the shaman and chief, looked thoughtful. They were listening.

''Ask yourselves why the English care to speak with me. Is it because they truly worry about the People and wish to drive the Long Knives from your land?'' Cutter shook his head in disbelief. ''I do not think this is so.

''The English want your people to fight with my people because my people have dared to stand up and say we will no longer be dogs to the English. I ask you this: if my people will not be dogs to the English, who will? Maybe the English are looking for new dogs. Would you have the Shawnee be the English dogs, doing their bidding?''

''The Shawnee are not dogs.'' Silver Fish stood up and folded his arms across his chest. ''We live the way we choose and do no man's bidding.''

''Whose bidding was it to steal my son and force me to talk to the English?'' Cutter asked softly.

''You cannot say my people are dogs to the English.'' Silver Fish loomed over Cutter, fingering the knife in his belt. ''Do not talk against the People.''

''I do not talk against the People.'' Cutter kept his voice

soft and low, knowing this was the most dangerous point he needed to make.

"I talk to warn the People. You must be sure that you do what is best for the People, not the English. Is it best for the People to hurt my woman or my son? How will this help the People? I am willing to sacrifice myself for the People because I recognize how great the Shawnee are. All I ask is that you consider these things before you make me leave this place we call home and go speak to the English. I ask you to consider these things when you decide what will happen to my woman and my son."

"The white face is afraid," one warrior said scornfully.

Cutter turned to face him, not daring to show any sign of anger or fear. "Yes, I am afraid. Just as all men fear for the safety of their women and children and old ones. That is what a man is. That is what makes a man a fierce warrior. For myself I am not afraid. I know I have lived my life in honor. Can each of you say the same?"

"That is what we must ask ourselves tonight," He Who Walks with the Clouds said before the warrior could reply to Cutter. "We will not talk on this anymore today."

The shaman rose to his feet once more, his bones creaking like limbs in a storm. "You and your family will be our guests this night, Cutter."

Cutter bowed his head respectfully so the shaman could not read the frustration in his expression. Guests tonight, but what of tomorrow?

Chapter 21

Emily knelt in the dirt outside the bark-covered lodge. Sharp stones dug painfully into her knees and the palms of her hands. Straining her ears to hear what was being said inside the lodge, she could faintly hear the even sound of Cutter's voice, and the much louder, angry tones of Big Fist. She could not make out their words.

Ignoring the stares of the Indians gathered around the lodge, Emily crept closer to the doorway, hoping to hear something. The rough bark walls scraped her cheek as she leaned in still closer. The sharp smell of wood smoke stung her nose and eyes. Bile burned the back of her throat as Emily battled against the wave of nausea that threatened to overtake her.

She would never forgive Cutter for barring her from the council that might well decide her life—and his. She almost hated him for pushing her away once again, for shutting her out of his life.

" 'This matter is between men,' " she repeated to herself to keep her anger alive. "How dare he?"

The truth was that Cutter dared, and he had succeeded in banishing her. Emily should have known that Indian men were just as controlling as white men, if not more so.

Big Fish shouted again, a long, unintelligible speech, and then Cutter roared in protest. Before Emily had time to react, Big Fist burst through the lodge doorway, dragging Tad behind him. Fear coursed through her as Emily wondered how Cutter would allow this. She dared not even think what had happened inside that lodge for Cutter to let the warrior lay hands on Tad.

Whatever had happened in there, Emily was sure of one thing: if Cutter would not protect Tad then she would. She knew firsthand the violence the warrior could wreak. She would not allow Tad to suffer anymore.

Emily threw herself at the large warrior with a furious cry. She kicked and hit at him with fists of rage until he released the boy. Roaring, he seized her arms and shook her until Emily's teeth rattled and her head spun dizzily. Her vision blurred, but she was aware of a crowd gathering around them. Their dark faces eagerly watched the fight, but no one intervened. Emily had not expected they would.

This was her battle.

Hers and Tad's.

She wriggled to free herself from the Indian's grip, but could not. He laughed, maddening her. Big Fist shoved her away, and Emily's head swam in a sickening motion. She sank to her knees and for a moment she thought she might vomit.

"Emily, are you hurt?"

Tad's anxious face hung over her, but Emily was too busy fighting the wave of nausea to console him. Big Fist shouted at her, reaching out a hand, whether to help or hurt Emily did not know.

Tad leaped on him with a fierce cry. The boy delivered a solid blow to the Indian's face, forcing Big Fist to shove him away, but the brave did not strike the boy. Emily was surprised the Indian didn't use more force, but she didn't expect that luck to hold.

Emily managed to stagger to her feet. "No, Tad. Stop."

Tad ignored her cry. He would have run at Big Fist again but an older Indian boy stepped in and caught Tad's arms behind his back. Tad struggled against the hold, but the other boy held firm.

Before Big Fist had time to act again, a sturdy Indian woman stepped between the warrior and the whites. She silenced the brave with a simple glare and a brief command. The slim brown hand she held up stopped the large man in his tracks.

The crowd chattered eagerly in response. Emily wished she understood what was happening. It was frustrating and not a little frightening to know they were discussing her fate and she could not comprehend a word.

Big Fist did not look happy either and shouted his protest at the woman. Emily expected the woman to back down before his fierce glare, but she cut him off with a brief sentence. The warrior stared at her for a moment, the entire crowd watching in hushed awe, before he turned on his heel and strode away. Emily's chest hurt, and she realized she'd been holding her breath in anticipation.

As she took a deep breath, another wave of nausea swept over her. Emily sank to the ground, unable to fight her body and keep her feet.

When she looked up again, Big Fist was swallowed up by the crowd of Indians surrounding them. The Indian woman still stood as before. She turned to face Tad. When she smiled at him the Indian youth released Tad. The Indian woman put a gentle hand under Tad's chin and tilted his head up to study his face. Seemingly satisfied that the boy was unhurt, she nodded and turned to offer Emily her hand.

Unsure what would happen next, Emily recognized that the woman had saved her a certain beating, at the least.

She took the woman's hand, surprised at the strength in the older woman's grip, and pulled herself to her feet.

Tad sidled closer to her, and Emily wrapped a reassuring arm around him, drawing comfort as well as offering it. She only wished she knew that Cutter was all right.

"My husband told me you had spirit, Cutter's woman, but only a fool challenges Big Fist when he is in a rage."

She spoke slowly, pronouncing her words awkwardly, but Emily was able to understand her easily. When she smiled Emily recognized Stands Firm's contagious grin in his mother's smile. This must be Silver Fish's wife. The boy with her also bore a marked resemblance to Stands Firm.

This family had once again stepped in to save her from Big Fist's wrath. The unbearable tension in her eased slightly at the knowledge that she was not as alone as she had once thought. She hoped Cutter was not alone inside the bark lodge.

Emily smiled back at the other woman. "Then you must be a fool as well as I, because you certainly challenged him."

The woman inclined her head in silent agreement. "That is so, but I knew there was no danger. He is my sister's son. I washed his bottom when he was young. He would not raise his fist to me. Still, when he is angry no one but his wife can be sure what he will do."

"Pity his wife." Emily shivered at the thought of being tied to a brute like that.

"No, Little Fawn manages him well enough. If anyone should be pitied it is my nephew. I think he will pay the price for his actions today."

"I cannot pity him. Not after the things he has done to me and Cutter." Emily shook her head.

Cutter! Remembering that Cutter might be hurt, or worse, Emily started toward the lodge.

The Indian woman caught her arm.

"No!" Her voice was adamant, her expression stern. "You must not go in there. The men must be left alone."

"Cutter . . ."

Emily's anguish must have reached the older woman, for her expression softened.

"He is all right. I am sure my man would let no harm come to him. The People have need of him."

"Your people already shot at him. He is wounded," Emily said scornfully as she stared hard at the lodge door, hoping for some sign that Cutter was indeed safe.

"Do you not think he is safest there with Big Fist outside?" the woman said reasonably.

The woman was right, but it was not enough for Emily. "Yes, but still I must see him. I should be with him."

"No, a woman shall not sit in on a council meeting. That is for the men."

Emily closed her eyes, fighting her exhaustion and fear. Blessedly her stomach seemed to be settled again, but her head still ached as she tried to think. She found it hard to believe that this strong, confident woman, a woman who stopped Big Fist's rampage with a simple command, would allow herself to be ruled by men.

Emily would not be so docile.

"Why? Why must I allow men to decide my life for me?" Emily did not bother to hide her scorn for such an idea. "I will stand up to those men and demand they listen to me."

"No. That is not the way it is done." The Indian woman shook her head and dismissed the idea with a wave of her hand.

"They are talking about me and Cutter, probably this very minute. Deciding what is to become of us. The decision may already be made," Emily protested, tightening her arm around Tad. She bit her lip as she stared at the lodge doorway again, half hoping to see Cutter emerge. They should be together now.

"Nothing is decided. The men will talk. The women will talk. Then a decision will be made."

"The women will talk." Emily echoed her as she tried to digest that amazing bit of information. Surely the Indians could not be more advanced about women's rights than her own kind? Not with brutes like Big Fist trampling about.

"Just as the men have a council, the women have a council. This is not the way of the Long Knives?" the Indian woman asked curiously.

"No, but we are making our own way now. The new way may very well change things." Even as she spoke Emily did not think it was true, but surely things could be no worse than they were beneath the English. "Why separate councils? Why not meet together as equals?"

"Women and men value different things."

"That I understand." Emily sighed, thinking about Cutter. Certainly they valued different things; Emily had learned that fact the hard way.

Talking with this woman gave her hope that some good might still come of their capture. At least now she knew their fate was not controlled solely by a group of bloodthirsty warriors. Emily could not be optimistic, though, not when she feared that even if they escaped this predicament Cutter would not allow them a future. She was so tired of fighting him.

"Cutter's woman, what is your name?"

It was strange to realize they had shared so much already, and still did not know each other's names. "My name is Emily, and this is Tad."

"Ee-mell-ee." She sounded out Emily's name slowly and nodded. "I am Willow."

Emily smiled. She felt a kinship with this woman and sensed they could be friends despite their many differences. For the first time since Tad was captured she felt her heart lighten. There was hope.

"Tad, you go with my son." Willow patted Tad on the shoulder as she smiled at Emily. "He and Running Bear are friends. They will be safe."

"It's okay, Tad." Emily gave him a little push toward the other boy. She felt her heart twist painfully in her chest as she watched Tad walk away without a backward glance. She was glad the boys were friends, but she was reluctant to allow Tad out of her sight. She allowed it only because she sensed that Willow wanted to talk with her privately. Emily wanted that as well. She had a feeling there was much she could learn from the other woman.

"Come, Ee-mell-ee. We will wash and we will talk. Then we will tell the men what we have decided."

Emily glanced down at her stained and torn buckskins, then looked after Tad as he walked with the other Indian boy through the village. Already the boy seemed to forget the violence they'd encountered only moments before and was talking animatedly with the other child. She wanted to talk with Willow but did not want to leave Tad or move away from Cutter.

"He will be safe," Willow repeated.

Emily had no choice but to believe her.

Willow led her through the village, calling out to women as she went. Emily reasoned that the older woman was warning them that an important decision needed to be made. Emily saw the searching looks, some angry, some curious, that the Indian women gave her as she followed in Willow's wake, and tried to school her face into a calm mask.

It was not easy. Despite the ease she felt with Willow, and the hope the woman's friendship offered her, there were too many uncertainties. Although Willow and her family had shown kindness, Emily had no reason to believe that was anything more than an exception.

She'd heard too many stories about the brutality of Indians, and witnessed enough violence firsthand, for her to feel completely safe. Still, her only alternative was to kneel in the dirt outside the lodge while the men decided her fate. She found it hard to believe the women had some power as well, but she would be a fool not to at least try.

They left the village and crossed through neat rows of corn and beans, then followed a winding path through trees. When the trees ended they stood on the banks of a broad stream.

The water arched in a wide bend, forming a deep pool among some rocks. The quiet lap of the water against the rocks was the only sound. A soft breeze made ripples across the water and cooled Emily's face.

Willow stepped into the water. Wading toward the pool she pulled her loose deerskin dress over head and draped it over a rock as she passed it.

Emily stared at her, amazed by the woman's lack of self-consciousness. Glancing around her quickly, Emily half expected to see a ring of dark faces watching her as they had in the village, but there was nothing but the trees and the quiet ripple of wind through the leaves.

"Come. The water is not cold."

Emily glanced down again at her stained clothing and grimy hands. The water looked cool and inviting. She wanted to be clean. After another nervous glance around her to be sure they were alone, Emily brought her hands to the fastenings of her clothes.

Emily removed her clothing and moved into the water so quickly she made a loud splash. A careful scan of the surrounding trees reassured Emily that no one but Willow had seen her.

Turning to face the Indian woman, Emily saw Willow staring at her with open curiosity. She reached out a tentative hand and poked Emily's shoulder with a finger.

"It does not come off?" she asked softly.

For a moment Emily stared back in confusion. Then she realized the woman was talking about the color of her skin.

She suppressed the urge to laugh, knowing that would offend the older woman. "No more than yours."

Willow nodded. "There have been many things said about the Long Knives. Some said that only your faces were white, but now I see you are white all over. Others said it was only paint."

"No paint," Emily agreed.

"Will your baby be white also when it is born?"

"Baby?" Emily repeated stupidly, once again confused by the woman's question.

"When will it be born?"

"I do not know." Emily moved her hands to her belly. Was it her imagination or was it more rounded than before?

Could it be true? Was she indeed carrying Cutter's child? A smile curved her lips at the thought. Glancing at Willow for confirmation, Emily saw she was smiling too.

Cutter's child. Their child. Filled with happiness, Emily wanted to run to him and share her news. Remembering where he was brought her abruptly back to reality.

In another life she might have celebrated her newfound knowledge, but at the moment it was only another burden, another worry. She desperately wanted Cutter's child, but just now her own life was in tremendous danger. There was no telling whether she would live to see her pregnancy out. She might live to see her baby born into captivity and ripped from her arms. Her baby might be born without a father.

Emily shuddered.

"Ee-mell-ee. What is wrong? Are you not happy about this child?"

Emily forced herself to smile stiffly at Willow. "I am very happy about the child, but I worry."

"It is good to worry. That means you take more care. You not so quick to pick fights with Big Fist." Willow smiled at Emily, obviously expecting her to enjoy the joke as well.

Emily bit her lip. "Willow. What will happen to us? What will happen to my baby?"

Before the other woman could answer, cries of greeting were called as more women came to the stream. As Willow answered them some came to join them in the water while others seated themselves on the rocks. Emily slipped as far down into the water as she could and still breathe, wondering how she would ever find the nerve to rise naked from the water in front of this many curious eyes. She was very conscious of the dozen or so unwavering pairs of dark eyes watching her, judging her.

Willow and the other Indian women bathing bared their bodies without shame. The younger women and girls pranced about in the shallows, naked as the day they were born, splashing each other and playing in the water.

After allowing the others some time to settle down, Willow called out in a sharp voice and the women quickly quieted down. Soon all their attention was centered on Willow and the white woman in the water beside her.

"I will speak in the language of the Long Knives so Ee-mell-ee can hear my words. Most of you understand enough to follow. These will help the ones who do not."

Willow gently touched Emily's shoulder and gave her a reassuring smile. "Stand, Ee-mell-ee."

"No." Just the thought of baring herself to these strangers sent a shiver of fear through her.

"They must see you." Willow pressed her lips together as she searched for the words. "They must know you are not bad."

Looking at the women staring at her, Emily felt her face flush in embarrassment. Most of them were naked. They were all women. Glancing from face to face, Emily let her gaze stop on a heavily pregnant woman seated on the rock directly in front of her. The woman's obvious hostility shook Emily and brought home to her once again that her life was at stake. She told herself that Willow wanted to help her.

"Ee-mell-ee, stand," Willow whispered urgently.

The woman in front of her smiled. It was not a nice smile. Emily smiled back and stood up. She did not move her gaze from the angry woman's. It was easier to concentrate on the woman's hatred, her anger, than to experience the eager curiosity the other women displayed.

Still, she felt their eyes drilling into her as the water sluiced from her body. Goose bumps rose on her flesh as the light wind skimmed across her wet skin. Emily fought the need to shiver. She did not want them to think her afraid.

Do not show your fear. Remembering Daniel Boone's advice helped soothe her enough to stand still.

"Look at this Long Knife. See her white skin. See how different she is from us."

Willow took Emily's hand in hers, holding their arms up so the others could see the contrast between the brown and white skin.

Emily stared at the angry woman, doing her best to stand up straight. She held her head high. She would not show them how afraid she was.

Willow put their arms down. "Look at her breasts. Are they so different from ours? Yes, they are white, but they are shaped the same. She has only two, as we do."

Willow put a warm hand on Emily's abdomen. Startled, Emily looked down, but quickly moved her gaze back to the angry gaze of the woman in front of her. "See her belly. She carries a child. A child her man put there just as Big Fist put a child in Little Fawn's belly."

Laughter skittered through the women, and a few reached out to push at the angry woman's shoulders.

This was Little Fawn. Now Emily understood her anger. Big Fist's wife would not be expected to like the white woman. Emily wondered how many of the women had cause to hate the whites. She swallowed nervously and moved her gaze above Little Fawn's head to stare at the trees.

"What is so different about this woman than other women? She is not of the People, but should we fault her for that?"

Many of the women murmured in agreement, but when Emily dared to glance at Little Fawn again the other woman's face was set and angry.

Meeting Emily's eyes, Little Fawn spoke. "No, I not fault her for not being of the People, but I blame her for being a Long Knife! Long Knives killed my son, and I will not rest until all Long Knives are dead!"

Emily felt the strength of the other woman's anger like a physical blow in the pit of her stomach. She clenched her hands into fists at her side, pressing her lips tightly together. She dared not answer the woman.

"Then you will never rest," Willow said slowly as she led Emily to the shallow water and reached for a dress one of the women was holding. Willow slipped the loose garment over Emily's head and gave her a reassuring smile. Emily managed to give her a tremulous smile in return. Covering her nakedness made her feel less vulnerable and gave her a measure of confidence to turn and face the other women once more.

"My man has killed many white men this summer. He will kill still more before the leaves turn and the snows are upon us," Little Fawn said scornfully. "If your man went on the warpath more and talked less, then there would be still fewer white men. We could drive them all from our land before my baby is born."

Willow slipped into her own dress and seated herself on a rock. She gestured for Emily to sit beside her.

"Ee-mell-ee, tell Little Fawn how many white men you have seen."

"What do you mean?" Emily did not think the Indians'

knowledge of English included the concept of thousands of people.

"The place where you came from. Did more people live there than in this place?"

"Yes," Emily said softly, still confused by what Willow wanted of her.

"Two times as many?" Willow prompted her.

"Yes."

Emily's quiet answer caused a flurry of response from the other women.

"Three times?"

"Yes. Much bigger than that."

"That is just one place," Little Fawn said scornfully. "We know Piqua Town is bigger than this town."

Willow dipped her head in acknowledgment.

"Ee-mell-ee, how many towns do the Long Knives have that are that big or bigger?"

"Dozens, I suppose."

When the Indian women did not understand, Emily held up her fingers, counting off by opening and closing her fists. When she was done they all sat silent for a moment.

"That is why we cannot fight. We cannot kill all the Long Knives. We can kill the ones here, but more will come. Then more. Each time we fight, some of the People will die. There are too many of them to fight," Willow said into the silence.

She leaned forward and took Little Fawn's hand into her own. "If Big Fist continues on the warpath, he will be killed. Is that what you want? Would you have the child you carry kill the child that Ee-mell-ee carries? Would you have her child kill yours? Is this what you want? That your children will fight as we do today? That they will never know peace?"

Little Fawn hung her head and did not look up. Emily was sorry to see the expression of pain on her face, and the woman's timeless gesture of covering her belly as if to protect the child within.

"The killing must stop." Emily spoke into the silence. She smiled when Little Fawn looked up at her. "We have much we can learn from each other. Let our children grow up as friends, not as enemies."

"How?" Little Fawn whispered. "How can we stop our men? To be a man is to make war."

Her words struck a chord of truth in Emily. She knew Cutter would fight to preserve his honor. She knew Big Fist would fight to release his anger, an anger she now considered justified. How could they stop the men from making war with each other?

"It is true that we do not have weapons such as the man has," Willow said and smiled at the women, touching Emily's and Little Fawn's shoulders with each hand. "Women do not have need of such weapons. We have better weapons."

Chapter 22

Cutter walked through the Indian village, drinking in the tranquil beauty of the scene. It was near dusk, and most families were gathered in front of their low, bark lodges. They sat cross-legged around fires, eating, talking, laughing, just as Cutter knew families were gathered at Fort Boonesborough.

The smell of wood smoke and the mouthwatering aroma of roasting meat and corn reminded Cutter how hungry he was. The intimate sound of a woman's voice as she talked to her husband reminded Cutter of a more important need, and he increased his pace. The desire to see Emily, to hold her, to know that she was all right, pushed him forward. He'd seen Tad hours ago, and knew he was safe, but he'd not seen Emily since the council lodge. They'd been kept apart all day. He had to be sure she was safe.

As he passed down the village streets, some of the people stared at him. Others called out greetings and invitations to join them for dinner. A few scowled at him when he looked their way.

Cutter thought about his mother, Mack, Reuben and Ruth, Daniel and Rebecca Boone, and all the other people crowded into the fort, preparing to battle the people he walked among now.

Both groups included good and bad people, people he cared for and people he despised. He did not want to see them destroy each other. If only there were a way to stop them from clashing. He'd spent countless hours talking about this with He Who Walks with the Clouds and Silver Fish.

There was not a way.

Clash was inevitable. They both wanted the same land. People would die. Cutter could do nothing to stop it, so he would do the only thing he could: he would protect the woman he loved and his only child from harm.

When he saw Silver Fish's lodge, Emily sat beside the fire, stirring something in the cook pot that hung over the fire. She was wearing an Indian dress. Her hair was pulled back into a single heavy braid that hung down her back. She was smiling as she listened to something Willow was saying. Then she threw back her head and laughed that full, throaty laugh that had first stirred his passion.

Cutter felt his heart swell in his chest. He loved her. He would tell her tonight. They had no future. He had no future. She deserved to know that at least he had loved her.

"Pa!"

Turning, Cutter saw Tad running in a pack of other young boys. His son's face was flushed with pleasure. How often had he given Tad the opportunity to be young? It was yet another thing to regret, another failure. Cutter smiled at his son, knowing there wasn't anything else he could give him.

"I shot a rabbit. Willow says we're going to have it for supper."

"I hope that's not all. I'm hungry enough to eat one all by myself." Cutter gently ruffled the boy's hair, noticing for the first time that his son's head nearly reached his shoulder. He'd missed so much, and there would never be a chance to make it up.

"There is plenty for everyone."

Emily's husky voice sent a thrill of pleasure jolting through him. Just having her near made him feel better. He had no future, but he had now. That was more than most men got. Cutter was determined to enjoy the time he had left with the people he loved.

"Did you skin Tad's rabbit for him?" Cutter teased her, remembering well her outright refusal to clean any of the game he shot.

"As it happens, I did." Her blue eyes glowed with pleasure, her cheeks flushed from bending over the fire.

"Playing favorites, are we, Miss Keating?"

"You know who owns my heart, Cutter." Emily stepped closer to him. She lightly touched the bandage He Who Walks with the Clouds had wrapped around his arm. "Are you all right?"

"I am now," he said and slipped his uninjured arm around her waist and pulled her close.

It was true. Seeing her safe and Tad unharmed was all that he needed to give him a sense of well-being. They were together, for this night at least. Seeing Emily and Tad accepted so easily into Silver Fish's family gave him hope that no matter what happened to him, his loved ones would be taken care of. Silver Fish would see that no harm came to them.

Emily was not so easily convinced. "But your wounds. You lost so much blood."

Emily bit her plump lower lip. Cutter wanted to kiss away her troubled look. He wanted more than that. Touching her side, he could tell she wore nothing beneath the deerskin dress. Knowing that, Cutter could barely think about his wounds. He felt strong enough to do anything.

"They were nothing but scratches," Cutter reassured her. "The shaman thoroughly cleaned and dressed them. He mixed some foul-smelling mixture that made me feel better after I managed to swallow it. No easy task, that. Then he gave me some kind of tea to drink that put me to sleep. I slept away much of the afternoon, and now all I need is something to eat."

"Then by all means, come and eat. We've been waiting for you."

Emily's smile chased any remaining gloom away, and Cutter was able to enjoy his meal and the company that came with it. For a short time both Indian and white sat down together and ate. They laughed as friends do, forgetting their differences.

When everyone could eat no more, Willow's daughters cleaned up the remnants of their meal. Tad and the rest of the children ran off to play while there was still some light remaining. Cutter lay back with his head in Emily's lap. Silver Fish took out his pipe and smoked as he watched Willow sew a pair of moccasins.

They sat in peaceful silence, listening to the village around them settle in for the evening. Mothers called to children. A baby squealed with delight as his father tickled him. The pungent aroma of well-cured tobacco drifted on the breeze. A handful of bright leaves skittered down the road as a prelude to fall.

Emily stroked his hair. Cutter closed his eyes, enjoying the gentle caress and listening to the village. He was content.

"What have the men decided?"

Willow's voice was low, barely disturbing the calm of the evening, but Cutter felt Emily tense as if the other woman had screamed. Cutter forced his body to relax, not wanting to reveal his own anxiety as he waited for Silver Fish's answer. He did not want the chief to know of his own unease. He trusted Silver Fish, but it was Cutter's life that hung in the balance.

He had spent a great deal of time talking with the chief and the shaman earlier this day, but did not know if anything had been decided while he slept in the shaman's lodge.

"Decided about what, wife?"

Cutter almost smiled at that. How like Silver Fish not to give a direct answer when another question would do.

Willow simply inclined her head toward the whites who sat on the other side of the fire and waited for her husband's answer.

They all waited.

Silver Fish drew on his pipe and held the smoke in for a moment before answering. "We have talked much, but not made a decision yet."

"What is in your mind, my husband?"

Silver Fish sent his wife a sidelong glance, which she met with a serene smile. He shook his head.

"The council will decide tomorrow. We have not made a decision."

"So you said, but I would hear what you think."

So would Cutter.

He knew the decision was supposedly up to the council, but Silver Fish and He Who Walks with the Clouds could lead the council to any decision they desired. The People knew they were their leaders and respected them. The People would listen to what Silver Fish and He Who Walks with the Clouds had to say and most likely do as they wished.

"We will take Cutter to meet with our English fathers, as I have promised them," Silver Fish said slowly and puffed on his pipe some more.

"I see."

Willow bent her head to her sewing once more, not showing any visible reaction to her husband's words.

Cutter felt his stomach twist into a knot. He'd known that was what Silver Fish wanted, but he'd still retained some hope that there might be another way. He should have learned long ago that there was no hope for him. Still, conscious of Emily's touch, he wished there were another way. Cutter took a deep breath and reminded himself that what happened to him was not important.

Cutter wished he dared look up at Emily. He wished he had been able to break the news to her himself. She'd always known it was a possibility, but it must have struck her harder than it did him.

If it had, Emily managed to keep it to herself. She still stroked his hair and did not make a sound. The only sign that she'd heard what Silver Fish intended was a single hot tear that fell from her face and struck his cheek.

Cutter wished he could comfort her, but Willow was not through speaking to her husband.

"What of his woman and son?"

Willow's question struck at the heart of what Cutter considered important. The only thing that mattered. It took all of his control not to show how very much it mattered.

They all waited while Silver Fish made a smoke ring and considered his answer. "My friend has said he will go to talk with the English if we let his woman and son return to the Long Knife fort in Kah-ten-tah. He will go and do as they ask."

Emily's quick intake of breath made Cutter wish he had told her himself about the bargain he'd struck with Silver Fish.

Cutter's life for Emily's and Tad's. Cutter considered it a fair bargain, but he had not consulted Emily. He doubted she would consider it fair.

She had to know that once he went to the British he

would not come back. He might be tried as a traitor and shot. He might be tortured for information he could give about Kentucky's defenses. He might be kept alive and used. However the British meant to exploit him, it was doubtful he would be able to return to Kentucky.

Cutter knew all these things, but it did not matter to him. What mattered to him was Emily and Tad. Their safety was all that was important. He would do whatever it took to keep them safe.

Maybe Emily had expected to go with him to Detroit, but Cutter did not trust the English to keep his loved ones safe. He trusted Silver Fish and He Who Walks with the Clouds. He would leave Emily and Tad here. Silver Fish and He Who Walks with the Clouds would see to their safety.

Emily knew these things as well. That did not mean she would accept his decision quietly. He hoped she would not make a scene in front of Silver Fish. Her hand trembled slightly as she stroked his hair, but she did not speak.

"The women talked today," Willow said quietly without looking up.

"Have they made a decision?" Silver Fish shifted his body so he could see his wife's face, but Willow's head was bent and her face was all but hidden by her hair.

"They have," Willow answered simply and continued sewing.

A ball made of hide and stuffed with pine needles rolled before Silver Fish, nearly landing in the fire. A red-faced boy, so young he was still plump with baby fat, ran up to Silver Fish. The chief leaned forward and picked up the ball. He weighed it in his hand while giving the boy a measured look.

"You must learn to take better care of the things that are important to you, boy. You might have lost this in the fire."

The boy stuttered an apology, and Silver Fish gave him

his ball. After he ran away, the four of them continued to sit in silence.

"The same could be said of you, my husband." Willow raised her head and gave her husband a cool stare.

Cutter felt Emily's hand still on his head as they both waited for what the other couple would say next.

"What is it I have not taken care of?" Silver Fish asked sharply, his eyes narrowing as he met his wife's look.

"You have not taken care of your friendship with Cutter." Willow motioned toward the couple on the other side of the fire.

"In what way, woman?" The chief's voice was gruff, and his expression was stern. He did not look at Cutter or Emily, concentrating solely on Willow's words.

Willow laid aside her sewing and leaned forward. "You are blood brothers, yet you stole his woman; then you stole his son. Now you will take him away from them. How can separating a family be a good thing? Is this the way of a true blood brother?"

"He can be with his family after he speaks with the English." Silver Fish's voice showed his growing irritation with his wife.

"Do the English wish only to speak with the Long Knife?" Willow stared at her husband expectantly. "Many of the People think the English plan to make war on the Long Knives."

"I am not of the English, so I do not know what they plan," Silver Fish snapped. "Who knows what the white-faces think?"

Willow shook her head so violently her silver earrings jangled. "You talk with them. What do you think they plan?"

Silver Fish turned his stony look on Cutter. The fire snapped and crackled, filling the ominous silence between them. The children laughed at their play in the village street. Cutter's mouth was dry, but nothing would induce him to move away from this circle to seek a drink.

"Truly, I do not know what our English fathers plan, but they are not happy that so many Long Knives come to settle in Kah-ten-tah. I think they would like to drive the Long Knives away. I have heard the English say they will drive them back into the big water."

Willow nodded as if she expected no less. "So you would give your friend to his enemies?"

Silver Fish's breath hissed as he glared at his wife.

"Be careful what you say, woman," Silver Fish warned with a growl.

"If you give Cutter to the English, men who have sworn to kill all Long Knives, do you think they will let him go home to his family?"

Silver Fish held his head proudly and did not answer. He did not need to. They all knew the answer.

"It is as I said. You are going to let Cutter go into the fire with no care for what will happen to him."

"I care," Silver Fish said stubbornly. "Cutter will go to the English. I have given my word."

"Your word." Willow spit to show her disdain for that. "What of your word as a friend? What of your vow as a brother?"

Willow's eyes blazed in the firelight. Cutter was glad she was fighting on his side. Now he understood why Emily was so willing to sit quietly and let others talk. She already had a strong advocate in Willow. As the wife of the chief, Willow was the women's chief, the peace chief. If the women decided they were against war, they had many ways of influencing the men.

Emily had rightly judged that Willow would have greater sway over Silver Fish than anything Emily or Cutter could say. He could see that Silver Fish was uncomfortable with the bargain he'd struck with Cutter, but would it be enough?

"What of my word as chief? If I do not keep my promises to the English they will not keep their promises to me." Silver Fish slammed his fist on the ground between him and his wife.

His show of violence did not disturb Willow, who simply shook her head. "What promises?"

Silver Fish made a sound of disgust in his throat. "You have seen their guns. You have seen the men marching with their uniforms the color of blood. Do you wish to see these men march on our village?"

"You should not deal with men such as these. They do not have honor."

Silver Fish sighed softly. "I did not choose it. You know that, wife."

Willow looked up from her sewing and stared into her husband's eyes. "Then, husband, maybe it is time you made a choice."

"What choice would you have me make? Would you have me choose to help this whiteface and see the blood of our people flow?"

"There is a way you can do both," Willow said in an even voice.

"How?" Cutter's question was out before he could stop it. Could the women have come up with a solution the men had not found?

"It is really quite simple." Emily spoke for the first time, her voice strong and confident as she outlined their plan.

"It might work," Cutter said slowly, still digesting her words.

"It can work," Silver Fish assured him.

"It must work," Willow said, meeting Emily's eyes over the fire. "We cannot lose friends such as this. The People will need our white friends, I fear."

"We will be there for you in your time of need, just as you are here for us in ours," Emily said softly.

Filled with hope, Cutter met Silver Fish's eyes across the embers of the dying fire. "I hope you value your wife, Silver Fish."

"As you should yours," the chief responded gravely.

Chapter 23

Emily's heart beat faster when the English soldiers rode out of the trees at the far edge of the meadow. As the redcoats crossed the wide, bowl-shaped green, she could not make out their faces. She contented herself with counting them. There were less than a dozen, just as Silver Fish had said there would be.

So far the English had kept their word.

Still, as a precaution, she tugged the fox mantle she wore despite the warmth of the day so that it hung over her face. The covering effectively hid her face—more important, her eyes—from view, but forced her to lean forward to peer at the approaching riders.

As if sensing her nervousness the bay mare shifted uneasily beneath her. Emily patted the horse's neck to reassure her. She'd been grateful to Stands Firm for nursing the horse back to health and was glad of the familiar mount today of all days.

She looked up again. The riders' faces were now pale

blobs beneath their tall black helmets, but still she could not make out their individual features.

Biting her lip, Emily glanced to her right at Cutter and Silver Fish. The men sat astride their horses, side by side. They stared intently at the group riding quickly toward them. Both men held their rifles in the crook of their arms with deceptive casualness, but the stiff set of their shoulders told Emily neither man was truly at ease.

Tad was seated on an Indian pony with Stands Firm and Running Bear flanking him. Stands Firm was struggling manfully to imitate his father, but the youth's hand trembled slightly as he stroked the rifle lying across his legs.

The two younger boys' eyes sparkled with excitement. They practically bounced on their ponies. Tad's fidgeting provoked his pony to snort and sidle toward Running Bear's pony. The second pony squealed in protest.

Cutter turned and gave his son a quelling look that stifled the boys' enthusiasm—for the moment.

Cutter shifted his gaze to meet Emily's. The smile he gave her warmed Emily to her toes.

They would be all right, she told herself. Surely life would not be so unfair as to let her find a love like this one and then take it away. There had been no time to be alone as they discussed plans with Silver Fish and Willow, then met with both village councils to determine if this was the path the Shawnee meant to take.

Days had passed while they had waited for a runner to carry the message to the British fort and bring an answer back. But those days had been busy. During that time Emily had been accepted into the village's daily life, and she found her days full, while Cutter spent hours closeted with He Who Walks with the Clouds and Silver Fish.

They had planned this carefully.

It had to work.

Cutter turned back to watch the English approach. Emily followed his gaze and moistened her dry lips with her tongue. Gently touching her hand to her abdomen, she hoped she was right.

So much could go wrong.

So much was at stake.

Emily looked past the boys to where Willow's erect figure sat astride a pony. Looking into the Indian woman's serene face, Emily found some comfort, but a lump in her throat made it difficult to swallow. A tight band around her chest made each breath painful.

She was so afraid.

The English stopped their horses a short distance away. Emily closed her eyes and offered up a quick prayer for the safety of the people she cared about. When she opened them, Silver Fish and Cutter were walking their horses forward to meet the English.

The English officer they spoke with was a silver-haired man with a harsh scar that ran the length of his left cheek. It made her uncomfortable to look at him, but Emily watched his every move closely, determined to judge for herself whether this man would keep his word to Silver Fish.

"It will be all right, Ee-mell-ee; you will see." Willow's quiet voice at her elbow startled Emily. Her attention had been so concentrated on the men that she didn't know the other woman had approached.

Emily's mouth was so dry she could not speak, but she clasped Willow's hand in her own, drawing comfort from its warmth and strength.

"Where is the man of God?" Willow whispered urgently.

Emily forced her gaze from the officer speaking with Cutter and Silver Fish. The minister was an important part of their plan. Searching the small group, she noticed a round barrel of a man whose bald head shone brightly in the sun. His white collar set him aside from the others— that and his poor horsemanship. Emily worried that the man might fall off his skittish mount at any moment. He was smiling at something one of the officers said when the leader motioned him forward.

"That one." Emily pointed out the cleric.

Willow snorted her disgust, obviously not impressed at the whites' idea of a spiritual leader.

"They come now," Willow said gruffly. "Keep your head down. Do not look up."

Cutter's mouth was set in a grim line. He was displeased about something. Looking over his shoulder at the English officer, Emily thought the Englishman was definitely angry.

They had already disagreed over something important. That knowledge increased the knot of tension in her stomach. She consoled herself with the fact that the first part of their plan was going forward. She'd been accepted as Silver Fish and Willow's daughter. The English were not going to question her identity. They would allow the marriage ceremony to go forward.

Emily kept her eyes lowered, knowing that if the Englishman saw her blue eyes he would certainly recognize that she was a white woman. Luckily it was dim beneath the stand of pines, the very reason Cutter and Silver Fish had chosen this spot to wait for the English. In her Indian dress, with the brown acorn stain on her visible skin and her eyes lowered, she might be able to pull this off.

She had to; this was too important to fail.

"Come, darling; it is time." Cutter stood beside her. His strong hands gripped her waist as he lifted her from the saddle.

Her legs shook a little when he set her on the ground. Emily took the luxury of leaning against him for a moment, within the circle of his arms, before following him to stand before the minister.

Cutter took her hands in his. Looking down at the nut-brown skin of her hands, she scarcely recognized those hands as her own.

"Does she understand English?"

The minister's kindly question almost made Emily feel guilty for her deception. She might have trusted the man if it was only her life at stake, but Emily would take no risks with Cutter's safety, or Tad's, or that of the child she carried.

"Yes," Emily whispered. They'd decided she should keep her voice low, but her throat was so tight Emily was surprised she could speak at all.

The minister dispensed with formalities, and the ceremony was quickly over. Cutter slipped a plain gold ring over her finger, then kissed her on the cheek. Willow started crying loudly and pulled Emily into a long embrace, with the boys crowding around her so the minister would have no more opportunity to look more closely at the bride.

As soon as the minister was safely mounted again, Willow released her. Cutter pulled her into his arms and gave her a fierce kiss that tasted of desperation.

"I love you, Emily," he whispered against her hair. "Always remember that I love you."

"Come back to me," Emily cried after him, but he did not answer as he mounted and rode away.

The first part of their plan was done. Now would come the most dangerous. Would the English believe Cutter was truly a Shawnee ally now?

Emily twisted her fingers together and turned the unfamiliar ring around her finger. She wondered where Cutter had found a wedding band in the wilderness.

Willow stepped to her side and slipped an arm around her waist. Emily leaned against the tall woman's shoulder, suddenly filled with the awful fear that she would never see Cutter again.

"Something is wrong." Willow frowned as she stared past Emily.

Emily turned so fast her head swam. She leaned on Willow to steady herself. When her vision cleared she saw two of the redcoated soldiers seize Cutter's arms and drag him from his horse. Even as Silver Fish shouted at the officer the soldiers bound Cutter's arms behind his back.

Cutter did not resist. He stared across the meadow at Emily. She felt his love for her fill her soul. Her love for him swelled in her heart.

She loved him. He must come back to her.

"Why doesn't he fight?" Emily asked desperately.

"He is doing what he said he would do. He is giving himself to the English to protect us," Willow said slowly.

"No." Emily's lips felt cold and stiff. She touched them, remembering how warm they'd felt when Cutter had kissed them only minutes before. Would he ever kiss her again?

"What of our plan?" Emily knew the plan was worthless, but she had to grasp at the frail hope that it might still work.

Then the silver-haired officer turned his back on Silver Fish, and Emily knew there was no hope. The English did not care that Cutter had sworn his loyalty to them. The English did not care that Cutter had married Silver Fish's "daughter" and had promised not to fight the English. The English were going to take him away. She might never see him again.

"No!"

Emily lunged forward, but Willow caught her with her strong arms and held her firmly.

"Wait, Ee-mell-ee; trust Silver Fish."

"I can't." A sob caught painfully in her throat as she watched two English soldiers manhandle Cutter back onto his horse. "I can't lose him."

"Do not go. If they see you, all will be lost. Think of your baby."

The English officer called his men to mount up, but Silver Fish urged his horse forward to block the officer's path. The officer sneered at Silver Fish's words. He raised a hand.

A flicker of movement at the far tree line drew Emily's
gaze. She sucked in her breath as she watched almost fifty
redcoated soldiers step from the trees and march in neat
formation toward the small knot of men in the center of
the meadow.

Silver Fish hung his head. Emily's heart beat so fast she
thought it might burst in her chest. She could barely hear
the voices of the men over the rushing in her ears.

Willow's hands tightened over Emily's arms, but she was
glad for the pain. It reminded her she was still alive.

Silver Fish raised his head. He glared at the white officer
and slowly lifted his arm above his head.

The trees around them suddenly came to life with warriors
Emily had never suspected were there. Dozens of warriors,
fearsomely painted for war, streamed past the women and
boys. Emily recognized some from the village; even Big Fist
was there. They came until they far outnumbered the small
cluster of white men on the other side of the meadow.

The Indians stopped and stared across the green
expanse at the redcoats. Big Fist raised his war club above
his head and delivered a mighty war whoop that started
the other braves to yipping until the sound of their cries
deafened Emily.

Clapping her hands over her ears, Emily stretched to
her tiptoes so she could see above the warriors gathered
in front of her. Although she stood higher on the gentle
slope, Emily could barely see the redcoats, and Cutter was
hidden from view entirely.

Her heart rose in her throat. She clenched her hands
into fists, her fingernails digging into the palms of her
hands.

Would there be a battle?

Part of her longed for the bloody destruction of the
English soldiers, whose only plan was to destroy the people
she loved, but Emily remembered too well the look of the
Indian boy she'd shot. The English were far outnumbered,

but they would not die alone. She did not want to see people killed, not for any reason.

There was also the knowledge that Cutter lay helpless in the hands of the English. They knew their doom stood before them. What would stop them from taking Cutter with them?

"Please." Emily did not know whether she was begging or praying.

The English officer and Silver Fish stared at each other as the yipping of the Indians died away. Neither spoke into the silence. Now the only sounds were the creaking of the boughs overhead.

Without looking away from the Indian chief, the white leader waved a hand. A moment later Emily sighed as she saw Cutter mount his horse again under his own power, his hands free.

Silver Fish then wheeled his horse around and turned his back on the redcoats. Defiant to the last, he did not urge his horse above a walk as he led Cutter back to the ranks of the Indians. The redcoats formed into neat lines and followed their officer into the trees.

Emily's knees suddenly felt weak as her world tilted and then turned black.

"Emily, my love, wake up."

Cutter's voice pierced through the darkness and brought Emily back to the light.

She smiled as she opened her eyes. He had called her his love. "Am I really?"

"Today and always." Cutter's relief was evident in his voice.

"Say it again," she whispered as she reached up to touch his cheek.

He bent to kiss her hand. "I love you, Emily Keating."

The rush of pleasure at that thought was stronger than

she thought possible. Emily lost herself in the green depths of his eyes, finding everything she'd ever wanted there, but still she had to be sure. "Not anymore."

Cutter frowned, afraid for a moment that Emily meant to reject him. Then he remembered and smiled. "I love you, Emily Cutright."

Just saying the words to her was not enough. He needed to touch her, hold her, to reassure himself that they were still together. He pulled her more tightly to his chest.

Cutter had been convinced his sacrifice was well worth protecting Emily and Tad, but when he'd been so helpless and then seen Emily's terror-stricken face across the meadow, he'd realized how very wrong he was. At that moment, when he'd thought he'd never see Emily again, Cutter knew he would give anything to hold her once more. Now that he'd been given that second chance he would never let her go.

"I love you." His voice shook a little, but Cutter could not be ashamed for that show of weakness. Not when he was with Emily.

"As I love you, Cutter." Her hand tightened around his. "Promise me you will never leave me again."

"I promise."

When he kissed her, the Indians yipped once more.

Chapter 24

Emily hesitated in the lodge, long after the others were gone. She smoothed her hands over the beadwork of the new deerskin dress Willow had helped her make. Her hands hesitated over the slight bulge of her stomach and she smiled.

She would tell him tonight.

Emily bit her lip nervously and touched her hair to see that it was still in place. She pinched her cheeks to give her face color. She was ready at last.

Closing her eyes and praying for courage, Emily stepped out of the lodge. The full moon rode high in the sky, bathing the village in a soft light. In the distance she could hear the voices of the People and the beat of the drum. The sweet scent of ceremonial tobacco wafted on the warm breeze that caressed her cheek.

Her stomach was a knot of tension. She hadn't been able to eat that night.

Tonight was special.

Emily touched the bead design that was sewn above

her heart, feeling each smooth, rounded edge until she'd traced the outline of a bird. She'd sewn a replica of this same bird onto Cutter's shirt. Remembering the pair of warblers they'd heard singing that morning, Emily hoped it would bring her luck—luck that would mean that tonight Cutter would choose her.

In the distance the People cheered loudly. It was time for the frolic dance. She hoped that Willow had managed to get Cutter to the dancing ground, as she promised.

Emily forced herself to take slow steps as she made her way down the deserted streets of the Indian village. She wanted to run, to hurry to Cutter, but this was a solemn occasion.

She would walk.

She heard the chanting of the people, the rhythm of the drum, the clack of the rattle-shaker long before she reached the dancing ground.

The frolic dance.

She felt the rhythm pulse to her through the warm earth and spread up her feet and through her veins. Her blood pounded in her ears, or maybe it was the drums. Emily toyed with the scarf tied around her waist, checking to make sure the knot was only loosely tied.

When Willow first told her about the frolic dance, how the Indian women chose their husbands at the dance, Emily knew she would dance with Cutter. Yes, they'd been married by the English clergyman, but to Emily a forced marriage was not the same as a marriage entered into freely.

She remembered Cutter telling her that he would marry her. Long ago he'd told her he would give her his name, but could not give her his heart. Now he'd given her his heart, but she wasn't certain she could trust it. It was so hard to trust with so much at stake.

Emily wanted more than his name. She wanted more than his love. She wanted a promise, that commitment drumbeats, while the old man with the drum was also singing his chant: *"Ea le lo we. He e yo he ya."*

The dancers echoed his chant: *"Ea le lo we. He e yo he ya."*

The chanter answered: *"O we a we a o e o."*

Through it all Emily was constantly aware of Cutter as he moved in front of her: watching the firelight play across his smooth skin, seeing the graceful movement of his long limbs, noticing the play of his muscles.

Forever or nothing.

The drums beat on, pulsing through her blood. The heat of the fire and the warmth of the night combined with her movement to make her skin hot and slick. Cutter's skin shone in the firelight. The memory of the slick feeling of his body against her created an ache in the cleft between her legs.

They danced on.

They were surrounded by other couples, yet her world was centered around the hard male body in front of her. Watching each movement Cutter made, Emily was reminded again and again of her intimate knowledge of that body.

As she danced around the fire, Emily's body grew still warmer and moister. She felt the rhythm of the drum, the rhythm of the dance, move, hot and pulsing, through her body in the rushing of her blood.

Staring at Cutter's smooth back in front of her, Emily imagined running her hands over that skin. She imagined the taste of him, touched faintly by wood smoke and tobacco from the fire. She imaged their bodies joining, throbbing together.

Forever.

Her blood pulsed in waves with every footstep and drumbeat. The other couples faded and she was aware only of the man in front of her.

And now came the singer's whoop, which was the signal for all the couples to touch hands.

Barely able to think, Emily fumbled with the scarf around her waist. She touched the knot and then remembered to let it be. When she looked up again most of the other women in the line danced with a cloth scarf in her hand. The scarf was to be used, or not, as a signal from the woman to the man.

Emily did not need a scarf. She reached up and took Cutter's hands. Her hands were bare, with no scarf between them.

This was a sign of acceptance.

It meant that their bodies should soon be touching like this, naked, no barriers. It meant still more to Emily. It meant that she was giving herself to Cutter wholly. There would be no barriers between their hearts, their very souls.

And so now he knew what her intentions were. It was his turn to show her his.

Forever, or nothing.

Emily's heart beat in her throat, and tears stung her eyes. She blinked them back. She would not cry.

At another whoop from the singer, the line of men dancers turned around and faced the women behind them, still holding hands, some couples joined only by the scarf, others standing bare-handed.

Staring up into Cutter's eyes, glittering dark in the firelight, Emily was suddenly afraid. He was not smiling. The lines of his face were etched in stone. If he had not held her hands Emily might have run away.

Her heart beat so violently in her chest that Emily thought it might burst. She looked down at their joined hands, conscious of the rough calluses of his hands on hers. His skin burned against hers.

As the other dancers shuffled forward, so did they, until they stood so close their bodies touched. The feel of his heat against her, the touch of his breath against her cheek, the scent of him, filled her and tormented her.

The singer chanted again.

This time they did not repeat his meaningless syllables but were meant to exchange love talk. This was the moment when the man would tell the woman of his feelings for her.

Cutter said nothing.

Emily thought she might scream from the torment. Now that the moment of truth was upon them, she did not know if she could bear it. She could not look at him. She did not want to know the truth. Not now. She could not bear to know the truth.

Forever, or nothing.

"Look at me, Emily."

Cutter's voice was soft and low. She loved that voice, but Emily could not obey. Her chest ached from the effort of holding her sobs inside.

"Look at me."

His breathing was harsh and ragged.

"Emily, my love." Cutter raised his hands to gently cup her face and tilt her face up to his. "Do you know the meaning of this dance?"

"Yes." Emily could manage nothing more than a whisper, but he heard her.

His lips touched her so gently it was nothing more than a whisper. Emily squeezed her eyes tightly shut. This was good-bye then. A single hot tear escaped her vigilance and slid down her cheek. She hoped he would not notice.

He touched the tear with his finger. "Why do you cry, Emily, my love?"

"Don't," she whispered. "Don't call me that unless you mean it."

"But I do, Emily. You are my love."

Emily opened her eyes, blinking away the tears so she could better see him.

"You are my love, Emily. My heart. My soul. My life."

The pain in her chest eased and Emily could breathe again, but it was so hard to believe it could really be true. "You will not leave me."

"Never."

Forever. He'd chosen forever.

Cutter would not lie to her. Content at last, Emily closed her eyes and leaned against him, swaying to the beat of the drum. Their bodies moved together.

"Emily, let me see you." Cutter's voice was hoarse with emotion, and his hands trembled as he gently traced the outlines of her face. He followed the pattern his hands had created with tiny butterfly kisses.

"When the music stops, Emily, if you go with me to my lodge then you are my wife. Forever. Is that what you want, my darling?"

"Yes, Cutter, that is what I want."

He kissed her, long and deep, creating a trail of fire wherever his hands touched her.

"Tell me why?" he whispered against her lips. "Tell me, Emily."

"I love you."

Looking into the emerald depths of his eyes, Emily finally believed that he loved her too. And she believed in forever.

When the music ended the lines of men and women stood facing each other in the firelight, breathing hard, eyes intent on each other. Some couples separated, the ones holding scarves, while others slipped off together.

"Come with me, Emily." Cutter held out his hand to her.

"Anywhere." Scarcely believing it was true, Emily took his hand and followed him off the dancing ground.

They walked hand in hand down the moonlit street. The tender whispers of other couples sometimes reached them on the soft breeze, but they were alone. The world faded and there were only the two of them.

He took her to a smaller cone-shaped hut near the edge of the village.

They were alone.

He laid her back on a bed made of furs spread across pine boughs and lifted her dress over her head. His sharp eyes searched her face and then seared her entire body with his hot gaze.

"I love you, Emily. Forever and always."

"I love you, Cutter. Forever and always."

He leaned over her and kissed her lips without touching her anywhere else. When she brought her hands up to cup his head he laced his fingers with hers and pressed them back to the ground.

As their kiss deepened and lengthened, Emily arched her back so the tender tips of her nipples grazed against the hair on his chest, but that was all the contact Cutter would allow her.

She moaned with regret when he pulled away from her.

"I love you, Emily. You are all I ever wanted, all I ever needed. I was a fool not to realize that sooner."

"Oh, Cutter."

Again tears shimmered in her eyes, but this time they were tears of joy. Cutter wiped them away and then kissed her again. She shivered with pleasure when he skimmed his hand along the length of her body.

"Are you cold?"

His love for her was strong in his voice, strong in his touch. It warmed Emily more than any fire ever could.

"No, I will never be cold again."

"Are you sure you do not want a fire?" His voice was husky with a promise that his hands were already fulfilling.

"Make me a fire, Cutter." Emily moved into his arms.

Epilogue

Cutter ducked his head through the lodge door and found Emily sitting on the bed mat. She secured the strap on a pack and glanced up at him.

The look she gave him made his heart skip a beat. He still could not believe she loved him. It was hard to grasp the concept that she would stay with him, love him always.

They would never be apart again.

She bit her lip and looked away from him, but not before he caught the glimmer of tears in her eyes. The pink cast to her nose told Cutter they were not her first tears of the day. He hated to see her cry, but at least he knew this time that her pain was not his fault.

Cutter went to her and pulled her into his arms. "I know, darling. I do not want to leave either."

"We have been so happy here," she said softly against his chest. "Tad is miserable at the thought of leaving Running Bear. I will miss Willow sorely. I am so afraid I will never see them again."

"It is time. If we do not leave now we will not reach

Virginia before winter sets in. You know we must do this for them.''

"Do you think we have a chance to help them, to make a difference?''

Cutter doubted their advocacy of the Shawnee would make a difference to the Colonial leaders. The Colonists were far too worried about the war they were waging against the British to care about the fate of the Indians. But however futile he thought it would be, Cutter owed too much to the Shawnee not to travel to Virginia, or Boston if necessary, to speak his piece.

He would show Thomas Jefferson a thing or two, and maybe, just maybe, someone would listen.

"I don't know, Emily, but we have to try.''

"Yes, we have to try,'' she repeated with a sigh.

As Cutter helped her to her feet, he ran his hands down her side and touched the slight rounding of her stomach.

His child grew there. The knowledge made his heart swell with love and pride.

"I do not like the idea of your traveling so far in your condition.''

"You will not leave me behind.'' Her chin lifted with that familiar stubborn look he loved.

"No, I made a promise and I aim to keep it.'' Cutter kissed her to prove it. "I will need your help.''

"We can get through this together,'' Emily said firmly and put her hand in his.

Looking into her eyes, Cutter could believe it was true.

Put a Little Romance in Your Life With
Fern Michaels

__Dear Emily	0-8217-5676-1	$6.99US/$8.50CAN
__Sara's Song	0-8217-5856-X	$6.99US/$8.50CAN
__Wish List	0-8217-5228-6	$6.99US/$7.99CAN
__Vegas Rich	0-8217-5594-3	$6.99US/$8.50CAN
__Vegas Heat	0-8217-5758-X	$6.99US/$8.50CAN
__Vegas Sunrise	1-55817-5983-3	$6.99US/$8.50CAN
__Whitefire	0-8217-5638-9	$6.99US/$8.50CAN

Put a Little Romance in Your Life With
Rosanne Bittner

__Caress	0-8217-3791-0	$5.99US/$6.99CAN
__Full Circle	0-8217-4711-8	$5.99US/$6.99CAN
__Shameless	0-8217-4056-3	$5.99US/$6.99CAN
__Unforgettable	0-8217-5830-6	$5.99US/$7.50CAN
__Texas Embrace	0-8217-5625-7	$5.99US/$7.50CAN
__Texas Passions	0-8217-6166-8	$5.99US/$7.50CAN
__Until Tomorrow	0-8217-5064-X	$5.99US/$6.99CAN
__Love Me Tomorrow	0-8217-5818-7	$5.99US/$7.50CAN